HEARTS
LIKE
SILVER

HEARTS LIKE SILVER. Published by Gold Pearl Press, LLC. Copyright © 2024 by Jamie Sheehan. All rights reserved. No part of this work may be used or reproduced in any manner whatsoever without written permission except in the case of brief quotations embodied in critical articles and reviews.

Library of Congress Control Number: 2024902632

ISBN 979-8-9898202-9-0 (paperback) / ISBN 979-8-9898202-0-7 (ebook)

Printed in the United States of America.

Edited by Caitlin Faith Miller

Designed by Jamie Sheehan

www.goldpearlpress.com

HEARTS
LIKE
SILVER

GOLD PEARL PRESS

For all who struggle to forgive or be forgiven.

SCOTLAND

C. AD 1100 — 1300

ORKNEY

MAINLAND

REDCASTLE

LOCH DOCHFOUR

BRECHIN

PERTH

DUNFERMLINE

FIRTH OF FORTH

EDINBURGH

SOUTH BERWICK

EILDON HILLS

JEDBURGH CASTLE

HAWICK

NINESTANE RIG

HERMITAGE CASTLE

BLACKWOOD HILL

DUMFRIES

LUCE ABBEY

EUROPE
C. AD 1000 – 1300

KINGDOM OF NORWAY

BERGEN

GREAT BRITAIN

KINGDOM OF SCOTLAND

KINGDOM OF ENGLAND

LONDON

DUCHY OF BRITTANY

ALIGNMENTS DU PETIT MENIR

NEOLITHIC CIRCLE

KINGDOM OF THE GERMANS

VERONA

REPUBLIC OF VENICE

BOLOGNA

REPUBLIC OF FLORENCE

FLORENCE

PAPAL STATE

CROWN OF CASTILE

TOLEDO

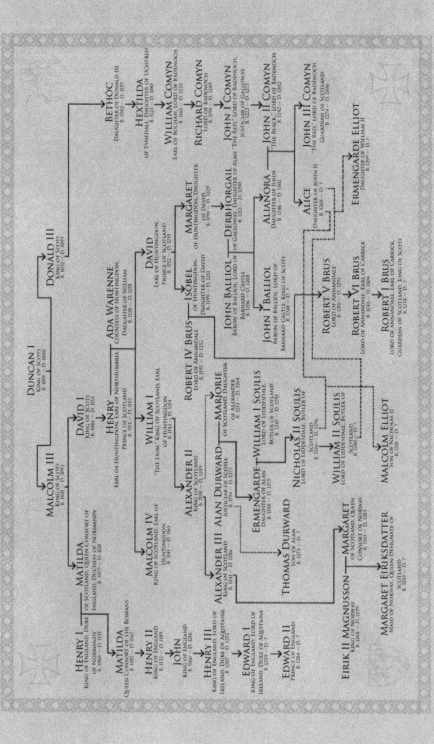

DUNCAN I
KING OF SCOTS
B. 1001 – D. 1040

DONALD III
KING OF SCOTS
B. 1032 – D. 1099

MALCOLM III
KING OF SCOTS
B. 1031 – D. 1093

BETHÓC
DAUGHTER OF DONALD III
B. 1062 – D. 1093

MATILDA
OF SCOTLAND, QUEEN CONSORT OF
ENGLAND, DUCHESS OF NORMANDY
B. 1079 – D. 1118

DAVID I
KING OF SCOTS
B. 1088 – D. 1153

HENRY
EARL OF HUNTINGDON, EARL OF NORTHUMBRIA
B. 1114 – D. 1152

ADA WARENNE
COUNTESS OF HUNTINGDON,
DAUGHTER OF WILLIAM
B. 1120 – D. 1178

HEXTILDA
OF TYNEDALE, DAUGHTER OF UCHTRED
B. 1103

HENRY I
KING OF ENGLAND, DUKE
OF NORMANDY
B. 1068 – D. 1135

MATILDA
QUEEN CONSORT OF THE ROMANS
B. 1102 – D. 1167

MALCOLM IV
KING OF SCOTLAND, EARL OF
HUNTINGDON
B. 1141 – D. 1165

WILLIAM I
'THE LION,' KING OF SCOTLAND, EARL
OF HUNTINGDON
B. 1143 – D. 1214

DAVID
EARL OF HUNTINGDON,
PRINCE OF SCOTLAND
B. 1152 – D. 1219

WILLIAM COMYN
EARL OF BUCHAN, LORD OF BADENOCH
B. 1163 – D. 1233

RICHARD COMYN
LORD OF BADENOCH
B. 1194 – D. 1249

HENRY II
KING OF ENGLAND
B. 1133 – D. 1189

ALEXANDER II
KING OF SCOTLAND
B. 1198 – D. 1249

MARGARET
OF HUNTINGDON, DAUGHTER
OF DAVID
B. 1194 – D. 1229

ISOBEL
DAUGHTER OF DAVID
B. 1199 – D. 1251

ROBERT IV BRUS
LORD OF ANNANDALE
B. 1195 – D. 1232

JOHN I COMYN
'THE RED,' LORD OF BADENOCH,
JUSTICIAR OF GALLOWAY
B. 1222 – D. 1277

JOHN
KING OF ENGLAND
B. 1166 – D. 1216

ALAN DURWARD
JUSTICIAR OF SCOTIA
B. 1194 – D. 1275

MARJORIE
OF SCOTLAND, DAUGHTER
OF ALEXANDER
B. 1215 – D. 1265

DERBHORGAIL
OF GALLOWAY, DAUGHTER OF ALAN
B. 1213 – D. 1290

JOHN BALLIOL
BARON OF BALLIOL, LORD OF
BARNARD CASTLE
B. 1208

JOHN II COMYN
'THE BLACK,' LORD OF BADENOCH
B. 1242 – D. 1302

HENRY III
KING OF ENGLAND, LORD OF
IRELAND, DUKE OF AQUITAINE
B. 1207 – D. 1272

ALEXANDER III
KING OF SCOTLAND
B. 1241 – D. 1286

ERMENGARDE
DAUGHTER OF ALAN
B. 1248 – D. 1275

WILLIAM I SOULIS
LORD OF LIDDESDALE,
BUTLER OF SCOTLAND
B. 1247 – D. 1292

JOHN I BALLIOL
BARON OF BALLIOL, LORD OF
BARNARD CASTLE, KING OF SCOTS
B. 1248 – D. ?

ALIANORA
DAUGHTER OF JOHN
B. 1246 – D. 1302

ROBERT V BRUS
LORD OF ANNANDALE
B. 1210 – D. 1295

ALICE
DAUGHTER OF JOHN II
B. 1268 – D. ?

JOHN III COMYN
'THE RED,' LORD OF BADENOCH,
GUARDIAN OF SCOTLAND
B. 1274 – D. 1306

EDWARD I
KING OF ENGLAND, LORD OF
IRELAND, DUKE OF AQUITAINE
B. 1239 – D. ?

THOMAS DURWARD
SON OF ALAN
B. 1273 – D. ?

NICHOLAS II SOULIS
LORD OF LIDDESDALE, BUTLER OF
SCOTLAND
B. 1266 – D. 1296

ROBERT VI BRUS
LORD OF ANNANDALE, EARL OF CARRICK
B. 1243 – D. 1304

ERMENGARDE ELLIOT
DAUGHTER OF WILLIAM II
B. 1229 – D. ?

EDWARD II
PRINCE OF ENGLAND
B. 1284 – D. ?

EIRIK II MAGNUSSON
KING OF NORWAY
B. 1268 – D. 1299

MARGARET
OF SCOTLAND, QUEEN
CONSORT OF NORWAY
B. 1261 – D. 1283

WILLIAM II SOULIS
LORD OF LIDDESDALE, BUTLER OF
SCOTLAND
B. 1280 – D. ?

MALCOLM ELLIOT
SON OF NICHOLAS II
B. 1280 – D. ?

ROBERT I BRUS
LORD OF ANNANDALE, EARL OF CARRICK,
GUARDIAN OF SCOTLAND, KING OF SCOTS
B. 1274 – D. ?

MARGARET EIRIKSDATTER
MAID OF NORWAY, QUEEN-DESIGNATE OF
SCOTLAND
B. 1283 – D. ?

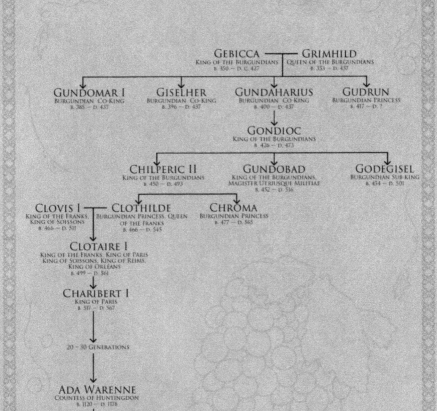

GEBICCA —— **GRIMHILD**
KING OF THE BURGUNDIANS | QUEEN OF THE BURGUNDIANS
B. 350 – D. C. 427 | B. 353 – D. 437

GUNDOMAR I
BURGUNDIAN CO-KING
B. 385 – D. 437

GISELHER
BURGUNDIAN CO-KING
B. 396 – D. 437

GUNDAHARIUS
BURGUNDIAN CO-KING
B. 400 – D. 437

GUDRUN
BURGUNDIAN PRINCESS
B. 417 – D. ?

GONDIOC
KING OF THE BURGUNDIANS
B. 426 – D. 473

CHILPERIC II
KING OF THE BURGUNDIANS
B. 450 – D. 493

GUNDOBAD
KING OF THE BURGUNDIANS,
MAGISTER UTRIUSQUE MILITIAE
B. 452 – D. 516

GODEGISEL
BURGUNDIAN SUB-KING
B. 454 – D. 501

CLOVIS I
KING OF THE FRANKS,
KING OF SOISSONS
B. 466 – D. 511

CLOTHILDE
BURGUNDIAN PRINCESS, QUEEN
OF THE FRANKS
B. 466 – D. 545

CHROMA
BURGUNDIAN PRINCESS
B. 477 – D. 565

CLOTAIRE I
KING OF THE FRANKS, KING OF PARIS
KING OF SOISSONS, KING OF REIMS,
KING OF ORLÉANS
B. 499 – D. 561

CHARIBERT I
KING OF PARIS
B. 517 – D. 567

20 – 30 GENERATIONS

ADA WARENNE
COUNTESS OF HUNTINGDON
B. 1120 – D. 1178

MARGARET EIRIKSDATTER
MAID OF NORWAY, QUEEN-DESIGNATE
OF SCOTLAND
B. 1283 – D. ?

"Above all else, guard your heart, for everything you do flows from it."
Proverbs 4:23

"...It is in truth not for glory, nor riches, nor honours that we are fighting, but for freedom—for that alone, which no honest man gives up but with life itself."
The Declaration of Arbroath
6 April 1320

COUNTESS ADA WARENNE

A standing stone with moonlit edges cast a shadow over the tarnished silver heart casket in Ada's hands. She looked from one body to the next. There were six of them, still breathing but unconscious, laid out like thistle petals before the stones.

She placed her hand on one of the cool rocks over whitish-gray lichen, sent her focus to its heart, and listened.

Teeth, the stone sorceress whispered to her, and the ground quivered.

A beige incisor bit through the soil, a loose tooth pulled from the depths of an earthy maw. More teeth bubbled up beside it and settled in three mounds, and the shaking ground relaxed.

A third of the teeth became agitated. Soft rattling sounded as they rolled into a circle, stacked and melded together, and formed a grotesque diadem. Marred silver dripped from the heart casket to decorate it, and the crown of teeth was completed.

Ada stared at it with wide eyes. The sorceress who spoke to her, she must have created it. But why?

From the now-thin-walled casket in her hands, she lifted a perfectly preserved heart—the heart of her father, William Warenne, 2nd Earl of Surrey, gifted to her once he'd died. Two more caskets sat on the ground at her feet and held the hearts of her and her husband's mothers.

She sank one of the dirty teeth into William's heart, set it in the centre of the stone circle, and stepped next to one of the bodies—a man in his forties, a labourer, strong and lean. She briefly wondered what his life had been like, where the sorceresses found him, and whether he would

1

be missed. But dwelling on the commoners' lives would only hinder her now.

From her wool belt, she pulled out a serrated, golden knife that had been passed to her in England after her mother's death. She'd never used it; she'd never killed anyone, and she wasn't sure she wanted to. But, after speaking with the coven, she harboured no doubt that she would.

"For my future son," she murmured with her hand on her stomach. He wouldn't arrive for seven or so months, but his reign would be the longest of any King of Scotland to date—and he and the country could enjoy all the glory, power, and stability that would come with such a reign.

This was what mothers did: they sacrificed for their children. Likewise, princesses sacrificed for their country, and this was her country now. It was why she was doing this, for him and for Scotland—or that's what she told herself.

But even as she thought it, something dark tugged at her heart: a want, a temptation. A thirst for blood.

She drove the knife into the man and ripped it back out. His flesh caught on the blade's jagged fangs, and blood sprayed onto her elaborate, sweeping sleeves.

She stabbed him again and again.

His blood left his body and surged toward her father's heart. Nightmarishly, muscle and skin crawled after it.

A man assembled—no, not a man.

A monster.

He was neither fully human nor fully alive. Not yet.

She cut into another sacrifice, a woman. Her blood swirled in the moonlight, black and glistening. It attached itself to the goblin's neck, William's neck, and flowed into a long cape.

Her father opened his murderous eyes. They fixed on Ada, and he smiled, revealing sharp canines and a row of powerful teeth. He was hungry, and he wanted her.

He stepped toward her, and she backed away, moving along the small circle's inner edge. She wanted to run from him, but the coven had locked her in. She couldn't leave the standing stones, not until she'd finished her task.

"I created you." Her voice broke, and she worked to strengthen it. "You can't harm me."

William leapt over two bodies and lunged for her.

She dove and rolled.

Teeth scraped her face. She saw canines—he had her.

It took a second for her to realize they weren't her father's teeth but the crown.

William's jaw opened wide, and he bent toward her.

She placed the diadem on her head.

Cries of despair, inhuman and human, rang through her head. She heard bones crunching and hearts squelching between teeth. She saw marked animals shredding corpses and felling primitive men, and she felt what she had before: thirst.

She felt what the ancient owners of the teeth once had, what her father was feeling now; this time, murder wasn't some dark, shameful want but a need. Necessary and natural. Perhaps not moral, but not immoral, either.

Ada fought the crown and focused on William, who was poised to eat her alive.

No. She pressed her will into the thought, which was so potent she wasn't sure if she'd thought it or said it aloud.

He turned from her to the four remaining bodies.

No.

William stopped.

Her fingers clawed into the ground, her breath and heartbeat gradually slowing. As she rose, she kept her gaze firmly on her father, or the thing that looked like him, knowing he wanted nothing more than to swallow her whole.

But he couldn't. She had the crown, and he couldn't touch her.

Two more. That was all—two more—and she could leave the circle. Two more, and her son would reign for many years, her family would thrive, and she would make herself forget this terrible night.

Ada took her mother's heart from the casket, dug a tooth inside it, and raised her knife over the next body.

CHAPTER ONE

Voices sounded panicked but far-off—the buzz of flies around a dead thing. But one word cut through the air: dying.

Someone said she was dying.

Margaret doubled over and vomited up what little food she'd managed to down that morning. Heavy rain mixed with it, washed her face clean, and soaked her clothes from above at the same rate cold sweat did from below.

She caught sight of the ship moored in the harbour and averted her eyes, afraid the mere sight of rolling waves might increase the churning in her stomach, and she clutched Bishop Narve's cope with clammy hands. Even after disembarking the ship, her body shook, and her insides fought her.

Her father, Eirik II Magnusson, had sent word to the Scotsmen that he would cross the North Sea with her, the seven-year-old princess. But he'd stayed behind and left her under the care of her teacher, the Bishop of Bergen, and her retinue, which included Baron Tore Håkonsson and his wife, Ingeborg Erlingsdatter. They were joined by two Scottish knights. One was skinny to the point of malnourishment; the other was older but brawny.

They gave her an odd feeling, those knights. They lingered nearby always, whispered low to each other, watched her with shadowed eyes and didn't look away when she stared at them. They made her uneasy.

She leaned against the bishop, pallid face pained. The world seemed dark, but her head felt light. Her ears rang and muffled the voices and splattering rain around her. Still, she heard her name and stared up at the bishop's concerned face.

Her eyelids fluttered. Through her lashes and lines of water, she saw the thin knight. He smiled, pivoted and left, and her head lolled to one side.

Margaret woke in the episcopal residence in Kirkwall, in a bedroom above the great hall. The storm had let up, but not much, and the sun was setting behind a thick layer of clouds—light like shaded silver seeped through them and bled through the room's thin windows, contrasted by a golden candle that gleamed on a stand beside her bed.

Though she'd dreamed of beasts, obscure, furred things whose teeth dripped into the ocean and became the islands of Orkney, sleep had cured her. Her stomach was settled. All signs she'd been seasick had gone. Not even the scent of cooked fish and seal, which wafted in from the hall, made her feel ill. She called for Ingeborg.

A chair creaked as someone rose from it. Bishop Narve.

He reached for her, and the candle gilded half his face.

His expression frightened her. He no longer looked like the caring teacher she knew. His features no longer showed concern; he looked like an eagle curling its claws to snatch up defenseless prey, eyes wide and fixed on a target. Fixed on her.

"I want to go home." Where was Ingeborg? She squeezed the blanket in her fists and drew it closer around her. "I want Pappa."

Bishop Narve's clawed hands closed around her arms.

He pulled her from the bed and out of the room, down a narrow stone hall. She heard two men speaking Norn nearby, a language she didn't understand.

Tears stung her eyes and red pricked her nose.

"I want Pappa!" she told them, but the Orkneymen didn't understand her words either, nor did they seem to know who she was.

Narve dragged her away. She tried to cling to the porous stone walls, and the bishop hissed, "Quiet! I'm bringing you to him."

Margaret brightened and willingly followed him, hurrying to keep up.

Once, she'd gone on a walk with Ingeborg. Dusk fell, and Ingeborg asked her if she knew how to get home. Turned around, she'd nearly given to tears, but Ingeborg put an arm around her and gestured to the water, an inlet from the sea.

"If ever you're lost," Ingeborg had told her. "Listen for the water. It will guide you home."

Margaret knew Eirik had stayed behind, but perhaps he also knew the secrets of the waters; perhaps he'd listened to the waves, and they led him to her across the North Sea. She would be glad to see him. He would know what was wrong with Bishop Narve.

They went down two low sets of stairs and out a door. Low-hanging clouds clung to the spire of St. Magnus Cathedral across the street.

Her father wasn't waiting outside, but two others were: the burly Scottish knight from the voyage and a girl. She was Margaret's age and height, with hair the same reddish blonde as hers, and she was wearing an extra set of Margaret's clothes—a fur-lined mantle and a gown embroidered with an exclusive design, worn only by royal children.

Margaret blinked and rubbed her eyes. They might have been sisters, or twins, except the girl's eyes were darker, her nose was larger, and her frame was thinner than her own.

The knight seized Margaret, mounted a horse, and set her in front of him. It happened so fast she didn't have time to ask about Pappa.

Bishop Narve said, "This is for your safety," and they galloped away.

Thus, the heir presumptive of Scotland's connection to Norway, to her family, to her human life, was severed.

CHAPTER TWO

The boy's fresh blood dripped from nine-year-old Margaret's fingernails and the corner of her mouth. She knelt next to his warm corpse, having slashed his throat and eaten a chunk of his face, and her cape drank in blood like a deprived lung sucking in air. Colour returned to her face, energy to her body, and her eyes blazed red and bright.

She consumed the rest of him, arms and head and legs. She ate everything but his entrails; those she left for her golden eagle, Magnus, who'd led her to him.

Satiated, she resumed her trek north and left Magnus to peck at the remains—he would catch up soon enough, and she didn't want to waste time. Nicholas might be following and, if he caught her, he would drag her back to the castle and lock her in for a month.

The River Slitrig ambled by, stark against her hurried pace. Its babble brought her both comfort and angst—she'd once loved the sound of water, but becoming a redcape stained her in more ways than one. It had darkened her heart and clouded her soul and, like blood poured into the sea, infused her fondness of water with fear.

Since leaving Bergen, Margaret had felt lost. Norway was her home, not Scotland, and she desperately wanted to find her way back. Back to Bishop Narve, strange as he'd acted. Back to Ingeborg and Eirik and her friends. Back to Bergen.

So, on their journey from the Orkneys, she'd listened for water. She'd gone so far as to ask her captor, who she'd come to know as William I Soulis, for the rivers' names when she saw them. He gave them to her, not caring if she knew where they were.

She found out later why he hadn't cared—it was impossible for her to leave the castle when ordered not to, as he knew it would be.

She turned her palm up and over to examine her fingers, which she'd licked clean of blood, and guilt pierced her heart.

Bishop Narve taught her about the Sacrament of Penance. She knew killing was wrong, that she should confess her sins and make amends for them. And she wanted to, but how could she? There was no priest who would hear her. Besides, she would kill again. To stay alive, she would have to.

She didn't know it when she'd left the castle, but because she'd killed outside of the stone circle instead of inside it, she now needed to kill every few hours instead of once a month; otherwise, the blood in her cape would dry out, and she would die. She didn't know how she would cross the North Sea like this. Where would she find a ship with a large enough crew to sustain her, and how could she pick them off, one by one, with no one noticing? Even if she could, no ship could sail itself, and redcapes feared water for a reason. But she didn't want to think of that. Her heart wept for Norway, for her father, and she would die trying to make her return.

William I had brought her through Hawick before, and she remembered its waters. She listened to the river and decided she was nearly to the parish, where the Slitrig would join with the Teviot.

A shrill call drowned out the gurgling river. Magnus had returned, and he was warning her of something.

The warning came too late.

Someone burst through the trees and shoved her toward the river.

Had Nicholas caught up with her? Or had she been found by murderous whitecapes?

Margaret watched the water rising to meet her in fear.

She reached out her hands. One of her palms struck a rock, and she cried out, but she kept her arms locked and held herself over the river, trying to keep her cape from getting wet.

The shover pressed down hard on her back, and she crumpled.

The river wasn't deep, but its current was fast. She could feel it sapping the blood from her cape and the life from her body. But even if the cape was washed clean, the water would keep it wet. If she stayed there, she would survive a short while longer.

There was a grunt and the weight on her lifted.

A man dragged her attacker to dry shore and returned for her, towing her with gentle hands.

Through slitted eyes, she mistook him for Bishop Narve.

Had he come to rescue her after almost two years?

She opened her mouth to confess to him her sins and saw it wasn't the bishop, but William I Soulis, wearing his crown of teeth and standing between her and his son, Nicholas II Soulis.

Margaret had lost too much blood to the river. The water had washed out her cape's oils and blood; as the water evaporated, she was dying. She struggled to follow the conversation, even to breathe, and her eyes blurred staring at Nicholas's knee, which was stained red from pressing down on her back.

"This is *her* doing, isn't it? *Ermengarde.* She wormed her way into your mind..." Nicholas's eyes were as dark as the crown of teeth on William's head.

"She's your mother, Nicholas—" William said something about Ermengarde, his wife. Something about a white cape and a silver sword.

And Nicholas did the unthinkable: he slung a knife, serrated and inlaid with human teeth, at his father's stomach.

Shock registered on William's face. He didn't look down at the blade stuck inside him. He stared at Nicholas in disbelief. Then, as if waking, he stumbled close to Margaret.

He used the last of his strength to yank the knife from his abdomen. A cape seemed to shimmer behind him, a white ghost. A trick of the light.

The crown unlatched itself and fell from his head.

Blood spurted from his wound, and Margaret's cape guzzled it up. She had no love for William, but in that moment, she felt she could have. It was the closest she'd come to it since setting foot in Scotland—but it didn't stop her from taking his blood and his flesh and gorging herself on his bones.

Invigorated, Margaret made to run, but Nicholas's voice echoed through her skull: *Don't move.*

She badly wanted to. She was still a child, but the cape gave her strength; her legs were muscled, and she knew she could outrun the wizard. But no redcape could fight the crown, which he'd taken for himself. Nor could she remove her cape, for it was anchored to her body like a fifth limb, attached to the flesh of her neck, and its amputation meant instantaneous death.

William I was dead, and she was alone with Nicholas. Without other redcapes to influence, with his focus solely on her, he could likely kill her if he wanted to.

She expected it; after all, he'd attempted it minutes before. He was less attached to her than his own father, and he'd killed him without qualms.

He took the knife in his hands and held it over her, noticeably distraught. But in the end, he spared her. She couldn't say why. She didn't understand it.

On the way back to the castle, Margaret caught glimpses of Magnus through the branches, free and flying, and listened to the river. *Where are you going?* it seemed to ask, and the canopy grew too thick for her to see her eagle.

Warm tears rained from her red eyes as blood had from William a half hour past.

Home had never felt farther away.

CHAPTER THREE

Friars in black copes trundled toward the priory like thick blood.

Margaret bumped into one of them, and he looked down at her. His nose was hooked and his mouth open; he had a slight gap between his teeth. His resemblance to Bishop Narve was strong and made stronger by his cope—a shadow against a gold candle, an invitation before betrayal.

She instinctively shied away from him, hid her face beneath the crimson hood of her cape, and pressed her lips together to hide her inhuman canines. He made no move toward her but may as well have for her horrified reaction.

Without a word, she sprinted from him toward the coast. He didn't run after her, nor did he sound an alarm. Perhaps he hadn't noticed her ever-present scent of blood and aura of death.

As she scurried through the streets of Edinburgh, Margaret kept away from people as best she could and tried not to meet anyone's eyes, for surely they would notice the red sheen in her own and think her a demon or a monster.

She lowered her lashes. Would they be wrong for thinking it?

For the thousandth time, she wished she could take off her cape. But for better or worse—likely worse—it was a part of her now. It had been for two years, and it would be until she died.

The Waters of Leith guided her to the town of Leith, where fishing yoals and dug-out canoes had been dragged onto the shingle beach. The ship bound for Norway was where her friend Robin said it would be, and she was right on time. Its sailors were hauling wooden crates on board and preparing for departure. With any luck, she could sneak on and hide away until they were on the other side of the North Sea.

She waited on a knoll of marram grass near a shell midden and hurried to embark when she saw an opportunity. Fear flooded through her with each crashing wave and gust of sea-crusted wind. Rippling water and creaking wood sounded as she walked onto the bridge. She gulped and swayed and took a cautious step forward.

Her stomach jolted. Was this seasickness?

She took another step and her head throbbed. Her brain numbed, and black overtook her vision. She lost control of her body, only vaguely aware that she'd fallen back to land and toppled over.

I can't, she thought, and a feeling like being trapped closed in around her.

When her sight returned, it came with voices. She half expected them to say she was dying as they had the last time she'd fainted near the sea, but they spoke of her cape.

"—soaked in blood!" one of the sailors exclaimed. Another said, "Look—her eyes!"

They reached for her.

There were so many. Too many. Could she fight them all? Maybe, but not disoriented as she was.

"Please," she stammered, but that made it worse. They saw her teeth, and her fear was realized.

"She's not human... a demon!"

There were shouts to kill her or to run, and Margaret pushed herself up with effort.

A man swung a club at her like she was a wild animal, and those who hadn't fled closed in from behind with various weapons or raised hands.

A red cape swirled before her. It belonged to Alianora Comyn, one of three co-alphas of Clan Elliot.

Alianora held a heart in her hands. She turned it to blood and sprayed it over the sailors. They stopped their advance and blinked up at her in confusion—she was tall for a woman, taller than most men—and she whisked Margaret away.

"What have you done to them?"

"I've made them forget us." Alianora pulled her farther from shore.

"I'm meant to be on that ship." She tugged against her, but not hard.

"You're a redcape, Margaret, made on Scottish soil. You can't leave Scotland, none of us can."

Some part of her knew it, had realized it when she fell back to the earth. "Nicholas can."

"You may call him Lord Soulis. And he's a sorcerer, not a redcape."

"And you're both," she realized, but the realization felt fuzzy in her mind, as if she'd forgotten sorcery existed... but how could she have when a sorcerer had changed her from an innocent girl to a bloodthirsty redcape?

Yes, the young William had changed her. She hadn't thought of that since... when? Since it happened?

Alianora sized her up. "Yes, but sorcery has its limits. I can bind flesh, memories, and objects..." she added wistfully. "Even time. But not even I can undo what's been done to us."

They rode back toward Edinburgh on bad roads and Margaret tried to recall what they'd spoken of. Alianora was a redcape and something else, but what?

The memory lay in a shallow grave, uncoverable if she knew where it was buried. When she couldn't find it, she accused Alianora: "You followed me here."

"Of course not. My brother's been summoned to England, and I accompanied him from Perth to Edinburgh. You simply weren't careful; a friar saw you. A loyal one, luckily."

She thought Alianora was in Irvine. Must have been the month before. "You said you can't go to England."

"No, I meant to part with him farther on, before the border, but I left preemptively to pursue you." Her breath tickled Margaret's ear. "It's been almost a month since my last libation. Yours must have been recent for you to attempt this... Nevertheless, it seems we're both Hermitage bound."

Margaret's shoulders fell.

Back to the clan she hadn't wanted to be a part of, the boy who turned her into a sanguivorous monster and damned her soul, and the Soulis's castle, where some ancient thing mingled with the earthy notes of moss and bone, something buried and resurrected in feeling: death. The castle, a place guarded by thistles and crawling with darkness that she could never truly escape.

CHAPTER FOUR

On the stones of a now-ruined castle, Nicholas II Soulis's blood ran. It streamed in smooth lines over slabs of rock and seeped into dirt, where waves of gore had surged months before when the English sacked Berwick and massacred nearly eight thousand children, women, and men—tradesmen, merchants, burgesses. Their corpses were gone now, buried deep below or taken by the sea, but the feel of tragedy weighed down the air like a black, oozing mass.

From Nicholas's lolling head, the crown of teeth loosened and fell, uninterested in capping a dead man, and called to William II, who stood over his father.

William's eyes were smiling, but they quickly changed and widened in horror. His body slackened, and a sorcerer's blade dropped from his hand. It was coated in bright, fresh blood.

This wasn't him. He hadn't done it. It was Abaddon.

He didn't remember travelling to Berwick. He didn't even know Nicholas would be there; after paying homage in Berwick a month prior, he'd gone to London with Edward I of England, and there'd been no word of his return.

William beheld his fingers and his clothes and felt his face. Red streaks and splatters were everywhere, drying on his skin, staining his soul.

Had Abaddon done it? William had prayed for this, hadn't he? Even if the demon possessed him to commit the actual act, he'd committed it first in his heart, and it would be a lie to say he wasn't glad Nicholas was dead.

Guilt's poison spread through him.

His grandfather was wrong. He could never be a whitecape. He could never be good.

He had killed his father, just as Nicholas had killed William I. In the end, none of them could escape the burdens of their line.

William bitterly took the diadem. His touch smeared its teeth with his father's blood.

He set it on his head, and it clamped down, but he'd retreated into himself, wallowing in darkness and self-pity, and the pain barely reached him.

Chapter Five

Caught in the rain under a slate-coloured evening sky, a man sought to take shelter in what looked like an abandoned castle, its door wide open as if it waited for him. He'd seen many a stronghold in his time, having travelled a good bit, but this one seemed particularly menacing and peculiarly dark—not just in view, but in feel.

The only comforting thing about it, to the man, was the grass along its edges—the fact that life flourished in a place where he could sense only death.

He went through the door into an unfurnished, gloom-filled room, of which he could see little. The dim light died soon after the threshold and was crunched by the high, open windowsills.

A rotten smell clogged his nostrils. He coughed, breathed through his mouth, and debated turning back, but he was already half soaked. He could endure the terrible smell for a while—until the rain let up—if it meant staying healthy. He could hardly walk miles through the fields if he fell ill.

A stifled cry echoed through the castle. It sounded like a scream.

He froze to listen, but all he heard was raindrops breaking on stone. It must have been a trick of fright, or maybe a bird humanized by his unease.

Still, he couldn't help but think he was trespassing on some black laird's domain. The very thought, in the waning light, made his heart beat faster.

He moved to sit down near the door and cursed his folly; his own footsteps made him jump, and even the water dripping from his hair and clothes seemed to splash on the floor too loudly. He felt hunted, though he kept telling himself he was alone.

Of course, he wasn't alone.

Gray light touched the entry, where the man leaned against a wall. In the gloom behind him, a figure crowned with antlers and draped in red slinked forward.

The man didn't sense the movement. He stared out over the bleak, ever-darkening woods and moorlands and saw something gliding through the sky: a golden eagle cutting through the grayness. It dropped low, flew around the side of the castle, and landed in a window.

Quiet against the heavy rain, the figure was almost upon him. The sound of damp fabric dragging on rock was too close not to hear; the man turned and saw the monster.

Clawed hands yanked out his teeth as he opened his mouth to scream.

He watched half his face disappear into a strong, bone-crushing jaw—the jaw of a human. A girl with animal teeth.

As his bones snapped into pieces between large, sharp canines, he saw no more.

Margaret, now fifteen years old, shredded the traveller's body. She tore into his bones and flesh, and her cape hungrily drank in his pouring blood. Before long, all that remained of him were his intestines, left for the common buzzards.

She held out her arm for Magnus, and from the darkness, her clan materialized. Their lust for blood was palpable, and she gladly led them from the castle to satiate it; she leapt forward with fresh blood shining on her cape, and her eagle took to the sky once more.

One of her antler-crowned co-alphas, Alianora Comyn, ran beside her, and the clan chased after. Margaret didn't look back, but she could feel them there, moving together as limbs connected to one body, one predator covered in teeth. A merciless hunter.

William II told them where to hunt, and they could go far. Nourishment was the only problem in travel for a redcape, as they could walk for days on end, although those with self-control weren't foolish enough to venture far from Ninestane. Or, if they were, they didn't last long before withering to blood. Sometimes, however, it was necessary, as Liddesdale had become known for its lawlessness. When people who went there were never seen again, others grew wary and made up stories about fairies living in the castle. The more realistic blamed wild wolves, so capes had to travel farther to find libations—though they occasionally happened upon beaters driving game through the forests, or the archers and spearmen they drove it toward.

William used to choose locations with the king, Alianora's brother, John Balliol, until he was deposed. Now he chose them with someone whose identity he refused to disclose; whether they based their decisions on politics, to keep the populace from learning of the redcapes' existence, or to ensure blood wells near home didn't run dry, Margaret didn't much care. There would always be Scots and Englishmen, at least for the alphas. If she didn't find it herself, someone would always bring her blood.

She preferred to track down and kill English officers, who did and took what they wanted and kept Scotland under their thumb as capes under a crown. But she also liked to participate in hunts with the clan, particularly those in areas she'd never been to like this one. William chose to send them to Erceldoune this time, a small village not obscenely far from Hermitage, farther north than Hawick and even Melrose. They would hit both towns on the way back so as not to take too much from one place.

Erceldoune wasn't so far for a redcape, but it would still take the night. As Margaret had given in to temptation and eaten the traveller, she needed to see to her cape's care or she wouldn't make the journey. So Magnus helped her find a straggler in the wildwood. She drew the boy to Ninestane Rig, ate him, and caught up with the others.

They took a predetermined route in order to pass over streams on redcape bridges or rivers on ferryboats. Redcape crossings were packed with Scottish soil. It was the only way for them to cross water, something

Margaret learned on her first far-off hunt three years after donning her cape. It was also the day she learned she couldn't trust anyone, not fully; until then, she'd trusted Alianora. That was the day she realized she'd lied to her. Alianora said they couldn't leave Scotland, but they could. With Scottish soil, they could. For two years after that, Margaret made several attempts to board a ship with a vial of soil and cross the North Sea to Bergen, but she'd never made it. She bridled the dream when Leith was captured by the English and gave it up when news of her father's death reached Scotland.

Her clan's timing was perfect. Beyond Leader's silver tide, they reached Erceldoune shortly before dawn.

Were they closer to Ninestane, they would eat their fill without care, but as they couldn't safely kill so far from the stone circle, this was more of a herd than a hunt, a picking off of unsuspecting villagers and saving them for later. They watched as the people of Erceldoune thawed and rose with the cold sun, which shone dimly in a sky clotted with clouds, and they worked to separate loners from the village.

A woman feeding her animals was swept away without a noise. Large hands snatched a child off the ground, and she released the twig she'd been toying with, too frightened to cry out. Margaret called to a man for help and, when he walked beneath a tree searching for the woman in need, he found himself trapped in the clutches of a redcape.

It took all the willpower Margaret had not to dig into their prey then and there. She could feel his blood pumping fast, the warmth of his skin... Her cape shuddered. She wanted him, now.

Robin, her friend and mentor, approached her with a worried expression.

"What is it?"

"It's Henry," he breathed heavily. "He gave in."

She rushed after Robin toward the west side of Erceldoune, crushing grasses and webs beneath her boots. Her cape fluttered like the dark leaves around her, moving over thorns and sliding between slim branches. Unwilling to be snagged, it dodged the obstacles of the forest along with her as a living part of herself.

Henry was a sharp-clawed, gory mess. He gnawed an arm in a frenzy, having already dug into the human's stomach and hollowed out her chest. Blood trailed down his neck and streamed back up, overruling gravity to join with the cape affixed to his nape.

Margaret kicked him hard in the back.

Henry fell forward, and the dead woman's ribs crunched, but he wasn't fazed. He scrambled for a detached rib, swallowed it down, and reached for another.

"You foul, lowly man," Margaret growled. She grabbed his shoulders so forcefully they might have drilled into his flesh, forced him around, and punched him in the nose.

His blood gushed and mixed with the human's, and he cowered from Margaret, raised his arm before his face, but she kneed him in the stomach and went for his face once more.

His eyelids flickered at the level of her boots, and he lay there, whimpering, as she asked, "Do you want to die?"

"No," he spluttered, blood bubbling from his mouth.

"Then why did you kill her?"

"I was hungry."

"We're all hungry, Henry." Margaret stomped on his left shoulder and imagined it was hers. She'd given in time and time again, but no one would punish her for it because she was an alpha, a queen among capes.

She ground her heel until she heard something break, then she turned back to Robin. "Get three more." That should keep him alive until they reached Ninestane.

When she turned her back on him, she heard Henry dragging himself back toward the corpse. She nearly turned again but snorted in disgust and walked forward.

Let him eat, the weakling. Let him eat and know he would be forever lost to temptation and darkness, and let him hate himself for it.

Margaret made her way back toward the bank of Leader Water to meet with the other capes.

In the village, a man held a wooden effigy in hands that should have been more weathered and wrinkled at his age, but the work in his life was of a different sort, so his hands were soft, and his skin seemed young for a man nearly eighty. His deepest wrinkle lay at an angle between his brows, and it had been there most of his life, cleaved deeper by each vision and every lie his smooth tongue wished it could speak.

He looked from the effigy to the redcape alpha, a slash of red cutting farther away. With glassy, knowing eyes, the Scottish laird said: "My sand is run; my thread is spun; this sign regardeth me."

He knew—the time had come for him to leave his tower, to leave his estate to the convent of Soltra, convene with the Brus, and pursue the Scots' lost lady.

CHAPTER SIX

Margaret strode into the hall in the southwest wing of Hermitage Castle. She ignored the humans' muted cries—they were crowded in the cellar, waiting for their inevitable deaths—and took her place on one of three thrones at the front of the room.

The thrones were made of polished human teeth and decorated with desiccated blood shards, cracked from dried pools, good blood wasted. They made her cringe every time she saw them; there shouldn't be three, but one. Hers.

After all, she was the heir to Scotland, a born queen. A throne was her birthright—her mother's final gift. If she couldn't have the throne she was meant for, she should at least have this one.

She hated that she had to share it, especially when Alianora seemed to care so little—as a sorceress, she could conceal what she was, to a degree, and live an existence outside of the one most redcapes were confined to. Alianora flitted back and forth between Hermitage and Edinburgh and who knew where else, and Margaret wandered the woods alone, watching humans from a distance. It was like watching ghosts, but worse, because her ghost was happier than she was.

And her third co-alpha, Alice Elliot, was an idiot through and through, prone to bouts of kindness and fits of tears. The only reason she was an alpha, whether she knew it or not, was because she was a harlot. Margaret knew she'd gone into William's apartments on more than one occasion, and Nicholas's when he was alive, and she was quite sure the girl Alice held in her arms, a human born months before, belonged to

25

William II. Her position had nothing to do with Alianora, who was her mother, because Alianora didn't care one whit about her.

Sadly, there had always been three alphas, the strongest women of the clan, with the exception, perhaps for the first time in history, of one: Alice. But Margaret's wish was for that to change, and why couldn't it? If she could find a way to eliminate Alianora and Alice, the clan would recognize her for what she was—a true leader. Their true queen.

She sighed. It was a dream, a fantasy. She'd fought Alianora before—many clan members had. No one could best her.

Alice perched beside her on the centre throne. At thirty-one, Alice was twenty-two years younger than Alianora, though she looked a mite older, and the same age as Margaret's father. For many years, Margaret longed to see him again, but, living in Hermitage Castle, where mothers raised children on their own and men were used to hunt and breed, she had learned to miss him less. Still, something about the sight before her brought phantom wisps of longing into her heart: there was a soft expression in Alice's eyes as she looked at her daughter, a protective closeness.

Margaret didn't say anything to her but picked dried blood from under a fingernail and consciously shifted her attention to the young.

They attacked each other violently among gnaw-marked bones, scratched at eyes and jabbed at ribs. One of the girls, four years old, was particularly vicious. Hours before, she'd killed a boy two years her elder.

It was the way of things. Male redcapes were weaker, and the boy hadn't grown fast enough to survive. The girl, on the other hand, was the dominant child in her natal clan and would likely do well when she was grown.

Alianora arrived and stood before the final throne. Her long, rose-blonde hair didn't stick to the bloodied fabric of her cape but remained unsullied and, in the dim, cool light, looked as metallic as the blood smelled.

"It's time," Alianora said. Time for their monthly libation and to welcome Alice's daughter, Ermengarde, to the clan.

Margaret and Alice rose.

The other redcapes ushered the humans—most of them from the hunt, a few that were sentenced to death by Lord Soulis—from the castle and followed the three alphas two miles northeast to the circle of nine standing stones. William met them there, his face hard as sarsen. The crown of teeth biting into his head emanated power and kept the redcapes from approaching him.

As night fell, Alice knelt in the centre with her baby.

This was Margaret's first joining as an alpha, which meant the choosing of the redcape sacrifice was in her hands.

She scanned the faces outside the circle, lit by the full moon. She gave Robin a half smile when her eyes met his. Though he was weak for a redcape—he looked borderline malnourished—he'd risen among the ranks and was well established. He would not die today. As her friend, he would not die ever if she had anything to say about it.

"Henry," she called.

Henry was one of the lowest-ranking men in Clan Elliot and the least controlled. No doubt he expected his end was near, but he stepped forward with his head bowed, submissive as a man should be.

"What you do not have." Margaret walked around Henry and severed his cape from his neck with her bare hands.

He collapsed, and his cape and body dissolved into blood. The ground drank it in. His heart remained a moment. It burst, and it, too, was gone, but something was left behind.

An ivory tooth from an ancient beast.

Margaret picked it up, held it in her palm, and whispered, "Will be taken from you."

And given to another, one more deserving who could strengthen the clan.

She knelt before Ermengarde and her cape settled around her in crimson ripples.

Alice smiled at the infant in her arms, but the smile didn't reach her eyes, and Margaret pressed the tooth into the baby's mouth. She swallowed it easily—a good sign, as so many choked on the teeth and died on the spot.

William brought one of the humans into the circle. Before Ermengarde, he ripped into the man's chest and sliced his veins wide. Blood spilled from his body and wove into a cape, which bonded with the baby's neck. Only a sorcerer could complete this part of the ritual, the cape fastening.

Ermengarde's eyes glowed red and her cheeks warmed. She didn't giggle as redcapes often did, but she silently turned her face into her mother.

"You did well," Alice praised her daughter.

Margaret raised her chin, pleased with herself, and the redcapes prepared to take their libations.

She'd eaten someone just shy of an hour before, and her mouth was starting to feel dry. If she went much longer without blood, after killing outside of Ninestane, she would die. But killing in the circle was different. The stone sorceresses fused the blood with their oily capes and allowed them to survive another month without libations; for that reason, it was risky to travel more than half a month's journey from Ninestane.

One by one, redcapes slaughtered humans, ate them in the circle, and soaked their capes in tides of blood.

CHAPTER SEVEN

"I don't want to do this again."

Grimhild's eyes were stony. "Do it, Gudrun."

She couldn't refuse her mother. She'd disobeyed her once and lost days of her life because of it; memories stolen in an instant, lost unless she could find some item or person or place she couldn't remember that could pull them back from her mind's abyss.

"Forgive me," she beseeched the girl gagged and bound next to her murdered brother.

Gudrun drove the blade into the girl's fleshy stomach. She then slit her throat, wishing she'd done that first, and grabbed her serrated blade from its place on the floor, where she'd left it after killing the boy. She used it to saw into the girl's chest, to separate the heart from the body, and specked the prayer rope on her wrist with blood in the process.

Once the heart was out, she ran her thumbs over its pericardium. It felt tough and tight, but she knew how to make it give.

The heart bled to nothing, and something within her bled, too.

"Another," she whispered.

Grimhild obliged and handed her the first heart: the boy's.

Gudrun felt its pull, or the pull of something dark within her. She knew she shouldn't partake. She *wanted* to leave it all behind, to stop practicing sorcery and forget she ever had. But she couldn't. Somehow, through Grimhild's urging or her own, she always found herself back here, gripping a heart, hoping she could resist the temptation and failing, knowing without remembering that she'd been there before.

She bit into the heart and moaned in painful pleasure. "More. "

"You only killed two."

Killed.

Red burst in her vision.

To hear it said out loud, so blatantly...

"I need—"

"Yes, I will take you," Grimhild said in irritation. "One day, you will stop begging to go and be pleased with what you have done."

Her mother brought her to the religious house in the centre of the city and thrust her in with the priest, who could reconcile her with the community. She was afraid to tell him what she'd done but, somehow, he already knew.

Her penance should have been lifelong and public, but Grimhild and the priest had an arrangement, substituting fines for punishment.

Fines didn't seem enough for what she had done.

A tear mixed with the blood on her hands. She'd half expected the blood to dissolve before her eyes, to wash away with her sins and leave her skin as clean as her newly purified heart. But it didn't, and her heart didn't feel clean. It felt marked with darkness like an adder coiled in her chest. If only she could cut it out.

"There, you're absolved. Now cease, your sobs grate on my ears."

Through the water and her quick-blinking eyes, Gudrun saw her mother produce another heart. She wanted to reach for it, to swallow it down and go back to confession. Before she could, Grimhild distracted her with a coin, silver and etched with the profile of a felled Arverni chieftain, and sprinkled her with heart blood.

"Come, Gudrun. We are to dine with your brothers."

Gudrun pressed her soaked lashes together and water streamed down her hot face. She couldn't remember why she'd been crying, so she dried her eyes and rushed after her mother.

Chapter Eight

A redcape was before Margaret one second and gone the next, murdered by a whitecape with blank features who guarded the entrance to the castle, where the portcullises gaped open. Never before had they infiltrated the castle, and they mightn't have if the portcullises had been lowered. Why weren't they?

Margaret sprinted away from him and whirled around a corner. William II Soulis was there with a heart in his hand.

They locked eyes.

Had she been in this situation with him before? She felt she had, but she couldn't remember when. At a cape attachment? No. But it had to have been—that was the only time she ever saw him holding hearts, or saw him in general.

Another cape flashed bright as a ghost in the dark, and a deep gash opened in William's stomach. He bit into the heart and the wound started to heal.

The whitecape went at him again.

William's massive fist sent the man reeling into unconsciousness. By the time he'd eaten it whole, there was no sign he'd been injured, and he bent over the whitecape with a sharp tool in his hand.

A second man with a large nose came at him from the side, weapon raised, momentarily distracting William from heart harvesting.

Margaret's arm hairs rose, and she felt someone behind her.

She ducked in time to avoid a blade slicing at her neck, an attempt to dislodge her cape from her body.

Her jaws closed around her attacker's arm, a woman with a round face and steely eyes. Delicious, if poisonous, blood gushed between her teeth. She sent her hand into the woman's stomach and wrenched life from her body.

"Margaret," a voice whispered.

Alice?

The alpha brought Margaret back the way she'd come. The whitecape with blank features was gone, but there was no sign of the violence he'd committed. No body or discarded innards from the redcape he'd killed.

She followed her a ways but turned when Alice didn't.

"There are three in the court," Margaret hissed. She'd seen Alianora there, taking out one after another like only she could do. "This way is safer."

"There's someone you need to meet. Hurry, before the attack is over."

She hesitated. That lightheaded woman might lead her to her death.

"Trust me."

Thanks to Alianora's lies, she didn't trust anyone, except maybe Robin, but she was intrigued. She let Alice lead her up the stairs to the Lord of Liddesdale's chambers in the largest tower.

William obviously wasn't there, preoccupied with whitecapes below, but two strangers were: a young man, a whitecape; and an old one, capeless. Another man, not much older than her, entered after them—the whitecape who'd attacked William from the side moments before. There was a gash in his shoulder, but it wasn't deep. He must have run.

Margaret tensed like a wolf readying to take down prey larger than herself and cursed her stupidity. Alice had led her to an ambush, and the timing couldn't be worse. The curse would strike her any minute, and it would leave her vulnerable.

"They won't hurt you," Alice assured her.

She gawked. Whitecapes hunted them, slayed them without mercy, and stole their heart teeth. There had once been sixty-five redcapes and smaller clans throughout Scotland, but thanks to whitecapes, they were down to thirty-seven and a single clan. Of course they would hurt her.

"Margaret," the young man said. His face was long, the space between his nose and longbow-shaped lips wide, and his hair was short and brown with hints of sun-touched gold. One of his hands was bloody from clutching his shoulder. "It's me. Malcolm."

She inclined her head and leaned away from the hurt on his face. She didn't fraternize with whitecapes, and she'd never seen this one before in her life.

The old man rested his arm on Malcolm's shoulder, the uninjured one. "Show to her the effigy."

Margaret backed up against the wall and pressed her hands against its rough stones. Her gaze flicked around the room, glancing off the cushioned chair by the fireplace, the wet windowsill, the guarded door, the weapons and torches hung on the walls, the papers on the table, and the letters pressed with William's barry of six seal.

Her stomach revolted and she doubled over. Her cape pulsed.

The white curse.

Blood spewed from her mouth and she coughed, tasting the whitecape all over again. The second time wasn't as pleasant.

She was fatigued. Her whole body felt sick. Her eyes were wet; they spilled tears of blood.

With her head hanging, the place her cape met with her neck was exposed. Why hadn't they killed her?

She looked up.

Malcolm knelt before her.

She was a pathetic sight, her pale face drenched in bloody vomit, an alpha brought to her knees by the white curse. But Malcolm didn't look disgusted as she thought a whitecape would. He looked concerned.

He glanced at the old man, who nodded, and he held something before her: a wooden effigy of Grimhild, a queen who ruled alongside Gebicca in the fifth century. She was also the first redcape. When she died, the redcape teeth lay dormant, hidden deep within the earth, for over seven hundred years, until Countess Ada Warenne, Cape Mother, dredged them up and brought Clan Elliot to life.

The old man cryptically said, "The name does not belang to he, hither come to plague the land."

Margaret didn't puzzle over that but over the effigy, for she had seen it before. Someone had made her forget, locked memories within her, but the effigy was the key—the last thing she'd seen when someone drizzled heart blood over her.

She stared at the grainy lines of Grimhild's aged, wooden face, at the Burgundian seax clasped between her hands, and memories splashed into her mind like rain returning to the sea.

William I Soulis had introduced her to his grandson, William II. He was ten when she'd met him and shorter than she was. It was strange to think someone so large had once been so small and sweet; for two years, he was like a brother to Margaret. They'd laughed and played, listened to his grandfather's stories, and dreamed of what things would be like when Margaret became Queen of Scots.

That was before she had become a redcape, before William I Soulis died. Before William II had turned dark and said horrible things, like saying he wished Margaret had died instead of the girl used to make her cape of blood. More than once after donning it, Margaret had wished the same thing, but it hurt more to hear it from him.

She took her eyes off the effigy.

"Look once more," the old man said, so she did.

William II gave her a foxglove. Its fuchsia bells cascaded in tiers, and Margaret said they looked like silky fairy dresses. She got sick soon after and was warned not to touch the wildflowers again, and William blamed himself. That gift was the last kindness he showed her, for they neither played together nor talked as friends again.

The memory was replaced by another, another, and another: Nicholas ripping hearts from still-warm bodies, William eating hearts lifted from black and silver caskets, Alianora spraying men with heart blood to make them forget Margaret's presence.

"Do you remember?" Malcolm asked. His eyes matched his hair, warm and molten.

She breathed, "Sorcery," and his face fell.

Who had made her forget it, and why?

Malcolm opened his mouth, but the old man said simply, "In time."

A final shard of a memory reached her, an image of herself with a bleeding heart cupped in her hands.

Grimhild gave up her life as a key and returned to being an effigy, and blood the colour of stale wine forced its way from Margaret's throat.

She smirked as she retched.

A sorceress. She was a sorceress. And now that she'd remembered, she could never forget it again.

"Margaret!" Robin the redcape thudded against the door, and Margaret charged at the man guarding it. But she was still weak, and he got the best of her. Malcolm protested, but she could feel a sharp blade against her cape, seconds from slicing it off.

"Margaret!" Robin yelled again, and Alice said, "She's not here."

After a pause, he left to search for her elsewhere, and his footsteps gradually quieted. With the knife threatening severance, Margaret couldn't call for him to come back. She dared not make a sound.

"Robert." The old man's voice was enough to stay her execution. As if possessed, he stood, and his eyes and tongue plated with silver like frost creeping over stones. He stared ahead with a pupilless gaze. "For thou that now a patient is, and seemeth to be bound, at liberty shall free be set, and with empire be crown'd." The silver receded.

Robert released her.

She rubbed the top of her cape and asked the old man, "Are you a demon?"

But he was halfway out the door, the whitecapes on his heels.

Malcolm met her eyes before he, too, dashed toward the door. His snowy cape melted from sight.

Why had they let her live?

Since the old man was gone, Alice answered for him. "He is Thomas of Erceldoune, a whitecape advisor. He was a friend of their last grand mistress."

"You know him?" Disgust curled within her, not just from the white curse but from the realization that Alice was a traitor. Did William know? Surely not, or Alice would be stripped of her co-alpha status and shunned, left to dry out and rot in their small pit prison, or killed to make way for a new addition to the clan. A more loyal addition.

"He's a renowned prophet. And the only man to take on Michael Scot and live..."

Michael Scot, the Wizard of the North. *Him*, she knew. There were legends about him drinking magical elixirs, summoning demons, and raising the dead. Stories too great to be true, records in the castle that hinted he'd taught sorcery to the Soulis line once upon a time, and perhaps even taught them how to attach the red capes.

Born in the twelfth century, he should have died years ago, but people saw him out or thought they did. He was rumoured to be in Aragorn or Portugal or Italy now, in Palermo or Granada or Naples, but he had ties to Scotland—ties that included an ancient vault of hearts.

Margaret was a sorceress... If she could find that vault, she could become the only queen. With hearts so old and dark as the ones Scot must own, she might be able to challenge Alianora and scatter the teeth of the two extraneous thrones. Or grind them to dust between her own.

Her cape wrung blotchy liquid out through her smiling mouth. A lack of blood made her head prickle and her vision double. Ironically, the abandoned effigy was the last thing she saw before she collapsed, and the shouts coming from outside the thin windows faded to nothing.

For three days, Margaret fought fever and expelled blood.

Alianora visited her once. Annoyingly, she was immune to the white curse. She could kill whitecape after whitecape and remain unaffected, so she was usually the one who fielded whitecape attacks while the others scattered and hid like frightened voles. It was the only downside Margaret could see to Alianora's frequent travelling—when she was gone, the attacks were brutal.

Aged hearts, black hearts, the sort Michael Scot collected, were the one hope she had of taking on Alianora and winning. With only the darkest heart could Margaret ensure the memory alteration would work against a sorceress as powerful as her, and she could think of no other way to fight her than from the inside out.

Once Alianora was out of the way, she would snap Alice between her teeth as easily as a dried, brittle bone. Acquiring or destroying the crown of teeth would be next, and she was certain she could do it: she could use the knowledge of her friendship with William to her advantage, lure him into a false sense of security, and steal the diadem. Then nothing and no one would be able to keep her from searching for the papers that proved who she was and the thing she truly wanted: her freedom.

She would do anything—whatever it took—to find a way out, to be free of the castle and William and Ninestane. She would escape, announce to the world who she was, and claim the queenship John Balliol took from her a decade ago. She would reign and never again feel imprisoned.

The clan members periodically brought Margaret blood to replenish what she lost until, finally, the pangs in her cape subsided and she could keep a fully grown human down. Her strength returned enough for her to travel to the standing stones, where she took a libation, having beat the white curse.

Margaret's eagle pecked at a rabbit he'd slain behind a stone, and she stared at the ground where a young woman had just died. There was no sign of blood in the grass, no stains in the dirt. The cape had sucked in every drop.

She could sense the standing stones all around her, sorceresses petrified thousands of years before. They watched her without eyes, and she wondered what their stories were, who had changed them, and why. Perhaps they'd done it to themselves, chosen to become a part of the earth, to exist forever half alive.

She felt she could relate to them, but she didn't know why. She hadn't chosen this life, William forced it upon her.

Why had he done it? Was it some sort of revenge, a scorned child upset at having ruined a friendship? Had his father put him up to it? Why did the Soulises attach capes anyway?

Her head ached. Try as she might, she couldn't remember exactly what had happened. Had someone made her forget her cape fastening? Had William?

She didn't realize how long she'd been standing there until Magnus's claws cinched around her shoulder. Like the blood, there was no trace of the rabbit; the eagle had eaten it completely.

His feathers brushed her ear as he gently preened. She tilted her head away from him and dislodged a thought. If Michael Scot truly had a connection with the Soulis family, the private library in Hermitage Castle might provide insight into where he'd built his vault.

Chapter Nine

Gudrun gulped in clean, spring air as she raced through the maze of bud-breaking vines.

She'd spotted her brothers and their armies from afar, moving fast toward the capital. There would be a feast tonight to celebrate their return, and she would pour Falernian wine down Gundaharius's throat and convince him to take her on the next raid. She was fourteen now, and a sorceress. She could be useful.

If they didn't allow her, she would go anyway. She would follow them and prove her power and intelligence or go to stay with Giselher's wife in Vindobona. Either way, she couldn't bear to be with her mother any longer. Grimhild was doing something to her, making her forget things... She couldn't trust her memory anymore. She couldn't trust herself. Sometimes, Gudrun felt she didn't know herself at all.

By the time she'd climbed the highest hill on the Rhine's left side, the one Borbetomagus was built on, pain was gnawing at her sides, and her lungs were crying out for air. She slowed to a fast walk, glancing sideways at the stone, rectangular buildings spaced within the city's walls. It had once been a Celtic oppidum, though none of their structures remained, then a Roman garrison turned city. Gundaharius took it a year after Gudrun was born. She grew up there, but she didn't care to stay. She wanted to be with her brothers, to help them fortify and expand the kingdom their father, Gebicca, built. And when she'd done all she could, she wanted to take up her home in the forest or the mountains. Somewhere she couldn't feel them all around—treasure-chest bodies protecting warm hearts, hearts that begged her to free them with every beat.

She scrambled atop the low, stacked-stone wall.

"There you are. You look monstrous."

Gudrun flinched at her mother's voice.

"We have to fix your appearance. There's someone here for you."

"Who?"

"Him. He is called Sigurd."

She followed Grimhild's eyes to the army drumming up the hill. Her brothers led the pack with someone else, a man she'd never met. She was immediately mesmerized by him.

His fair hair was long and parted in the centre. It flowed behind him like golden water. His perfect teeth shone at the eldest of the three Burgundian kings, Gundomar I. His reins were caught between large, callused hands, and his lion-capped sword seemed to be sheathed in a soft, white comet.

He was a stag among beasts, beautiful and bright, as if light pulsed through his veins instead of dark human blood. Could he be one of those fabled few? Someone with a pure heart, a heart that could safeguard another?

She'd never met someone like that. What would his blood taste like? What would it do to her?

No, he was too perfect. Besides, she'd never killed anyone and she didn't want to start now—that was her mother's realm. Grimhild supplied the hearts and Gudrun didn't want to know where she got them.

Gudrun took in Sigurd's every detail as he approached: his straight-backed torso, his muscular arms, the goldwork dragons on his linen tunic. His hair and skin were gilded by the afternoon light. What colour were his eyes? She couldn't tell from afar but imagined they were clear-sky blue or flawless silver to match—that was what he was, blue-glowing silver beside dull copper or dented iron.

She didn't want just his heart; she wanted all of him, for him to be hers. She wanted to know him.

Grimhild smiled smugly and pulled her from the wall.

She didn't argue. She didn't want to meet Sigurd looking like she did. Her rosy hair had escaped its coiled chignon long ago, her sleeve was torn, and her round face was specked and smudged with dirt.

No, she wanted him to notice her. For that to happen, she would need to look as beautiful as he did.

All thought of leaving Borbetomagus left her. For the first time, she didn't drag her feet as she followed Grimhild; she glided eagerly behind her, carried by some sun-infused breeze.

CHAPTER TEN

"I need access to William's library."

"Ask him for it. I don't see why he should object."

"He'll ask questions."

"You want access without him knowing you have it. Why?"

"I know you can get the key," Margaret said in a low voice. "If you don't help me—"

Her teeth snapped the sentence in two. She wouldn't go so far as to tell William that Alice was a whitecape sympathizer, that Margaret suspected she was the one who kept the portcullises raised and let the white vermin into the castle. She didn't want to involve him in redcape business, not when she planned to take care of the problem herself, eventually. And to threaten physical violence might earn Lord Soulis's wrath, as Margaret didn't give empty threats. Then again, it might not; William was habitually apathetic.

"I'll do it; there's no need for threats."

Alice was thick, but even she had a sense of self-preservation.

Alice pushed herself off her throne and scooped Ermengarde up from where she sat with her natal clan and Magnus, who had taken a liking to the child and pecked at anyone who came too close to her. He flew to Margaret when she held out her arm.

Curious as to Alice's motivation for siding with the whitecapes, she decided to voice her suspicions about the portcullises—why shouldn't Alice give answers as freely as her time? So she did, then asked, "Are you afraid of them? Is that it?"

Alice laughed. "No, I'm not afraid of them."

Margaret flushed. She wouldn't have blamed her for it. At least that was a thing she could understand. "Then why would you let them in? And if you're on their side, why are you so willing to help me with this?"

"Because I'm on your side, too. I know you better than you think. You're a lot like me and," she paused, ignoring the offended look on Margaret's face, "my son."

"Andrew." She'd heard about him a few years before, a young man named Andrew Moray. Alice left him and her husband behind after donning her cape and spoke of him only because he was wounded at the Battle of Stirling Bridge and news of his death reached her.

"No. A different son."

"I didn't know you had another."

"You..." Alice held her eyes a moment before her gaze dropped down. "Wait for me here."

The door muffled Alice's and William's voices and Ermengarde's ten-month-old babble. It was but a minute before she returned with a silver key, and Margaret tailed her to the library on the floor beneath Lord Soulis's numerous apartments.

The library hadn't changed since she'd gone there as a child with William, something she'd forgotten until seeing the effigy of Grimhild. It was strange being there, like stepping back in time or into another life. She could see books falling open in William's hands and herself seated before him on the floor, staring at the inked words upside down. She'd never minded reading, not during her schooling in Norway and not when she had the occasional chance here, but she preferred when William read poems and stories and snippets of scholarly research aloud to her.

"Margaret?" Robin stood in a corner of the room, a stack of books beside him. "What are you doing here?"

If she'd known he had access to the library, she would have asked his help instead of Alice's. She trusted him far more than her co-alpha.

"I can take it from here," she said to Alice, who hesitated before walking back out the door. "I need to find information on Michael Scot."

The inner corners of Robin's eyes twitched almost imperceptibly. "The wizard?"

"Yes, you've heard of his vault..." She explained to him her newfound sorceress status, asked him not to tell anyone. He agreed without pause; of course he did, he was her greatest supporter. He believed that she could wrest them both from Hermitage, even before she had a decent plan for doing it.

"Have you read anything that might help?"

He started to shake his head but scrunched his eyebrows instead. "There might be something..."

He led her around a case, past chairs and a table stained with something dark, to a black-painted armaria crowded with scrolls. Labels were written beneath each, and they scanned them carefully.

Margaret drew a scroll from its sheath, labelled not with words but with three chevrons, the arms of the Soulis family.

The scroll documented the lives of the Lords of Liddesdale. It told first of Ranulph I Soulis, of his and his fellow Normans' recruitment by the Prince of Cumbria, David I, of their journey from France to Cumbria and Ranulph's from Cumbria to Great Doddington. David gave Annandale to Robert Brus, and Liddesdale to Ranulph, where he built Liddel Castle in the typical Norman, motte-and-bailey way and sparked the growing of the village of Castleton. Ranulph's brother, William, had followed him to Scotland; William's son, Ranulph II, succeeded him as the Lord of Liddesdale.

Ranulph II was the first practicing sorcerer in the family, taught by Michael Scot. He was murdered. Next was Fulco Soulis, one of the factions of the Comyns. He was also murdered. Then there was Nicholas I, the princerna regis of Alexander II. Not only did the scroll identify Alexander as King of Scotland, but also Grand Master of Whitecapes.

Who was their current grand master? She'd dwelled on the whitecapes before, but she'd never known who any of them were.

How many kings had been whitecapes? John Balliol certainly wasn't, or if he was, he wasn't like the others. He'd married a sorceress, and Alianora had once hinted at his past involvement with the Soulis lords and Clan Elliot. Was Alexander that sort of king, the sort who used sorcerers and redcapes to his own ends? If that were a goal of whitecapes, why did they hunt reds at all? Were there many whitecape clans, each with a different purpose? When did whitecapes originate anyway?

It didn't matter. They were there now, and they would keep coming for her. As long as she had a crimson cape, she was a target.

Her eyes refocused on the script. Nicholas I built Hermitage Castle, and Michael Scot later fortified it with the help of a summoned, unnamed demon. As were his black-hearted predecessors, Nicholas was murdered, and William I became Lord of Liddesdale. He married a whitecape named Ermengarde and was murdered.

Margaret remembered it like it was yesterday. He'd saved her life. It seemed odd to see his own laid out in a few lines of ink, like he hadn't been living flesh and flowing blood a few years prior. Like he was nothing.

She skipped over Nicholas II, because he really was nothing. William II succeeded him, and the scroll paused there.

A few mentions of Scot, but nothing useful.

"Do you have anything?"

"I might. Look at this." Robin quickly walked to the stained table and unrolled a different scroll. "It was penned by Ranulph II Soulis."

Robin pointed to a paragraph and summarized what Margaret was partway through reading: "Michael Scot battled Thomas of Erceldoune on Eildon Hill—Hills, now. Ranulph watched him wield a demon. In the course of the fight, he split the hill in three and tunnelled into black rock. Thomas couldn't find where he had escaped to, a cavern like those Scot visited in Salamanca and Toledo."

"There's a cavern in the Eildons?"

"It would seem so."

It had to be the vault's location unless the rumours were wrong and Scot built his vault in Castile or France or wherever else he'd been instead of Scotland. All she could do was hope they weren't. "I'll go tonight."

"I'll come with you."

"You won't be going anywhere." A hard voice stilled Margaret's heart. She felt the crown before she turned. William's eyes were as hard as his words; she'd never seen more resolve there.

"My Lord," Robin started, but William charged: "You will not leave the Hermitage. You will not go to the vault."

The crown of teeth sharpened the order, cut it into her heart. Her jaw clenched against it, but she nodded. She couldn't refuse him. She couldn't leave the castle, not until he left it and the crown's influence lessened or he gave up the command.

Lord Soulis stepped out the door but halted on the other side and shuddered. His resolve gone, he said, "Disregard our order. Go."

Our order?

It was obvious then: something was wrong with William.

He left.

Margaret thought she would feel the crown's release, but her heart was tight, held inside a wraithlike maw. He hadn't freed her, he couldn't. He'd simply given her another order.

On the south side of the Tweed, the Eildon Hills stood as great, frozen beasts stuck in their riven moment—when they were torn by a force stronger than the earth. They seemed on the brink of movement as though they'd strained to reunite before relenting and settling into their new lives.

She climbed the slopes with Robin through gorse patches layered with dark green and budding gold, and they reached the southwesterly summit. They wandered about the hill, searching for some entrance inside, moved on to crest the mid-hill next and, when they didn't find anything, dragged themselves to the top of the north hill—the largest peak. From there, they could see forests and fields for miles, waning in the distance.

A shepherd's delight sunset bloomed across the horizon, cold purple and dry red, but the colour didn't warm the air. A human would seek shelter for the night, but Margaret could survive the temperatures of winter without too much trouble, and she was happy to search the hills until it was time for her next libation.

"You can't remember anything else? Anything you might have read about Scot and the Eildons?"

"Not Scot, no, but..." Robin toyed with his short beard. "Thomas, perhaps."

She raised her eyebrows and tilted her head forward, pressing him to go on.

"I'd forgotten until I saw it, but there was something about Thomas and a tree..." He looked pointedly at the tree that stood in the centre of the peak. It was an eldern oak with weathered bark lined with green moss, and its branches were high enough off the ground that a battle horse and its rider might pass untouched beneath. It was an extraordinary tree, but only because of its age and beauty; there was nothing otherworldly about it, no demons lingering about, ready to tithe them to hell or lure them to the fair queen's realm.

They inspected it separately. Robin went so far as to climb into its branches and methodically rap on its wood as though he might happen upon the right pattern and open a magically hidden door.

Scarlet light glinted on something between the tree's thick, exposed roots. Margaret knelt and pushed freezing, loose dirt and grasses aside to reveal a dragon made of clouded silver. She took hold of the curve of its long body and yanked upward. More dirt tumbled off the slab of striped metal and wood as she lifted, and the door tilted up on its pivoting strap hinge, where stone steps lead down into the hill.

Robin was around the trunk, concealed from sight, so she called his name. He entered the tunnel after her and the door thumped shut once again.

A spiraling staircase lined with blazing torches. Someone had lit them, but who else would be there? Michael Scot?

Margaret gave Robin a look and he nodded, silently agreeing to proceed cautiously.

The stair curled down and down and grew gradually wider as it went. Shelves were hewn into the rock near the end, holding books and trinkets: arrowheads, feathers, medicinal plants, pine marten bones, and bowls of old, unshelled hazelnuts. At last, they took the final step into a cavern.

No one was there, though there was another tunnel leading east toward Eildon.

The cavern looked similar to the library in Hermitage but crowded with more books. It was sparsely furnished, filled mostly with literature and art, and a hook cut into the wall held a bugle horn. Two more hooks were beside it; a sword might once have been mounted there, but they held nothing now.

The one thing Margaret expected was missing: heart caskets.

"This isn't the vault."

Robin's silver, garnet-set finger ring glinted. He was rifling through book pages and torn, scribbled-on parchment, clearly searching for something.

Margaret narrowed her eyes. "You knew."

"Yes."

"You lied to me." Her head felt heavy, pressured by tears she wouldn't let come.

Robin's shoulders sagged as he faced her. "I had to."

Her lower jaw jutted out. She was going to leave, to turn her back on him like she had other capes who'd betrayed her over the years. She didn't become an alpha by forgiving but by punishing. By keeping and enforcing strong, unyielding standards.

"I'm dying."

Her light feet rooted. That, she hadn't expected. "What do you mean?"

"I changed the record Ranulph II wrote to say Michael Scot hid from Thomas of Erceldoune here, but it was the other way around. This is Thomas's cavern. I'm sorry I tricked you, but I knew you could find this place, and I needed to come here... I believe Thomas has the recipe for a medicine that can cure me."

"I don't understand. How do you know that? How can you be dying? And why couldn't you find this place without me?"

"Because of your mother, she sealed—"

"My mother... you know who my mother is?" Only the Soulises and Alianora knew Margaret's true identity, or so she thought. He'd known this whole time? And what did her mother have to do with anything?

His ears perked. "Did you hear that?"

She wasn't sure. Had something echoed through the tunnel? Were footsteps thudding down the staircase, or was she imagining sounds because Robin heard them?

"Listen," he hissed. "I do know where the vault is. I've worked it out—Luce Abbey. We'll go there next. But please, keep watch while I search for the recipe."

Could she forgive someone just once? She might have done the same thing if she were dying and desperate.

"All right. But I'll look, too."

He seemed to stop himself from protesting and she rummaged through Thomas's things, records on wars and elves and religions. The books were piled along the irregular cavern walls, and they branched out in a maze of stacks from there.

Against the far wall, Margaret found herself before an iron pedestal painted with glittering dragons. It held a broad tome with an ivory-carved cover that depicted a man with a sword who faced a great dragon. Figures in cloaks gathered behind him under a gold moon and a silver sun, and between them was a verse:

The heart of a bright warrior,

On regina leonum will be bestow'd,

Then shall God's sword sweat mortal dross,

A new empire behold.

The edges were embossed with lions and serpents and short, four-legged, furred creatures the likes of which Margaret knew she'd never seen but somehow felt she had.

She tried to lift the cover, but she couldn't touch it, so she interrupted Robin, immersed in his own reading, and said so.

"Break this over it." He gave her a heart, watched, but didn't follow.

The heart bled over the tome, chipped away at something unseen, and dissolved. She traced the verse and brushed her fingers down the cover, suddenly able to touch it as if an invisible case had been broken.

She took hold of a section of pages and let them fall off her thumb, producing a sound not unlike the soft susurration of an aspen, a slight breeze stirring its leaves into a fluttering frenzy.

The tome was full of prophecies broken up by paragraphs of history and ramblings, family trees and diagrams, legends, and fairy lore. Fact, fiction, delusions. Its letters and sketches were silver all the way through.

Margaret stopped the flow of paper to look at a drawing. It was an animal like the one on the ivory cover, with large, rounded ears and teeth remarkably similar to her own. A shred of paper was stuck in the pages. It read, "A man may dig his grave with his teeth."

She flipped to the next sketch. This one wasn't just silver but splashed with red in a circle made of nine stones. It wasn't Ninestane Rig; the stones were shaped differently, and it was in a large field, not a woodland clearing, but it may as well have been. A woman stood tall in its centre over several dead bodies, and she wore a cape coloured with their blood.

Shimmering words dripped down the adjacent page over an illustration of King William I:

Scotland be sad now and lament,
For honours thou hast lost,
But yet rejoice, in better times,
Which will pay the cost.
Tho unto thraldom you should be
Brought by your enemies;
You shall have freedom from them all,
And enjoy your liberties.
The grave of the most noble prince,
To all is great regret,
The subject to law, who both leave

The kingdom and estate.
O anguish great! where every kind
And ages doth lament;
Whom bitter death has ta'en away,
Shall Scotland sore repent.

On the next page, Queen Grimhild and King Gebicca's bloodline was laid out. Margaret traced it with her finger: Gundomar I, Gudrun, Giselher, Gundaharius, Gondioc, Chilperic II, Godegisel, Gundobad, Clovis I, Clothilde, Clotaire I, Chroma, Charibert I...

The names stretched over three pages as ringleted scratches. Counts of Hesbaye, Worms, Burgundy, Bar-sur-Aube, Hainaut, Mâcon, Soissons, Orléans, Vermandois, Rennes, Meaux, Tours, Boulogne and Lens, Luxemburg, Holland, Flanders and Bidgau. Dukes of Neustria, Normandy, Lorraine, and Brittany. Earls of Northumbria, Bernicia, and Huntingdon. A marquis of Pont-à-Mousson, a bishop of Tours and Paris, and a king of Frisia. English princesses and Scottish queens. Princeps of Burgundy, Thuringia, Normandy, France, and Scotland.

A few names Margaret recognized: David I, Henry, William I. Henry was married to Ada Warenne, the woman who brought the redcapes back to life and whose own lineage could be traced back to the patricians.

After William I was Alexander II, Alexander III, and Margaret's mother. She gasped when it dawned on her: Grimhild's blood was hers. Her ancestor was the first redcape. Was it a coincidence that she was one now?

She skimmed several more pages until her eyes snagged on the words "elixir of life." A paragraph detailed a theory as to the elixir's origin; if it existed, it was likely discovered by Gundobad, who was King of the Burgundians for a few decades in the fifth to sixth centuries. Had he taken it, he could have lived hundreds or thousands of years. He may never have died.

The elixir's exact properties were unknown, and the writer had only speculations on how to create it. But could that be enough to save Robin? Did it extend the lives of the healthy, or could it cure the sick as well?

"I may have found—" she began, but when she looked to Robin, she saw they weren't alone.

Thomas of Erceldoune had returned. His eyes flicked to the tome Margaret cradled, and Robin stabbed him in the stomach. The wound was thin and torn at the end as if a sorcerer's blade had pierced him, but Robin's hands were empty.

The elderly man crumpled. Blood drooled from his mouth and made his words sound like gargling river water, but they were intelligible.

"I do suppose, altho' too late, old prophecies shall hold." His eyes swam again with silver, his tongue a scale flashing in the torchlight. "Hope thou in God's goodness evermore, and mercies manifold."

The silver hardened and stayed. Someday, a thief might happen upon the cavern and harvest them, or a sorcerer might melt and shape them into a heart casket. But his real eyes were gone with his breath, never to see or be seen again.

"Why did you do that?" Margaret whispered. Secretly, she'd hoped to see the man once more, to discuss how he'd known about her memories, torture him into revealing his secrets if need be. What if she had other memories hidden somewhere and he knew about them?

"Does it matter?"

Only Robin would dare speak to her like that. Based on the events of the night, she was beginning to wonder if she had allowed him too long a rope.

"You forget your place," she said, still staring at Thomas's metallic eyes.

"I apologize. It won't happen again."

He seemed sincere, so she nodded, turned her gaze from Thomas's lifeless one, and let it go.

"You found it, did you not?"

"Not a medicine, but something else that might help..." She showed him the entry on the elixir.

"Margaret, friend." He took her by the shoulders in a surprising bout of affection. "You'll save my life yet."

53

She didn't want to waste valuable time dragging a human to the stone circle, so she was careful not to get close enough for her cape to drink in Thomas's spilled blood.

They left his silver-flecked corpse to chill on the cavern floor and entered another darkness, this one of night.

At Hermitage Castle, William II Soulis knew Margaret had gone, which meant one of two things: someone was taking his memories, or Abaddon had taken over and let her go. He hoped it was the former. Otherwise, it meant the demon had plans for her, and his plans were always evil.

William shut his eyes and built another wall around his heart.

Chapter Eleven

Gudrun spurred her horse onward to keep up with Gundaharius, who sped up as soon as the tower was in sight. Sigurd raced beside her on his sorrel steed, sun-touched and perfect as always.

Atop the hill, Gundaharius dove from his horse before it came to a full stop and scrambled toward a tower. It rose high on a rocky cliff and peered over trees and the cold, blue lake below.

It was true what they'd been told: a fire circled the tower. It whirled and flared, more alive than the trees around them.

"We can't get through." Gundaharius closed his eyes and tilted his head away from the heat toward the ground.

"Yes, we can," Sigurd said.

Gudrun grabbed his arm. "It could kill you."

His glossy eyes sparkled with flecks of silver, and he caressed her cheek with a hand. "I'm not afraid."

He rushed at the fire, held his breath, and leapt.

"I am," she breathed, but he was already through.

Staring through the flames, she couldn't tell if he'd been hurt, but she saw his flickering form disappear into the tower and that reassured her. Still, she had a terrible, sick feeling in her stomach, like when her brothers would leave without her for war. Like losing someone alive.

It was a long while before Sigurd returned. When he did, he wasn't alone. He held a woman in his strong arms. The minute he stepped from the tower, the fire fell to the earth and was gone.

The woman gazed up at Sigurd adoringly, and he looked at her much the same.

Gudrun's gut wrenched so hard she thought she might vomit.

He'd only just begun to look at her differently, to brush stray hairs from her face and offer small tokens of affection. Their relationship was a year in the making; how could she lose him to someone he'd just met?

Sigurd set the stranger down near a tree and she leaned against it appreciatively. Gundaharius introduced himself, clearly as smitten as Sigurd, and the woman gave him a sultry smile. That eased Gudrun's fears, if only a bit, as she seemed more interested in Gundaharius than Sigurd.

She was young, a year younger than Gudrun, and she called herself Brynhild. Her hair fell to her knees, and her voice was sweet and innocent—it made Gudrun wish she could lock her in the tower, call back the flames, and make everyone forget she existed.

Perhaps she should have; Gudrun didn't know it yet, but Brynhild would be her bane.

CHAPTER TWELVE

Magnus flew low overhead as Margaret made her way along the Hermitage waters, which ran southeast beside her. The newly fallen snow was thin, and the going was easy, but against the white and blue landscape, her cape was noticeable, and she had few places to hide if a group of humans passed by. She'd rather not get bogged down by a fight; she just wanted to find a suitable, lone human and get back. She needed one before her trip to the Abbey of Luce, and she was hoping to leave the next morning.

A child's laugh was swept up by the wind. It danced over branches and bubbled over hills; the lack of foliage did nothing to swipe its zeal, and Margaret shifted direction toward it. If someone vulnerable was there, not far from the castle, she might not have to travel to the nearby village to trap her next libation.

The source of the laugh was a shock. It was Ermengarde, and she was with one of the whitecapes Margaret met in William's apartments, Malcolm. But where was her mother?

Alice shouldn't have left her alone, except with other children, until she was fully grown. Redcape mothers were notoriously protective. If another adult approached their child, even if it was another mother—and especially if it was a male—they had a tendency to lash out, or even murder, the offender.

Yet, here Ermengarde was, alone with a *whitecape*. What kind of mother would allow it?

He couldn't have kidnapped her. If she wasn't with her natal clan, she was with her mother, always. Unless he'd killed Alice—a real possibility—but, for a reason she couldn't grasp, Margaret didn't think he would have. Alice must have given Ermengarde to him willingly, which was a testament to her trust in him.

For the life of her, Margaret couldn't understand how he'd earned that trust. She didn't trust anyone like that. If she had a daughter, she would never leave her side, not if the whole whitecape army were against her. But Alice was a dunce. Maybe she'd have handed her child off to anyone who asked.

Malcolm tossed Ermengarde into the air, and she giggled in glee, smiling wider than she ever did in the castle.

He smiled, too, and there was something in him that reminded Margaret of Alice—how she'd looked at her daughter that night in the stone circle and every night after. It was tenderness, or love, something many redcapes never experienced.

Margaret had, but that was years ago. There was no one to love her now and no one for her to love.

She watched Malcolm and Ermengarde a second longer, then took a step back.

Something crunched beneath her foot.

She'd wanted to sink into the forest and resume her mission without being noticed. She was usually more careful than this, and the snow was soft enough that she should have been neither seen nor heard, but she'd given herself away in her distraction. Malcolm saw her.

He set Ermengarde in a cleared patch and Magnus swooped to land beside her as if to keep her in the circle. She took to playing on its edge, grabbing handfuls of snow and throwing them into the air, unmoved by the cold temperature. She babbled happily to herself as loose clumps rolled off her fingers and flakes stuck in her hair, sprinkled powder like ground bone. Her cape was safe in the clearing; it wouldn't wash out unless Ermengarde swam through the stuff.

Quick as a fox, Malcolm bent down and threw some weapon at Margaret.

She winced and dove away. She was right not to trust him. She should have rushed him as soon as she saw he had Ermengarde and—

Snow hit her in the stomach. It wasn't hard, but it startled her.

He could have aimed at her cape, but knowing it might leach blood from the material, he went for the tougher shot.

"What was that for?"

He laughed and threw another snowball, which narrowly missed her head.

For a moment, she forgot herself. She reached down and cupped snow between her hands. It lost half its size in the air, as it wasn't wet enough to stick properly together, but the ball found its target.

She skidded across the snow, pelting snow at Malcolm, until he slipped and fell with a thud.

She didn't think of why she did it, but she hastened to his side to see if he was injured.

He wasn't—the wind was knocked out of him—but he sucked it back in a loud gasp.

"You win," he surrendered, and Margaret smiled a genuine smile, one that wasn't incited by blood or victory or plotting.

Magnus nuzzled Ermengarde's cheek as he so often did with Margaret, and the child clapped her hands and blurted, "Dada!"

Margaret shot away from Malcolm, afraid William had arrived.

"Don't mind her," he said, sitting up. "It's the only thing she knows how to say."

Margaret brushed white from her sleeve.

She didn't look at Malcolm. She didn't want to feel the warmth inside her. She couldn't.

Redcapes couldn't fall in love. They mated to replace weak links and strengthen the clan; they didn't have human relationships. Love would make them vulnerable. Many redcapes would never experience even a sliver of it.

Margaret remembered Ingeborg and Tor's marriage, the loving looks between them, how they held each other. She remembered how she loved her father, hearing that her mother loved her before she'd been born. William I saving her life at the end of his. But Margaret didn't deserve love, not anymore. Not unless she could lose her cape, if that were possible. Maybe not even then.

And Malcolm... he was full of life and light and joy, all the things she wasn't. She hated him for that and for bringing out in her, for a short time, that innocent, childlike self she'd once been but could never truly be again.

She scowled at him.

"What did I do?"

"Be careful with her." She pointed to Ermengarde and stalked away from him. She called for Magnus, and he flew to her, albeit a bit reluctantly.

"Wait!"

Though she willed them to move, her feet stopped of their own accord. If she didn't know better, she would have thought he possessed the crown's power of influence.

"You came looking for me, didn't you? I knew you would."

She could hear the grin in his words, and she clenched her fists, angry at him and herself and the wrongness of it all.

He had the wrong idea about them.

"As if I would. It's my hope to never see you again."

She turned to see the hurt on his face, but it wasn't there. If anything, his grin grew wider.

"Thomas..." His grin fell with the mention of the old man. Clearly, he knew of his fate. "He told me I shouldn't, but I have to tell you. We know each other. Or we did, a long time ago..."

This again. "I don't know you."

"Alice said she's tried—she's searched the castle for things that might make you remember... but nothing has."

She bored her eyes into his, the dark side of the moon looking at the bright. "I do not know you."

She said it with force because she wanted to believe it. The thought that someone had stolen something so precious from her filled her with revulsion. She didn't want it to be true, but she knew in her heart something was missing.

"I'll find whatever it is." His voice didn't waver. "I promise you. You will remember me."

"I assure you, you will never be anything to me."

She left him and Ermengarde, her heart in her throat, and she marvelled...

If she had seen him, how could she forget those eyes?

Chapter Thirteen

The sun spilled into the valley as molten gold and cool shadows splashed against Luce Abbey's cruciform. Margaret dove into the shadows and let them carry her to the south transept, Robin swift beside her.

Above the crossing, a lantern with a gabled roof had been set, and it rose high above. Magnus settled on its top, which Margaret couldn't see from her place on the ground—she was too close to the walls. But she could see the sandstone building's beautiful, traceried windows, their moulded ribs new and strong.

"This way," said Robin.

She followed him from there—he was the one with the theories, and he seemed to know the abbey from his studies. Judging from his confident movements, he must have found the layout drawn somewhere.

According to Robin, Michael Scot had spent time at the Abbey of Luce before or during the time he trained Ranulph II Soulis in the way of sorcery. Only Scot knew where his vault was hidden, but Robin believed he'd have built it either in the sacristy, the monks' dormitory, or the scriptorium—he would have spent the greatest amount of time there, which made it the most likely. But would Scot have done the most likely thing? Robin believed he would, perhaps thinking others would assume he wouldn't.

Margaret had suggested searching beneath the graveyard, but Robin said tunneling was Thomas's area of expertise and Scot wouldn't have burrowed into the earth like a common shrew.

"Wherever it is, we will find it," Robin had said, and Margaret agreed wholeheartedly. "We'll take the abbey apart by stone if needed and search the surrounding area inch by inch."

They entered the precinct through the slype and nearly turned left but heard something thud and retreated into the plain chapter house through an archway with a stone architrave.

Realizing the thud had been a clump of wet, fallen snow, they slid back onto the east walk and scudded beneath the beam of the cloister roof, which was held by wooden, notched corbels seventeen feet up. Thin icicles jutted off the roof's sides like fangs, bleeding water droplets into the cloister garth. Aside from the drips, the abbey was quiet, seemingly vacated.

When at last they encountered two white-clad monks of the Cistercian order, they stilled in the waxing darkness and remained undetected as redcapes were wont to do. The monks marched down the walk toward the chapels in the transepts or the quire.

On the west side of the garth, men headed to the lay brothers' quarters—labourers of the estates, converts, serving brothers, other non-clergy members who stayed there, the men not clothed in white tunics.

"This is the stair," Robin indicated, and they took it to the upper floor.

A second later, a gong rang through the abbey, and a large group of monks appeared behind them, obediently ambling from the refectory to the dormitory like a drift of snow, exchanging not a single whisper among the lot of them, oblivious to the scarlet capes that slithered around the corner ahead and escaped through the dormitory into the scriptorium, which stretched over the chapter house and sacristy.

"In the daytime, monks will be here, copying texts or decorating books with colour and flourishing designs, bustling to and fro to complete their work," Robin said quietly. He'd chosen the right hour to visit, for the sun's last light had drained. "The room is now empty and will be until morning—or until a monk passes through to descend the circular stairs there and say their offices in the church, which they do three times every night. But hopefully none will until after we've gone."

He took a cresset from its slot on the wall and Margaret raised an eyebrow. The dark was a hindrance for humans, but redcapes had excellent night vision. He shouldn't need a lamp, and a monk might see the light from the dormitory; a fact he surely knew, but he didn't explain himself—nor did he light the cresset, but he held it as he began his search.

She shrugged it off and joined him.

A manuscript with still-wet ink lay open on a lectern beside a goose quill, which was mostly stripped of its feathers and stained black at the sharpened shaft's end. The writing wavered between English, Scottish Gaelic, scattered Latin, and a language Margaret didn't know. It read as a prayer of sorts and led into a warning against cavorting with demons.

Around the lectern, the floor was bare—as it was under the shelves and chairs and every angled desk she inspected, save a few parchment frames stretched with skins, which leaned against a stark wall.

"Here." Robin's quiet voice drew her eyes to his face.

Margaret crossed the drafty scriptorium and ducked the folded paper leaves hung on lines above, folios that netted sections of the room like butterflies draped over spiderwebs.

Against a windowed wall was built a small desk enclosure, one of three carrels in the scriptorium, and Robin was pointing at an intaglio in the stone beneath it: a white serpent, its paint oddly fresh-looking. Robin pushed and the wall gave, revealing a secret stair.

His timing could not have been better; a monk entered the scriptorium from the dormitory. Whether he was on his way to the stairs in the transept's angle or had heard the stone wall swing open, they didn't wait to find out. They crawled under the desk, shut the hidden door behind them, and Robin finally lit the cresset—for there wasn't a shred of light there, and even capes couldn't see without a hint of it.

Built into the wall, the stair was steep and so narrow Margaret's shoulders bumped against the occasional stone. It led directly downward into an equally secret, closed-off room on the north side of the chapter house—Michael Scot's vault.

They'd found it.

Shelves hewn into the rough walls held scores of caskets in varying states of tarnish. The blackest caskets contained the darkest hearts, the ones Margaret had come for.

She eased one from its place on the shelf and reached toward the heart inside but remembered William with a heart in his hands and blood on his clothes, and she hesitated.

"So I was right."

Clutching the casket to her chest, Margaret whirled.

Alianora was looking at Robin, not her, and it was he who innocently replied, "How do you mean?" Shadows danced across his wan skin, spurred to life by the cresset.

Alianora's eyes gleamed. "It's you."

Margaret's fingers felt stiff around the casket as if she'd been holding it tight for longer than she had.

Whatever Alianora was doing there, whether she'd followed them or found the vault on her own, it didn't matter. This was her opportunity; with so many hearts at her disposal, Margaret could take her. And with Alianora distracted by whatever she had going on with Robin, gaping at him like he was a dead man risen, she had the perfect opening.

Wariness forgotten, she grabbed the heart, bled it on Alianora, and willed her to forget how to use sorcery.

Using the heart was a warm rush, a feeling she could get drunk on. It made her want to cut one out of a breathing person, use it fresh off the body.

The blood didn't melt into Alianora's skin and dissolve over her vine-embroidered dress like it should have. Instead, it slid off like oil, and she chuckled. It was a deep-throated, disheartening sound.

Margaret scrambled for another casket, but her co-alpha was on her before she could tear its lid wide, and it fell to the ground.

Alianora's strong hand wrapped her throat and forced her backward.

Her head hit a hard shelf and her back pressed against the cold metal of a casket. She could feel its edge through her cape.

She wanted to kick through Alianora's stomach or claw at her throat, but the sharp nails cutting into her own held her still. One wrong move and she'd be dead.

She was dead, anyway.

Alianora could have killed her at any point. There may have been three alphas, but they weren't evenly matched. She could have disposed of anyone she wanted to; more than a few times, she had. And now she had a reason to kill Margaret.

She released her throat.

Margaret looked down in shock.

Her abdomen was torn open, her own guts and blood spilling out. She hadn't felt it, but now that she saw it, she could.

Pain exploded in her head. Lightning zagged through her core.

She crumpled and landed on the second casket. It didn't hurt. Then again, everything hurt.

A biting cough drummed through her, expelling more liquid from her body, which she desperately tried to seal with her hands. But she'd lost too much.

It didn't register that she was dying, but she was. The wound was fatal. Her cape blanched as it gave her blood that rushed through and out of her. Her breaths were numbered, and her mind was brimming with so much pain there wasn't space for thought.

A warm mass met her lips.

On instinct, she opened her mouth and bit down. It tasted better than anything she'd eaten. And, somehow, worse.

It was giving in to the darkness; it was life laced with sin. It was the blackened heart from the casket beside her, fed to her by a demon with a red cape.

As her breathing normalized and her vision cleared, she saw it was Robin who saved her, not a demon. But he may as well have been.

"More," she whispered, and he gave her another. "Alianora..."

"She's gone."

Margaret checked herself with shaking fingers. The heart had sewn her skin together, replenished her blood and reconstructed her insides.

"There's something else…"

"What?"

"Alianora, she made us forget something."

Though the colour had returned to Margaret's cape, it left her face at that. "How do you know?"

"When it's done to you enough, you start to notice. I'm not sure what, but Lord Soulis has made me forget many things."

He was right. Lately, Margaret could tell her mind was missing pieces.

"What would she want to make us forget?"

Robin shook his head, thinking. "Her reason for coming here? A weakness?"

It was possible. They might have figured out any number of things: how to kill her, how to destroy the crown, how to lose their capes…

Margaret stood. She glared at Michael Scot's heart caskets and a mixture of anger and fear welled in her chest.

It was supposed to work. She should have been able to chip at her mind—the heart she used was like pitch, dark enough to seep into anyone, even Alianora.

"How did she fight it? Why didn't she forget?"

Robin looked puzzled. "Do you not know?"

Red returned to her face, so she kept it facing the shelves. "Know what?"

"Alianora has a pure heart."

Margaret scoffed, "If she has a pure heart, I'm the Queen of Scotland."

"Not *her* heart. She carries one with her. Pure hearts protect their wearers from sorcery."

She'd never felt so stupid. Had she known that once?

"I need one."

She scanned the caskets, but Robin interrupted: "Even Michael Scot has only one. They're extremely rare."

Again, he was right. Of all the caskets in the vault, not one was untarnished. No pure, shining silver—no pure hearts.

"Where did she get one?"

"She dug it up in an abbey, I don't know which."

Margaret's fingers curled.

She knew Alianora had made her forget things—but how many times had she done it? How many times had William, or Nicholas before him?

She couldn't allow anyone back into her head. She didn't want to forget anything, not ever again. She hated it—that someone could bind her mind and steal her last, precious shards of freedom. How could she find a way to be free when others could control her very thoughts?

"It is said your mother was pure," Robin said. "If only they had saved her heart..."

"They did." Her grandmother had. She'd seen it hung around her neck. Scot may not have a pure heart, but she knew where one was—in Bergen. "But the elixir, you said you need me to—"

"I can wait. You need to do this."

Margaret agreed. She would go to Bergen, get her mother's heart, find out what Alianora took from her, and never forget anything again.

Chapter Fourteen

Cold gusts swept over Bergen's rocky shores. Water from the cold sea splattered rocks with spots like dark blood, and the scent from clusters of pale flowers with tooth-shaped petals mixed with brine, sweetness with salt, carried in on bouts of wind. Margaret closed her eyes and breathed it in, a jar crammed with Scottish soil held between her hands.

The trip took days—days of being trapped belowdecks, hiding from the crew in corners—but the briny North Sea winds hadn't dried out her cape and she hadn't been sickened by the sea. It made her wonder: if she were human, would seasickness touch her as it had on her first journey? Or was it something else that brought it on, magic or poison?

She supposed she would never find out; as a redcape, without soil, she would always be sick by it, and she would never be human again.

She left the vessel when it was safe and held her breath as she crossed from sea to shore. The land felt familiar but faraway, like walking through memory, half vision and half feeling. New buildings had been put up, but the small town and salted air shook pictures loose in her head: gray herons waiting for fish in shallow waters, white cod drying on wooden racks next to rows of salt-glazed stoneware jugs brimming with oils. Ingeborg's hand in hers, leaves dripping into quiet water on a warm afternoon. Men placing illegal bets on wooden dice carved with concentric circles. Her father, young and laughing, sweeping her into his arms while people around them danced the Halling. Fishing boats and traders from the northern coast bobbing in the harbour, driven in by summer winds. Freezing waves rinsing loneliness from her skin.

Loneliness. When had she felt that?

She didn't want to think of that side of her past but had the sudden urge to feel at home. So she made for Holmen, the stone fortress that held a cathedral, monastery, and the royal and episcopal residences, and tugged her hood over her head. As long as she kept her mouth closed, she could be mistaken for a human.

Though she stood out in her cape, she had a way of melting into nothingness, and there were many shadows to fade into. She searched the fortress and its faces but recognized none. Perhaps her friends and family were travelling. Perhaps they'd moved on—there weren't nearly as many people as there had been when her father was alive, and the residence felt caught between occasional use and abandonment.

The path to her quarters in the tower was as she remembered it, but the rooms were different. Her things were gone—not replaced by someone else's, just gone. The one addition was a statue next to the window, painted with gypsum and chalk, but even the bed had disappeared. No one lived there.

She hadn't expected a shrine, particularly since her father died, but she had expected... something. Some feeling of belonging, a sense of what she'd felt when she was young. The warmth of coming home.

Instead, the last bit of light and warmth within her flickered and extinguished. All she felt was a lonesome cold.

This wasn't home.

Her heavy heart yanked her from the royal residence. She forged past wooden houses and wended her way southeast, along the water, far enough from it that spume wouldn't spray her. She listened as Ingeborg Erlingsdatter told her to so many years ago, but the waters didn't guide her back to Holmen as they once had.

When the sea turned south and then northwest, so did Margaret, and she found herself on the peninsula called Nordnes, searching the skies for her eagle, though she'd left him in Scotland.

A woman's question froze her in place: "Did you search the cathedral?"

To kill someone in Norway, to consume a single drop of blood, would mean her death. She might be able to kill without spilling any, but it would be a risk; if any did spill, her cape would reach for it, and there weren't enough men on the ship to eat one every few hours, certainly not while going unnoticed in the lower decks.

"Margaret?"

It took the saying of her name for her panic to subside—for her to realize the question had not been asked in Norwegian, and that she knew the voice. It came from an Elliot, one Margaret knew well. Alice.

Seeing a redcape against the backdrop of Bergen added a new layer of strangeness to an already surreal expedition. It was the past she missed stirring with a present she'd never wanted.

"I know you came for the queen's heart. Did you find it?" Suspicion overtook her, but Alice held her hands open and said, "I came to help you."

She gave her a fake smile. "Why?"

"I know what you think of me." Alice walked closer. A vial swayed on a leather thong around her neck, crammed with Scottish earth as Margaret's was. "But we have more in common than you think. I know what it's like to feel lost, to want to go home... and to be manipulated by a sorcerer."

"I won't give you the heart."

"Why would I want it? I wish he'd make me forget."

Why would anyone want to forget?

Movement drew Margaret's eye. Loud people flocked to a monastery at the height of Nordnes, a place she'd yet to search for the queen dowager. As if urging her to leave it, the sea to her right grew violent.

"You can trust me, Margaret."

Something in her face or her voice reminded Margaret of Malcolm. Like him, Alice was different—in a good way, a way she wanted to understand. Maybe she wasn't as dimwitted as she came off back in Hermitage.

"Fine."

They left the sea to climb the hill toward the monastery.

Shouts grew louder as they neared the top and skirted the masses. Thanks to the hordes of people, they couldn't see what was going on.

Margaret couldn't risk speaking and didn't want to push through the crowd, so she leapt onto a house. Its roof was covered in dirt and fresh grass. She clambered to the edge and saw someone she'd all but forgotten: her uncle, Håkon V Magnusson.

He shared features with her father—nose, lips, and eyes—but his face was wider and his forehead smaller, and he had a harsher air about him.

Would he be glad to see her? Would he want her to stay?

What if she could stave off her bloodlust and live a relatively normal life like Alianora? She could travel back and forth between Bergen and Ninestane. She could have a family again.

She nearly leapt down, but her overwhelmed ears held her in place. There were too many people. She would find him alone as soon as she could.

"There's Robert's sister, Isabella."

Margaret had barely noticed Alice joining her on the roof, but she followed her gaze.

Beside Håkon, who was now King of Norway, two women not yet thirty stood. One had flaxen hair, and the other's was darker than most Norwegians'. The dark-haired one was the woman Alice looked to.

"Robert..." Margaret's eyes widened. "Brus?"

"Yes."

"That's the man who tried to kill me?"

Robert Brus, the Earl of Carrick. Margaret knew of him; his grandfather was among the claimants to her throne. She didn't remember where she'd learned it; most of what she knew about the outside world, its politics and kings, she'd heard from Robin and Alianora, from eavesdropping on humans in the wild or lurking about battlefields with the other redcapes. It wasn't much, but she did know many competitors vied for her throne after she'd been kidnapped. Likely, this younger Brus was after it now. It was a wonder he hadn't cut off her cape and her head in the castle.

"He wasn't going to kill you. He wouldn't have."

She didn't believe that for a moment. Margaret felt it—his wanting. His hands shook as he itched to slice into her, drain her cape and her life. She didn't know why he hadn't, but he'd wanted nothing more.

"Why is she here?"

"You don't know?"

Clearly, she didn't.

"She's King Eirik's widow."

Her father remarried? She'd heard of his death, but not that.

Screams pulled her attention to the left.

Distracted by Alice and Håkon, she hadn't noticed what he and everyone else was staring at: a woman being dragged before the king.

She spoke, and Margaret tried to wring the words from her memory. It had been so long since she'd heard the melodious language—time had watered it down, tried to drown her knowledge of it.

But she did hear one thing: her name.

The woman said it plainly: "Margaret Eiriksdatter."

Mixed cheers and shouts rang through the air, and Margaret's breath caught in her lungs.

This was about her?

Håkon said something, called for proof, and the woman responded in a hysterical, high-pitched voice, her cadence too quick to understand.

The body was identified by his brother, Håkon said, or something to that effect, and Margaret realized what was happening.

The woman was an impersonator. She was pretending to be the princess, his niece. Pretending to be *her*.

Margaret was eighteen years old, but this woman was over twice her age, and she looked nothing like her. It was ridiculous but infuriating nonetheless. She felt a staggering desire to bore her fingers into the false Margaret, feel her blood ooze from her body and crunch her bones between her teeth.

Håkon had ideas of his own.

Royal hirdmen strung her to a pole, lit a fire beneath her feet, and beheaded a man before her. Someone close to her, no doubt, a friend or a spouse.

The woman began to sing, though golden tears hot as flame ran down her face:

Veni, Creator, Spiritus,
mentes tuorum visita,
imple superna gratia
quae tu creasti, pectora.

Margaret's breath rushed from her as she remembered the day she left Norway for Scotland so many years ago, for this hymn was the one the clergy sang then. It had ended just as she was taken aboard.

Qui diceris Paraclitus,
donum Dei altissimi,
fons vivus, ignis, caritas,
et spiritalis unctio.
Tu septiformis munere,
dextrae Dei tu digitus,
tu rite promissum Patris,
sermone ditans guttura.

People in the crowd tried to rush forward. They yelled in protest, but they were held back, and the fire's prongs reached higher still.

Accende lumen sensibus:
infunde amorem cordibus:
infirma nostri corporis
virtute firmans perpeti.
Hostem repellas longius,
pacemque dones protinus:
ductore sic te praevio
vitemus omne noxium—

The false Margaret's singing turned to screams that faded into smoke as she burned alive, never to finish the hymn.

The real Margaret closed her eyes, thinking of what Håkon said, that her father saw her body... The world spun as she recalled her kidnapping and the girl who seemed so like her.

Margaret always thought her father held out hope for her. She imagined he'd refused to believe she'd succumbed to sickness and sent people overseas to search for her. But how could he hold out hope when he saw her fate with his own eyes? He believed that girl's bloated corpse to be hers. Like the rest of the world, he believed she'd died in Orkney.

Who was behind that plot? Narve, William I, Nicholas II?

She'd lied and lusted and betrayed, killed men and women of all ages, but she'd never felt as guilty as she did now. That girl... she should have saved her. She should have seen it coming. She should have known. If she had prevented that death, she would have prevented every sin since.

She watched the smoke before the monastery, watched it rise toward gray clouds, and envisioned her flesh searing, flaking off and wafting as ash toward the sky in place of the pretender's.

"The heart wasn't in the other church, is it in this one?"

"No. They didn't bury it with her. I remember seeing it when I was young..." A small heart casket on a silver chain looped around her grandmother's wrinkled neck. Back then, she'd thought it gaudy jewelry, but she recognized it for what it was now. "The queen dowager had it."

The dowager had never been partial to Margaret. She would strut about with her favourite cousin-in-law and do her best to pretend Margaret didn't exist. She made it known, without directly stating it, that Margaret would do what she said, that she was the one who held the power, and Margaret would never have any final say, or much to say at all, even after being coronated as queen. If Margaret did something wrong or uncouth, which was often as she was a young child, her grandmother would smile and say she was just like her mother.

"You think she still does?"

"Yes. But I don't see her here."

The queen dowager would be quite old now, bedridden, perhaps. And if she wasn't in Bergen—it wasn't the royal hub it once was, so she might not be—then Margaret didn't know where to look.

"You know this Isabella woman? Will she tell you where the dowager is?"

Alice flexed her jaw, visibly unsure.

"We'll go together." And Margaret would make her forget after. She had only a few hearts, but keeping their identities safe was worth one.

They dropped from the roof, skirted the barely contained crowd, and snuck into the door a ways behind Håkon. After crossing the aisle, they waited behind a marble statue of King Øystein I, which stood tall in the apse at the head of the monastery.

Her uncle entered first. Margaret wanted to reveal herself to him, but what if he didn't believe her and tried to burn her on a pyre like the false Margaret? Her father sent papers with her to Scotland as proof of who she was, but they were back at Hermitage—the Soulises had taken them and refused to give them back, and as long as the crown could control her, she couldn't search for them. Even if Håkon did believe her, he would see her too-wide mouth and inhuman teeth, the red in her hair and her eyes and her bloody cape, and he would fear her, or hate her, and order her death. The chance that he would accept her was poor.

So she held back as he knelt and exited, and Isabella entered with another woman, the plump one with flaxen hair who'd been with Håkon. Margaret waited for the other to leave, but the young women knelt together.

She hesitated. She didn't want to be wasteful with her hearts here, where she couldn't kill for more, and there were other options. She could follow Isabella and wait to get her alone, or they could corner someone else. The queen dowager was obviously well-known; where she was might be as well.

With glazed-over eyes, she wasn't prepared to stop Alice, who left the statue's cover. Margaret lamented her inevitable loss of hearts and stalked after her.

The companion finished praying and looked up. Her eyes widened as she beheld the redcape before her. Her hand shot to Isabella's arm, and she opened her mouth.

"Euphemia." Isabella, who was shockingly calm, shushed her, but her attention stayed fixed on Alice. She tilted her head and the inner corners of her eyes twitched. "What do you want?"

Alice answered, "A small favour."

"You know these..." Euphemia struggled to say "people" but gave up the effort and shrank from the redcapes.

"No. I don't."

The words held a weight that Margaret didn't understand.

"We won't hurt you." Margaret's assurance sounded shallow and didn't assuage Euphemia's fear. "We only want to know where my... where the dowager is."

Euphemia squeaked, "Dowager?" She was fixated on Margaret and Alice's capes.

Isabella rose. She drew herself up before Alice. Most humans would never dare to get so close. "What did I do?"

Alice's head angled toward her shoulder.

"To make you hate me, what did I do?"

"Hate you? How could you think that?"

"You wouldn't see me. Even when you knew I was leaving, you refused to come. And Robert said he gave you my letters, but you've never written. What was I supposed to think?"

"I ruined your family's future, the capes', and mine... how could I face you after that?"

Horror spread over Euphemia's face as she realized their capes were doused in blood. Before Margaret could stop her, she screamed.

Margaret produced a heart and crushed it over Euphemia. Isabella didn't protest that, but she said, "You need to go."

She endeavoured not to break Euphemia's body open and reminded Isabella, "The dowager.

"She's dead."

Margaret knew she was old, but she hadn't expected that. Her grandmother always seemed untouchable, a looming, condescending mountain she couldn't move. It was strange to think mountains could crumble.

Alice asked, "Do you know what happened to Queen Margaret's heart?"

"Eirik had it, but he gave it to his brother, who insists it remains with his newborn, Ingeborg." She glanced behind her. "She's being cared for in Holmen now, but she and Euphemia return to Oslo tomorrow. Go!"

The sound of doors being pulled open sent the redcapes reeling backward.

Before they were out of earshot, Isabella said to Alice, "Forgive yourself. I have."

Men chased after them. Margaret and Alice split up and tucked themselves into dark recesses, hoping to hide until they could escape the monastery.

Margaret's cape pounded in time with her heart as she scrunched against a wall in the crypt. Her knuckles brushed carved crucifixes and runes as she pulled the fabric closer to herself.

Three men barrelled by, unaware they'd passed her. They searched the room, which kept records and furniture, vestments and relics.

Their noises faded and her adrenaline gradually slowed. She waited a bit longer before peeking around the corner.

There was no one there, so she peeled herself from the crypt and glided down the side of the monastery's single aisle, dashing from pillar to pillar.

A warrior rolled around the side of a pillar and angled a spear toward Margaret. Four others circled around her. They backed up, startled when she bared her teeth, but they didn't lower their weapons.

She reached for a heart.

Alianora could have used one heart to make them all forget, but she wasn't as strong a sorceress. It would make them forget temporarily, at best, or disorient them, at least. Either way, it would give her time to escape.

She spun, throwing the melted heart in their faces, and ran from the monastery, where she came face to face with Håkon's day guard. The man himself was in their midst, with a clear view of Margaret. He stepped in front of Isabella to protect her from the red-caped fiend, should she break through his henchmen, but Isabella's expression was serene. Maybe she didn't care what happened to Margaret or knew what would. Maybe she had remarkable control of her emotions.

Margaret's awareness was on her last heart, but even that wouldn't do her good against so many.

The men waited for Håkon's call to strike—to lance her with their spears or string her on the pyre. But he didn't order her death, not yet. He spoke in a low voice and Margaret made out most of it—either her understanding of Norwegian was trickling back in, or she remembered the order, or found his meaning in his tone. He demanded they imprison her in the cellar of the tower where Eirik had lived in Holmen. There, he said, a bishop would attempt to cleave the demon from her soul.

It took several of them to subdue her. They brought her to the cellar, bound her in irons, stole her remaining heart, and left her alone in the dark.

CHAPTER FIFTEEN

"I am so sorry." The voice was from a long-lost dream. It sounded like lifeblood seeping through a haphazardly bandaged wound, like time-suppressed hope.

Margaret stared at its owner, the Bishop of Bergen, who had descended to meet her hours after she was thrown into the cellar. His face was lit by a beeswax candle set in a bronze holder. He looked worn out, too old to be hobbling into cellars and meeting with redcapes. Surely he was nearing the end of his life.

Of all the people she thought she might see in Norway, Bishop Narve wasn't one of them.

"Should that mean something to me?" She flexed her fingers into fists, grinding her wrists against the iron they'd bound her with. A similarly made, iron collar chafed against her neck and her cape. "You gave me to them! You condemned me to this life."

"No!"

"You knew where I was. You could have come for me. You could have told my father what happened. You could have done many things, but you chose to do nothing." She slumped against the wall behind her. "He thought I died. He'll never know something far worse happened to me because of you."

"We did it to save you."

"Well, you didn't."

"King Eirik was worried about sending you to Scotland; he knew you wouldn't be safe there. There were too many noblemen who wanted you dead, rumours a demon had called a storm to slay Alexander III... The

Soulises were supposed to protect you. They said they could hide you from the evil one." His eyes wandered to her cape in dismay. "And they swore they wouldn't do this to you. You were their assurance. You were supposed to remain... human."

King Eirik was worried...

We did it to save you...

"Do you mean to say my father knew of this deal with the Soulises?"

"The plan was devised by the queen mother. So yes, he knew."

Margaret's heart seemed to stop. Her vision grew fuzzy as if her brain lacked blood. She felt light of body and heavy of mind.

He knew? He sent her to live with monsters, never tried to contact her, and let the world think she was dead?

The iron shackles didn't hold her up. She foundered and let her head fall against the hard, cold wall.

"We too are plagued by demons... Eirik feared you—and himself—and what you were doing to each other. What the demons were doing to you. I wish I could help you remember, but I am also grateful you don't. The Soulises were well-versed in sorcerous arts, and Eirik thought..." Bishop Narve took a step toward her but shied away before he got close. "Truly, Margaret. I am sorry."

Demons and sorcery in Bergen? Narve had never spoken of such things.

"We mustn't tarry." Isabella Brus rushed to free Margaret from the irons.

"He knew," she told Isabella. "My father knew."

"We all did. Håkon, too. But he's never seen one of your kind in person before, and he doesn't understand what you need. He won't let you return to Scotland on your own. He wants to keep you here until you are made human again and then use you and my home country in the war against England. He doesn't know it isn't possible. He doesn't understand how much blood you will need to survive here."

Even after she was able, Margaret didn't move. "Why do you care?"

"I may not wear it here, but like my brother, I am a whitecape. And I loved your mother very much." She lowered a silver chain over

Margaret's head. The heart casket it held clinked against the vial of earth—she'd retrieved it from the infant Ingeborg's blanket-laden crib. "She would have given this to you if the choice were hers. The queen mother made sure it wasn't." Isabella shook her head in disgust. "After taking her life, that woman had the gall to keep her heart."

"Her life?"

"Margaret—your mother—was twenty when she married Eirik. He was seven years her junior. She was unhappy; she didn't want him, and the queen mother didn't want her. She feared Margaret's influence over Eirik and the court. She felt threatened by her... I didn't know it until I came here, but Margaret's death was her doing. She made it seem she died in childbirth. Your mother's last act was to save you. She gave you to Bishop Narve. He made sure you were safe and watched over you after her death." She looked at Narve, gratitude in her eyes. "He has been a great ally to us both."

Margaret wrapped a hand around the ovular casket. It gave her the strength to stand.

"I pray every day for your soul," Bishop Narve said. "I pray you will never have to take another heart."

Her eyebrows bunched.

Another? She had never taken one. Unless he didn't mean harvesting hearts with a sorcerer's knife but tearing them out with her hands and eating them.

Narve left first to distract the guards.

She didn't say goodbye to him. Somehow, as if his blood called to her like a thick river, she knew it was the last time she would see him. He would be dead in years, sooner than she would return—if she ever did. She hoped he would forever remember her like this and regret his part in making her that way.

But a different part of her, the part that was like a blood-coated, neglected sword, didn't feel the sharp sting of betrayal she once had. The rust, the blame, was dissolving, the grudge she carried for the bishop slowly lifting from her shoulders.

Perhaps she didn't hope he would regret it. Perhaps he *had* saved her.

That part of her hoped he would find peace.

Never releasing the casket from her grasp, Margaret let Isabella lead her from Holmen and give her directions on where to go. Thanks to her father's widow, her mother's friend, she found Alice in a secure house beside the sea, and they waited for the time they could board an England-bound vessel, which came to port days later as Isabella said it would.

This ship was larger than the last, a cog stuffed with cargo. In the hold, Margaret and Alice huddled between barrels of cardamom wine and crates that exuded the fresh, spicy-sweet aromas of sawn redwood and whitewood and listened for the coxswain's order to shove off. Even with their excellent hearing, his voice didn't make it to them; nevertheless, the cog heaved itself from the harbour.

What if they ran into a storm as Margaret had outside of Orkney? The small fear blossomed and died. What could have gone wrong on the voyage to Norway hadn't: there had been no storm, her uncle hadn't burned her alive, she hadn't killed someone overseas and doomed herself. Worrying that a new storm might take her would do more harm than good.

Margaret imagined the mountains, coniferous forests, fjords, and shores falling away behind them. She wondered if she would see them again, but the loss didn't cut. She'd felt it already, the first time she left and in Holmen days ago.

"You miss Bergen," Alice remarked astutely. She ventured, "You miss being human?"

"No."

"I can see that you do." The ship leaned as they veered away from the wharf. "Not all Elliots see it as such, but we do—it's a great loss."

"I've endured many losses." The ruin of innocence when she'd first killed a man who'd done nothing. The death of her father. And the thievery of her memories, a deprivation she hadn't felt until recently when she discovered they'd been tampered with.

But Alice was right. The displacement of her humanity was a great loss. The greatest.

Margaret didn't recall becoming a redcape. But she did remember waking up as one and experiencing, for the first time, a rapacious hunger for blood. The predacious desire to hunt and kill. A suppression of emotion, the inability to care for humans as she once had.

Only recently had certain emotions begun to surface, though she couldn't determine why.

Alice drew her back to the cog when she said, "As have we all."

"Isabella was one of yours?"

Alice nodded.

"You said you ruined her family and the redcapes. What did you do?"

"The whitecapes trusted me with their most valued possession. I trusted the wrong person and... I lost it."

"What was it?"

Alice inhaled long and slow before she spoke. "A powerful weapon. One that could save us all."

Margaret repeated aloud what she'd so often told herself, "We're red-capes. We're beyond saving."

"It's time for me to show you something. First, I'll answer the question you'll inevitably ask: no, I am not a sorceress, and I did not take this from you. I protected it so that, one day, when I knew you wanted it, I could give you proof that it's possible for us... to be human."

Margaret believed her soul would never be saved. But a ribbon of hope, wound in disbelief, remained inside her—hope that one day, she could achieve the impossible and get rid of her cape. That ribbon clogged her throat and weakened her voice. "You have proof?"

Alice pulled down her sleeve to reveal an armlet of twisted gold with an Arabic inscription.

Her brow drew together, unsure how it was proof of anything. Then she was in a memory, her memory, watching a boy she'd just met but had also met long ago.

She did know Malcolm.

He was there when she arrived at Hermitage Castle as a girl, before her cape took hold. He was nine, then, and she was seven.

He was different than the Malcolm she knew now. His eyes were wrong, his teeth were too large, and his cape was... red.

Margaret gasped and looked away from the armlet.

It shouldn't be possible. Blood capes were permanent.

Yet, she had seen him. A human with a white, removable cape.

She refocused on the armlet and her memories.

Malcolm was a vicious redcape. He killed violently and often and would have grown to be a high-ranking male in the clan, except he lost his lust. His appetite waned, and he began to starve himself. The water called to him like it called to Margaret, and they bonded over that. Once, he went to it. He almost died, but Alice dragged him from the stream.

"You're his mother," she murmured, but she kept her gaze on the armlet. She'd known that once, before she forgot him.

Margaret had been there when he changed.

He was fifteen. A sword was in his hands, its sparkling hilt adorned with lions. The blade itself was silver caught between liquid and light, with a long, thin blood groove on its flat side.

His eyes turned first; they lightened and lost their red luster. They were clearer and more beautiful than any eyes she'd ever seen. She was mesmerized by them.

Malcolm breathed in a peaceful breath, and his cape released him like a scarlet hand unfurling.

The hope within her swelled and she felt light, as if she'd already shed her mantle. It was possible.

"Why did you keep this from me?"

"Others have tried to leave the clan before and been killed for it. I had to be sure you wouldn't go after him... I had to protect him."

Margaret had punished disloyal capes, weak capes—capes who spoke out of turn. None had outright tried to defect while she was an alpha; certainly, none had succeeded except Malcolm, unless there were others the Elliots were forced to forget. But if any had attempted it, they would have been executed. Even if they were an alpha—which was why she shared her plans and hopes with only Robin up until now.

"What makes you think I won't?"

"Because the water calls to you. Because you want to be saved." She took one of Margaret's hands in hers, a gesture more intimate than any they'd ever shared. Her hands were warm, the hands of a mother. "Because I am sure now. You don't want to be what you are. You don't want to hurt my son, or anyone. You want to be better."

It was true. She wanted to be better. She always had, even when she believed she couldn't be. Even when she committed horrible, despicable acts. She'd always felt some level of guilt or regret, of knowing she was making the wrong choices but being too far in the darkness to see the light.

The sword Malcolm held... it was that light. Could it save her, too?

"That sword... it's what you lost."

Alice's eyes were the colour of shadows under green sea waves, dark and moving. "Yes. The Sword of Living Waters. It could dispel the teeth within our hearts if we had it."

Margaret tore her hand away.

Who would ever trust Alice with something so valuable? Of course she would be the one who ruined life for everyone else, the bumbling fool.

"Where is it?"

"When the King of England took the Stone of Scone, the regalia and the Black Rood of Scotland, he took the sword as well. It's in an abbey in London."

"If you know where it is, why haven't you retrieved it?"

"It's held by a sorcerer's seal."

"Who sealed it?"

"The whitecapes think it may have been Michael Scot. We can't know for certain."

The elusive Wizard of the North. His connection to the Soulises ensured Margaret knew who he was, but the more she searched for a way out of her cape, the more his name seemed to crop up. Was he meant to be her saviour—Scot?

Questions lingered on her tongue, but her worn jaw barred them. She settled more comfortably into her place, savouring the scent of wood from her home country, and the cog's sway eventually lulled her to sleep.

The overloaded cog docked first in Shetland, around six hours after its departure, before arcing east to England over the course of several days, at the end of which its men lowered its single sail and rowed into the River Hull. When they reached York, at the confluence of the rivers Ouse and Foss, they beached the flat-bottomed boat, paid the wharfinger, and failed to notice Margaret and Alice, who had crept from the hold and slipped into the shadow of the aft platform. Men walked to and fro before them, even glanced in their direction, but no one really looked. They were too focused on their tasks, too eager to complete them so they could spend their sea-won shillings on land and return home after weeks of maritime labour.

When the opportunity to cross the walnut deck and disembark beckoned, Margaret took it by the hand. She glided from the cog and quietly wished she could drag a box of whitewood with her—or one of the men, so she could hear his language whenever she wanted and never forget it again. Of course, the thought was silly and fleeting; if she took a prisoner, he wouldn't last long in Hermitage, and he would slow them down on the way there.

Dusk washed over the land with its dark kind of light, and they escaped into it, following the river north. They didn't know of any redcape crossings in England, so they had to jag back and forth across the country, finding bridges or building makeshift ones when they could. It made the going slow, so slow as to double their period of travel, but they found Scotland's border with days to spare—though their hunger had already set in—and they traversed its sheep-spotted, rolling hills through light, swirling mist.

"Why do you kill? Why don't you just die?" Margaret asked Alice as they carried two unconscious, elderly women toward Ninestane. Their bones would be thin and brittle, but better than nothing. "Malcolm was willing to."

"He's a good man. He's better than anyone I've ever known, especially myself." Alice's lips pursed and shadows swam in her eyes, "But for my children, I would have chosen death long ago. And I would like to right my wrong and see the capes saved before I go, though it's a lofty dream. I'm working to find a way."

Margaret wanted to save herself, but Alice wanted to save the others.

A query rose in her mind. "Why did you allow Ermengarde's cape fastening?"

"It wasn't my choice. William commanded it."

In that moment, or perhaps the one before, she was sorry she'd thought her a fool and she was glad her plans had changed, for all desire to murder Alice had gone.

Standing back to back, they killed the old women in the stone circle and gulped down their flesh and bones. Sounds of ripping and crunching and greedily slurping rang in Margaret's ears, buoyed by the silence of the woods around her.

She drank her libation, guiltily reveling in the warm, tangy blood as it saturated her cape and secured for her another month of life. It tasted like poison-laced honey.

Chapter Sixteen

Gudrun stared at Brynhild across the room. She sat on a bench next to Sigurd, so close their arms touched, and tipped back her cage cup. The ring Sigurd slayed a dragon for was on her finger, its thick, silver band set with a polished garnet. Its colour was so deep it looked black, but it glistened scarlet in the light.

She met Gudrun's green eyes with a maleficent smile, her lips stained blood-red from the wine, and Gudrun looked away.

Sigurd denied it, but she knew he and Brynhild were in love.

She'd watched it happen. When they met a year ago, his attraction to her was obvious. They spent as much time together as anyone could, shared tender moments and stole kisses when they thought they were alone—or when Sigurd thought that. More than once, Brynhild had caught Gudrun's eye mid-kiss, though she never alerted him to the intruder.

Sigurd had pulled away from Gudrun. The glances he once threw her ceased, and what she'd thought they had vanished without a mark as if she didn't matter. As if she'd never mattered.

When Grimhild told her Sigurd planned to wed Brynhild, she understood how victims of a sorcerer must feel. It was as if Sigurd had sawn her heart out with a knife and offered it to Brynhild. Their wedding night, when the deed was done, Brynhild would crush it in cold blood, knowing how it would hurt Gudrun. Love lost to another was the most vile, torturous kind of sorcery.

Scorching tears blazed in Gudrun's eyes, and she realized how much she hated her. She'd envied her at first sight, but she didn't hate her for that or for snaring Sigurd when she hoped to claim him for herself.

She hated her because Brynhild hadn't wanted him, at first. She'd been interested in Gundaharius, but he would have been an easy conquest. When she discovered Gudrun desired Sigurd, she began to return his sentiments instead. She was the worst kind of person, the sort who took simply because she liked taking and wanted to see if she could. The sort who didn't just need to be chosen but had to be chosen over others. Who wanted to feel she was better than other women.

Gudrun couldn't help it: her gaze drifted back to the pair. Sigurd was talking to the man on his other side, and Brynhild caught her eye once more.

"I've won," the light-haired woman mouthed, and Gudrun's tears swelled heavy and fell. She ducked her head so no one else would see.

Grimhild saw.

"Stop," her mother commanded.

She dried her eyes, though the command made her want to bawl. Grimhild often told her to stop crying. She wished she didn't feel so weak inside.

"You are not helpless. Nor are you innocent, though you may think it." Under the table, Grimhild pressed a warm, moist mass of muscle into Gudrun's hands. "There are other ways to handle this if you refuse to kill her."

"I couldn't kill," she whispered.

"If you did, I would make you forget."

The tears resurfaced.

From comments like that, Gudrun knew she had. She didn't remember, but she knew.

"No. I've never," she lied and washed it down with truth: "I won't."

She did want to kill Brynhild. Her fingers itched to strangle her, throttle the life from her body. She would relish the fear in her eyes. But, like Brynhild accepting Gundaharius, that would be too easy.

She squeezed the heart with her hands. After a series of squeezes, it began to beat on its own, and its pulse skipped to match her own.

Gudrun wouldn't kill Brynhild—she would best her.

She would win.

Chapter Seventeen

Robin did not look well. If Margaret hadn't believed him before, it was apparent now: he was gravely ill. His skin and cape were grayed and papery, his eyes afflicted and a flat, iron gray. He said, "I was worried you would not return in time."

He lay in Lord Soulis's bedchamber. Everyone knew he was a favourite of William's, second to Alice, but it was still unusual for him to be there, especially because William didn't seem happy about it. William leaned against a wall and glowered at Robin for a time after Margaret's arrival before stalking from the room without a word.

Once he was gone, Robin told her to close the door and raised a shaking finger to point at the tome from Thomas's cavern, the one with the ivory cover. It was open, and he'd scratched notes in spaces around the theory for the elixir of life.

"I have figured it out," he croaked. "Will you make it for me? Will you save my life?"

"Tell me what to do."

He coughed, and dark blood dribbled from the corner of his mouth. "I collected hearts from the abbey. We'll need to take them to Nines-tane..."

She took up the bag of caskets and the tome and helped him from the bed. His weight felt like nothing to her, like his bones had hollowed. He leaned on her as they went down the stairs and mustered what strength he had to walk out on his own so the others wouldn't stare or call to replace him.

Margaret hadn't seen Alianora since the stabbing at Luce Abbey, and she didn't see her now, but she was watchful. With an enemy like her, she had to be.

Still, it was comforting to know her head was safe from the sorceress, thanks to her mother's heart.

As they left the castle, Magnus swept from the forest to Margaret's shoulder. Ermengarde must have been close—Malcolm had cared for her, his little sister, while Alice was in Bergen and was likely returning her now.

Margaret tilted her head to touch the eagle's side, thankful to have him back.

They headed for Ninestane Rig and, by the time they were close, Margaret was half dragging Robin. She left him a ways from the circle, deposited the hearts, and carried him the rest of the way.

It was odd to bring someone to Ninestane to save them instead of eat them.

Robin's breathing was hard and gnarled. After expending his energy on the short journey, he was closer to death than life, a coal sloughing to ash.

The caskets weren't the only thing in the bag; there was also a small earthenware bowl and a stick that had been sharpened to a dull point.

The bowl was glazed over with turquoise and had two layers of twelve lobes each. It looked like a seashell moulded into a goblet by a sea goddess, a vessel a ceasg might fill with children's blood. Margaret set it in the centre of the stone circle at the tome's instruction—Robin was too weak to help much, but his notes were thorough.

With the stick, she mimicked what he'd drawn on the page: she traced a square around the bowl and melted three hearts over it. She then drew a triangle; it apexed at the square's eastern point and its base overlapped two of the square's sides. For the triangle's three corners, she melted three more hearts over the bowl.

Robin lay beside her, his eyes fluttering with urgency. The full moon above, framed by knucklebone clouds, nearly mirrored the one in his drawing. It would soon be overhead.

Margaret sprinkled warm, loose earth from the circle into the bowl. The blood devoured it.

She felt each line of ink with her finger, read it through once and once more. Again, but frantically.

The instructions ended there.

"What do I do next?"

Robin's eyes were closed, his breathing ragged.

She shook him.

"Robin!"

His eyelids snapped open.

A tremor ran through her, fast as a cold front.

Not since she was a child had she been truly afraid of another redcape. They were vicious and bloodthirsty, but Margaret was strong, and they hadn't marked her for death. She had never been the target of their thirst.

She was the target now.

Robin's eyes fixed on her with a deep, murderous, insatiable greed. He didn't want to eat her, but he wanted her life. She could feel it.

Too quick for her to block him, his hand shot toward her chest.

Something tore. For a second, she thought it was her skin, but it wasn't. It was her clothes. He ripped them and yanked the heart casket from her neck. It lit gold in the light from the moon.

She cried out and lunged for it, and Magnus swooped at Robin repeatedly, forcing him flatter against the ground, but it was too late. He had already undone the clasp.

The heart, pure as its discarded silver casket, fell and submerged in the blood concoction. It began to pulse. With each pump, it soaked up more and more blood until it had blackened and swelled to the point of bursting. It settled in the bowl, a shadow under the brilliant moon, and Margaret reached for it.

Against her naked chest, Robin pressed a gold knife with a serrated edge. A sorcerer's blade.

This one was elaborate, ancient, and curved like the jawbone of an age-old beast. Though Robin was still weak, it wasn't. There was no doubt it had taken countless hearts, and Margaret didn't want it to have hers. She motioned for Magnus to leave her. He didn't, but he took to the sky and circled them in worry.

So she watched as Robin took her mother's heart in his willowy hand and bit into it.

He closed his eyes and she tried to move away, but the knife jerked and kept her in place as he ate the entire heart, every single drop of blood.

Strength replenished, he smiled at her. "You saved my life after all. Now, you are useless to me."

He jammed the knife into her sternum and her bone splintered. He began to saw.

Her pain was immense. Each movement brought a hundred agonizing stabs, like he was ripping her heart out and shoving it back in, only to rip it out again.

Black spots blotted out the moon above, cratered the standing stones and Robin's contorted face. They danced and merged into visions of the future—of Robin finishing the cutting, taking the heart from her bloodied body, and swallowing it whole like a snake.

At least she would join her mother in his stomach. And wasn't this what she secretly wanted—to get the punishment she deserved and be free at last?

Robin's face suddenly changed.

The sawing ceased.

"You are not useless to *me*." Robin relinquished his hold on the blade and left it in her chest. "As long as you use Īzebel."

His face left her blotchy vision.

The knife stuck out of her at an angle. It felt wrong inside her, and she desperately wanted it gone, but she couldn't move her arms. If Robin thought she was going to save herself, he would be disappointed.

Her lungs were ablaze. Every breath left her feeling strangled. She gasped in air and her heart threatened to plunge from her half-sawed chest.

The pain left her when the moon snuffed out, and all she could see were tarnished silver stars.

It returned with a strike to the face.

Someone's hand cupped her chin and forced her to chew.

A figure rippled before her, tall with swamp-coloured eyes. They fled in an instant before Margaret's eyes had time to clear. But they left the bitten heart behind and she downed the rest of it.

Her cleaved bones and skin wove back together, and her body forced out the foreign gold knife, which hit the grass with a soft thump. She picked it up.

Disgust curled in her heart, and she dropped it, but it called to her like shadowed water.

"Īzebel." The knife's name dripped from her tongue in the form of satiny foxglove bells, beautiful but dangerous. She slipped her fingers beneath it again and gingerly cradled it in her hand. She didn't want it. But she kept it.

The earthenware bowl was gone, as were Robin, his tome, and the caskets, save one. Her mother's casket still lay open on the ground. Margaret clicked it shut and refastened it around her neck.

Another heart lost. Another thing she would never forgive herself for.

She cursed herself for falling prey to Robin. She should never have trusted him. He knew more than he let on—about her and her mother and who knew what else.

It had been his plan all along, hadn't it? For her to find her mother's heart. After all, he was the one who told her it was pure, and he urged her to go to Bergen before helping him—not for her benefit, but his. He'd used her.

Which meant he had known she was a sorceress before she remembered the fact. But if he needed one, he couldn't be a sorcerer, and he couldn't have taken her memories.

She had so many questions, and she planned to make Robin answer them.

Maybe she would use Īzebel to do it.

Margaret hunted Robin for two months. She searched as much of the castle and the surrounding area as she could for the first and staked out Ninestane Rig for the second. He should have needed a libation—every other cape cycled through. But Robin never showed.

He'd disappeared.

She wanted to pursue him further, but a different problem arose. The whitecapes attacked once more, compelling Margaret to tend to her alpha obligations.

"Where were you?" Cecily, a redcape who would have been in her natal clan, had Margaret been born here, let seven heart teeth fall into her hand. Cecily said they'd killed four more but were able to snatch those teeth before the redcapes could.

Eleven dead. Alianora was still gone; that was why they lost so many in one morning.

Were any of them killed by Malcolm?

Margaret closed her fingers around the rescued teeth, letting them dig into her palm. Then she slipped her hand around Cecily's neck and pinched the top of her cape. A pained groan emitted from her lips. "I decide who lives and dies. Keep that in mind."

She removed her hand and the girl lowered her head in submission.

Though Cecily had attempted it first, Margaret was the one who killed her mother and sister and ascended to the third alpha position. If any redcape hated her, it was Cecily.

Margaret constantly had to put her in her place, remind her why she was an alpha while Cecily was second to three. She had as many bruises as the low-ranking members of the clan, so abused was she by Margaret.

She could practically feel Cecily's eyes burning through her cape as she walked away and took the stair at the north end of the cobbled courtyard.

"Lord Soulis." Her rapping caused the door to open a smidge. She pushed it the rest of the way and found him huddled by the cold fireplace in his solar. Seeing him like this, a grown man curled against the wall, reduced to half his size, felt like a transgression.

He barely lifted his head to acknowledge her, and she made a point of looking away from him when she spoke.

"I'm going to look for candidates. We'll be at the circle by nightfall."

His head fell back against his muscle-corded arms. The sound he made was something between a grunt and a sigh.

"You'll be there." She meant to make it a question, but he seemed a child, so it came out like a weak order, almost a plea.

"What does it matter?"

"We can't fasten capes without you."

"But what does it *matter*?" His head came up this time, rested against the wall and rolled toward her.

"It matters for the clan's survival."

She began to wonder if this was some sort of test and he was only acting broken to confuse her. But then she remembered how much time he spent in his private quarters, his door closed, shutting everyone out. How he travelled less often than he used to and waffled between seeming alive and half dead.

"Perhaps I don't want the clan to survive." A treasonous thought, a death wish, on any lips but his. His head turned away from her, but his eyes seemed to come alive as he said, "Come here."

She couldn't refuse. She knelt before him and glanced up at his diadem. Could she move faster than his thoughts and tear it from his head? She could slam it into the wall and it would shatter; among splintered, tarnished silver, teeth would thud onto the wooden floor, and she would crush every one. William's scalp would likely come off when she took it, but his death would be quick.

"I know what you're doing."

Her eyes froze open.

"You're looking for a way out of your cape."

How did he know that? Did he know about Alice's treachery, too? If he did, why would he let them live?

"It won't matter if you find one."

She wanted to ask why not but didn't want to confirm what he said—though he hadn't said it like an accusation, just a fact.

"We used to be close, you and I."

"I remember."

"I wouldn't mention it if you didn't." Arms on his knees, he leaned forward. "How I yearn for those days. We were innocent and free, or we thought we were. I loved you like a sister."

Her nose pricked with heat. She felt it for him, too, back then.

The idea of tearing off his scalp suddenly seemed so repulsive her stomach roiled with bile. It burned her throat, and she swallowed it down with difficulty.

"We can never be free now."

"You're already free," she choked.

He laughed pitifully. "No sorcerer is free. Least of all me."

"You are. You can leave. You can stop killing—I can't."

"You think it's so easy?" He laughed darkly. "No. We're trapped together. Even if I lose this crown, even if you lose your cape... we're unreachable. Lost in darkness, forsaken. We can never be free."

She resisted, but tears stung her eyes as he voiced the fears she tried not to hear.

"I used to fight him—"

"Who?"

"—but I've given up trying. Because nothing matters. We're all lost." He slumped back against the stone, beneath a tapestry stitched with a bloodied unicorn on a battlefield. A shadowy, snarling animal towered over it, victorious. "Leave me."

For once, she didn't want to leave him, but the crown of teeth compelled her to. It stabbed at her heart with urges to move, urges so overwhelming that they crushed any desire she'd felt to stay.

The crown forced her from his apartments and down the stairs. She waited for her face to clear before she reentered the hall and led a group of redcapes from the castle.

When no one was near, she buried Robin's knife in the woods.

The redcapes and their sorcerer gathered at Ninestane Rig.

Lord Soulis wasn't the depressed man he'd been in his solar; he was the same as he always was at Ninestane: imposing, inscrutable, prepared.

Margaret was the only alpha in attendance. Alianora had been spotted days ago taking her monthly libation alone and riding off on a horse after, and Alice was pretending she'd killed a whitecape and was afflicted by the curse, which Margaret would have believed not long ago. But she knew Alice now—she didn't want to participate in the turning of humans.

The Elliots found four young, robust women and a few lean men to replace what dead they could, along with seven sacrifices to complete the ritual. Fear rendered the humans mostly silent, though a few sobbed to themselves. Their sobs fell on deaf ears.

"You will be first." Margaret indicated the tallest woman, whose eyes twitched to the red deer antler crown upon her head. The antlers were thick, highly developed, and aged, humus brown. Their tines branched in every direction, and their grooves were lined with dried blood.

A redcape shoved the woman and the teenage boy, who would become her cape, forward. Lord Soulis followed them, passing between two standing stones.

"Swallow this."

The woman took the incisor by its point so as not to graze Margaret's fingers. Her eyes darted from the tooth to the redcape, and her nose wrinkled. She swallowed it.

William did his duty: he sliced the boy's throat wide and fashioned his blood into a cape for their newest member. There was no indication of what he'd said hours earlier, no sign he might want Clan Elliot to fall. On the contrary, there was a glint in his eye, a pleasure on his parted lips. Like he rejoiced in spawning monsters.

Screams tore from the humans outside the circle. A few were frozen in place. Others tried to run. They didn't get far.

The process was repeated five times.

As the last would-be redcape, a man who'd fallen to his knees in fear, was heaved into the circle, an alpha intervened. Alianora had returned, and she had a human with her.

She strode into Ninestane Rig, opened her maw wide, and gruesomely chomped down on the man's face. She gobbled down his head and broke down his torso. He was finished in seconds. But she didn't soak up his blood; she let it run freely.

Margaret's cheeks sparked red as her cape as emotions swirled inside her: fear at seeing her, annoyance at feeling afraid, anger that Alianora ruined the one night she had as the clan's sole alpha.

"Tooth." The sorceress held out her hand.

Margaret clutched it a long while, a show to the others that she didn't *have* to give it to her, that she wanted to, though she did, and she didn't.

Alianora motioned to the man she'd arrived with and he rushed to her side, unconcerned with the redcape onlookers. She gave him the tooth and he eagerly downed it.

William, unbothered by who was turning as long as someone was, attached fresh-blood fabric to the latecomer's nape, and it was done.

The three of them, Margaret, William, and Alianora, stood in Ninestane with seven bloodless corpses and as many new capes. With four heart teeth lost to the whitecapes, their clan capped at thirty-three, there was no way to grow it. And if they could, would Margaret want to? Did she want the whites to eradicate them all?

She couldn't bring herself to care about the rest, as long as she was saved, and Alice. Maybe William.

His words haunted her: *We can never be free.*

She pictured him by his fireplace, crushed against the wall, spiritless. Pitying himself.

He had given up. All the times Margaret thought she would, she listened for the water—for life. And she kept going.

Redemption could never be hers, but until all paths were travelled, she would strive for freedom.

Margaret took charge of completing the ritual, ordering the new seven to lower their heads before her. It was how alphas asserted dominance, how inferior redcapes greeted their superiors.

Flanked by Clan Elliot, the alphas and sorcerer led the way from Ninestane Rig, leaving the new capes to scavenge the dried bodies they left behind.

Chapter Eighteen

The melting sun's orange glow clung to the woodwork on the ceiling, faint light on rubescent wood, and traced the arabesque motifs on the stucco walls with soft fingers.

When Michael Scot voyaged from Sicily to Toledo clutching a manuscript against his chest, the *De Animalibus ad Caesarem*, the first piece of furniture he acquired was a cedar table. It was worn and nicked, but it was still where he'd placed it under the window, which looked over an enclosed garden where Scot had once studied the planets and stars, the moon and the sun. Poppies were recently planted there among grass that had bronzed slightly from a cold night. Scarlet celosia and white camellia flowers lined the garden walls, welcoming autumn. The jacaranda and orange trees had lost most of their leaves, but they would explode in flurries of lavender and white come springtime—the florets would blanket the ground like fallen snow and stray petals would drift into the house through open doors and windows.

Beyond the garden, past narrow streets and brick, patio-connecting arches, was the house owned by the Order of Solomon's Temple, where Scot had spied on whitecapes—including the Queen of Castile and Toledo, Eleanor, daughter of King Henry II of England—and culled valuable information about the location of reds and contemporary sorcerers. Southeast from there was the School of Translators, where he'd worked with Moorish astronomers, studied the heavens, wrote and read and translated.

He turned from the view, red cape lagging behind his cerise, gold-hemmed, tight-waisted Moslem dress. He wasn't there to admire the garden or reminisce but to retrieve the trephine he'd stowed upstairs.

A keyhole arch led to a hall lined with black and white azulejos that linked together to form a tiled, white serpent. Its tail began on the right side of the arch, and its body spanned the hall, snaked around, and ended on the left, where its orbed eyes were glazed red.

Scot pressed against the base of its head and the wall budged. Stone ground against stone as he shoved it wide, revealing a secret stair like others he'd built. Closing the door behind him, he climbed the stair and lit a nine-branched candelabrum, which caused the vaulting on the ceiling to flicker—it resembled glistening honeycombs. The glass alembic next to the candelabrum came alive with saffron light as if liquid gold boiled inside it.

His laboratory was unchanged. No one had discovered it since he left Toledo to return to the court of the Holy Roman Emperor, Frederick II, in the 1220s.

Here, he had studied and practiced chemistry and metallurgy, delved into recipes for the making of silver and gold—in some cases from mercury and copper—poured and fashioned caskets for hearts, and worked with all manner of materials, many of them rare. They were set on stained shelves, most bottled: Cumaean and Sardinia salt, ground carcha and coral root, Roman alum and vitriol, Arabian gold, Italian black marble, copper, lead and tin, Egyptian garnets and pebbles from the Indus, Cyprus and Barbary earth, sand from the shores of the Red Sea, soapstone and flint, talc, arsenic, sulfur, mercury, pulverized bone and oxygenated blood and other treasures. Here, he'd translated pieces of *Liber Luminis Luminum*, among other works, and penned *De Alchimia*.

Scot pushed aside a mortar and a small, ceramic crucible so he could see the wall behind a shelf, where a wide tapestry was hung, embroidered with the al-Qasr in Palermo before the Normans won the palace. He'd brought it with him from Sicily. It had once hung in plain view, but he'd used it to hide a compartment behind this shelf when he left, for he'd worried about bringing certain items with him to the Imperial Court.

He drew the tapestry open, reached into the dark hole, and grabbed the first thing he touched: a Celtic bronze hand mirror, its back dented and decorated with double spirals. In its polished metal, he didn't see his own reflection; he saw a face more perfect than his, symmetrical and bright, impossibly clear in the bronze. It was the face of the demon whom Scot had let in at a young age, who'd come and gone as he pleased since then and wore a crown of gold. That serpent of old, Abaddon.

Abaddon gave a brief smile before his beautiful, blue-violet eyes faded and gave way to Scot's face, to his broad nose and wide-set eyes. It was a face he'd known for centuries, one that had many names over the years, including Michael Scot, Robin Elliot, and Gundobad. Before that, before he'd been incarnated as a man, he'd had a different body and a different name, that of the sorceress Grimhild, Argentum Maga, Queen of the Burgundians—the first redcape.

Scot placed the mirror beside the crucible, reached back into the compartment, and felt for what he'd come for—the thing to harvest bone, for he'd used all he had and couldn't manipulate sorcerers without it.

When he couldn't find it, he swept the shelf's contents to the floor. Glass shattered and metal clinked as he ripped the tapestry from the wall and thrust both hands inside.

Nothing.

He seized the candelabrum and brought it close enough to see clearly but not so close as to set anything afire.

The compartment was empty. Someone had found his laboratory, after all, for the trephine was gone.

Chapter Nineteen

To protect their teeth after the devastating ambush, William ordered the redcapes to patrol the grounds and send their eagles to the skies, and he sentenced them to autumn in Hermitage, kept a watchful eye, and succeeded in fielding the whitecapes; they had attempted a few attacks, but they hadn't made it into the castle, and they'd failed to assail the reds on their trips to Ninestane Rig. No one had been lost, and the flashes of white on the surrounding hills or in the marshy woodlands abated.

The man Alianora brought to the last cape fastening later proved to be her son, John III Comyn, rival of Robert Brus and former Guardian of Scotland. He took his libations with the high-ranking females of Clan Elliot, a thing Margaret didn't approve of, but he was an alpha's son, so she allowed it. Besides, she was still wary of Alianora, though the woman had made no more attempts on her life. They both acted as if the incident at the abbey never happened.

Margaret had done what she could to search for Robin—leafed through books he'd read, checked every stone and corner for hidden clues. But there was no mention of the elixir of life in any of the library's scrolls and no sign as to where he might have gone or what he might do next. She doubted he was dead—he was too clever for that, and she'd helped him heal himself. He'd likely soaked his cape at Ninestane while she was shut in the castle.

Someday, she might avenge herself; perhaps when she was Queen of Scots and had greater resources. For now, she had to let him go.

Two months after the cape fastening, William sealed himself in his room. The suggestion to stay in the castle was still there in the back of the redcapes' minds, but he couldn't control all of them at once. When he couldn't see who was trying to leave, who to focus on, his control was all but lost. Margaret took the opportunity to visit Lucy Abbey. To her chagrin, Michael Scot's vault had been cleaned out. No casket or stray paper had been left behind. She returned to Hermitage Castle empty-handed and, on a damp, clammy day, she did the thing she'd been dreading: she sought out Alianora.

After hours of searching, she found her less than an hour north of the castle on the edge of a morass with John III Comyn. Margaret had charged into it years before and gotten sucked in. She would have died if Alianora hadn't been there and pulled her out, wrapped in mud.

"...understand," John said. She could barely hear from far off. "Look at what I've done for you—"

"I didn't want you to." Alianora turned away from him, shoes squishing on the spongy peat, brown rushes rustling.

"I thought you did," he said softly.

Margaret was close now; they'd both seen her.

"Leave, John."

Her hairs rose when he left them alone. If Alianora came at her, she was ready to fight back, though she would lose again. But she didn't attack, nor did she threaten to. As this was their first time alone since, Margaret suspected she might bring up the incident at the abbey, but she didn't so much as allude to it.

"What are you doing here?"

"Do you know how to break a sorcerer's seal?" spouted Margaret.

Not hunting Robin allowed her to explore the possibility of freeing the Sword of Living Waters and freeing herself with it. As William wouldn't speak with her, or anyone, Alianora was the only person Margaret could think of who might know how.

But Alianora traipsed past her and flicked her wrist, dismissing the question. "Don't waste your time. It can't be done."

"There must be a way."

Before she got too far, Alianora stopped. Her tone was flat. "You've been acting odd lately. Did something happen?"

"You know what happened."

She cocked her head. "Something with whitecapes, I assume. Or Norway? Yes, I know you went back."

"I meant what happened at the abbey."

"What abbey?"

"Luce Abbey. Where you left me for dead." Margaret's words slowed as she saw the truth lined in Alianora's face, and likely the reason she hadn't attacked again, "You don't remember."

"Tell me."

"It was a misunderstanding. Robin and I were at Luce Abbey. You arrived. I was hurt. You left."

"You're lying." Alianora searched her face. "I hurt you. Why?"

"How should I know?"

"You must have attacked me. I wouldn't have otherwise." She frowned. "Wait, who is that?"

Margaret's gaze flitted back and forth in practiced movement, scanning for signs of life. She didn't see anyone. "Who?"

"The person you were with... Robin. You said you were at Luce Abbey with Robin."

Her skin flared.

Another of Robin's lies. He said Alianora made them forget something, but it must have been him. He'd plucked moments from them both, but why? And if he was a sorcerer, why did he need Margaret to create his elixir of life?

"Do you remember why you went to the abbey?"

She narrowed her eyes. "No."

"Robin is a redcape. He must have made you forget... but how? He said you have a pure heart."

Alianora's fingers flew to her chest, where a thin casket must have lain beneath her cotton top. Her voice was a trifle more than a whisper. Her skin had gone flake-white. "You can bypass the protection with a heart and a sorcerer's trephine. Only a trephine can make you forget twice."

Before she could ask, "A what?" the sorceress had fled over the low, blue-brown hills and left Margaret alone with the mire.

In the first-floor hall, Ermengarde's small feet padded after Alice. She was almost three years old with spades of energy. She could outrun everyone in her natal clan, so she fought infrequently and spent much of her time playing with her mother, who broke from her when she saw Margaret. Magnus took her place, dodging Ermengarde as she jumped to brush his marbled tail feathers.

"I spoke with Malcolm," Alice murmured. "The whitecapes want to meet with you."

"Why?"

"I don't know."

Margaret chewed her lip.

What would it be like to see Malcolm again?

"When? During another attack?"

"No, they want you to go to them. Will you?"

Truthfully, Margaret was already pondering it. Robin was a dead end, neither William nor Alianora would help her, and she didn't know any other sorcerers. She was at a loss for what to do, but the whitecapes were an avenue she had yet to explore. They condemned sorcery, but surely they knew things.

"Yes. I'll go."

With instruction, a hand mirror, and her sheepskin cloak, she exited Hermitage to hunt with Magnus. He soared through lightly drizzling rain as she moved over the moors.

High above, he looked at her, swept his right wing down, and flexed his talons. It was a signal: he'd found her a libation.

She climbed a small, grassy hill and passed under a rowan. A ways later, she saw what Magnus found: a stream between a wood and a pasture where laundresses gathered. They went back and forth on both sides of the stream, washing clothes and hanging them over branches and bushes or spreading them out in the pasture.

Margaret made her way through the wood and hid near the drying clothes until a washerwoman wandered over by herself to hang a tunic, then yanked her behind a thick-trunked tree and clamped a hand around her throat. The woman's scream broke against the crushed bones of her neck and was too weak, at its end, to escape Margaret's other palm, which was fitted over her mouth.

Margaret easily dragged her back through the wood to Ninestane and made short work of her before beginning her journey north.

CHAPTER TWENTY

LOCH DOCHFOUR, KINGDOM OF SCOTLAND, NOVEMBER 1301

Margaret stole a horse near Perth a few days after leaving Hermitage Castle, and hours north, she slept for the first time. She didn't know for how long but overestimated to be safe, as keeping track of days was a redcape necessity.

On the edge of a wildwood thick with pines, a wood too dense to enter, the horse finally tired and she left it behind. It was a sad affair; the animal was particularly useful for crossing small streams, but Margaret found other ways across: forgotten bridges or fallen logs. In some cases, she had to travel far to ford rivers, but it was faster than waiting hours for the horse to regain energy when she needed rest less often—one perk of her cape she would be sorry to lose.

She followed Alice's directions to a cruck-framed house at the edge of Loch Dochfour and waited before it, feeling out of place. She wasn't used to making her presence known and was quite unsure how to go about it.

Magnus let out a weak, high-pitched call, and fabric rustled behind her.

She turned too late. A hand caught her throat and a dagger tasted her skin. It slid from her throat to her nape and pressed sideways, about to cut through. They were going to kill her.

"Wait—Brus—" she sputtered and struggled to pull her cape and cloak back so they could see the mirror tied against her waist with slashed cloth. Its back resembled a flag, but not one she'd seen elsewhere. It was etched with a red-painted rampant lion in the centre of a blue cross-and-crosslets and carefully sanded to reveal pure silver beneath, which accented the image in swirls. Alice said it belonged to Robert and gave it to her as a precaution; a ticket to board whitecape ferries, a metal letter of safe conduct. "Robert Brus sent me."

The dagger let up as the door swung open to reveal a woman in a brown kirtle laced up the front over a light shift.

Her eyes went wide. Through her teeth, she said, "What are you waiting for? Kill her."

The person behind Margaret, a man, judging from his voice, ordered everyone inside. Before he closed and locked the door, Magnus swooped in and perched on a curved oak beam above the long room.

The man let Margaret go and stood with his two companions. He said, "You're Margaret, then?"

They knew her name... did they also know her story?

The woman whispered a heated accusation—that the redcape probably killed Robert and pried the mirror from his still-warm hands—and the man hushed her. Margaret waited impatiently until, at last, they introduced themselves as Agnes, Maud, and Randolph of Clan Grant.

Their agreement to ferry her across the loch had an addendum from the angry one, Maud. If Margaret had lied, she told her, as redcapes were wont to do, Maud would hunt her down herself, dump her in the middle of Loch Dochfour, and let her washed-clean body drift down River Ness to the sea.

Margaret smiled at her threat, vexing the woman. With Magnus, she followed Agnes to the loch's edge, where she stood far from sunlit waters.

"We're ready," Agnes called from the boat. "Randolph will carry you out so your feet don't touch the water."

She clutched her cape with tight fists and sickness ebbed in her chest as she watched the boat sway. A large ship where she could find shadowed hideaways was one thing; unsettling, but doable. Getting in a ferryboat was another. She wasn't sure she could do it, but she didn't squirm when Randolph grabbed her. In seconds, they were over the water, and she was acutely aware that if he let her go, she would submerge and be forced to eat one of them to survive.

She dug her fingers into his arms, clung so hard he cried out in protest. She almost dug in harder and fought to hold back. If she drew blood, she couldn't stop her cape from inhaling it.

He heaved her into the boat and got in himself, and Margaret was surprised to see the ferry was coated in earth, moss, grasses, and twigs. They'd either done it in anticipation of her arrival, or they ferried other redcapes. Alice, maybe.

The three humans, whitecapes not wearing their capes, picked up their oars and rowed slowly so as not to spray her with water. Maud was the least careful and, on one occasion, she purposefully flicked water at Margaret, who barely dodged it. Despite Maud, the rocking of the boat, and her fear it might tip over, Margaret's sickness had dissipated.

Woodland birds chirped on either side of the loch. Margaret searched the trees for them, distracting herself until she made it safely across, having lost but a few blood drops from water spray.

Randolph carried her to shore and deposited her in a place between trees and thick bushes, frightening a moulting red squirrel into the thinning undergrowth. He and Agnes bade her a terse farewell while Maud watched silently from the boat.

Margaret was glad to be on her own again and, while walking through forested swamps and wet heathlands, glad of her leather boots, which were reinforced at the seams to keep water out.

As Alice told her, there was another whitecape ferry at the River Beauly. Margaret approached with the safe conduct mirror raised this time and supplemented her credibility with Agnes, Randolph, and Maud's names.

This boat was attached to a rope that spanned the river; using it, the whitecape hauled her across, and Margaret made her way around the western edge of Beauly Firth.

She crossed a field half covered in stones and half in broom and, near the firth's shore, saw a triangular, sandstone castle that rose above a variety of trees. Her destination, Redcastle, was built on the site of Edradour, which was once a redcape hunting seat constructed and fortified by William the Lion.

Bluish white flashed on a fighting platform in the waning light. They'd seen her.

She climbed the slope to the main entrance and three of them met her there: Malcolm and a man and woman she didn't recognize.

Margaret held up the mirror protectively, but Malcolm grinned and she lowered it. She crossed the threshold beside him with a whitecape ahead and behind and had to remind herself that Alice trusted them. But then, Alice admitted she'd trusted the wrong people before.

They're not the enemy, she assured herself, but she didn't believe it. Whatever Alice thought, whitecapes didn't save redcapes, they killed them. They were the enemy; they always had been.

Yet, here she was, consorting with them. What did that make her?

Malcolm caught one of her glances with his rich brown eyes and didn't look away. Warmth bled through her.

She couldn't imagine he would hurt Alice, Ermengarde, herself, anyone. She couldn't fathom blood staining his pure white cape, splattering his perfect, mauve-rimmed smile.

She was safe with him. Or as safe as she could be among whites.

They entered the hall, which was strewn with rushes, and walked the length of it, passing banners stitched with the same design as Robert's mirror. It was clear, now, that it was the whitecape banner, not some crest or image of the House of Brus.

At the end of the hall, several whitecapes waited, conversing in Norman French. A boar roasted on a spit in a huge, open fireplace behind them. The heat expanded the humans' blood vessels, brought colour to their flesh. How easy it would be to tear them apart, shove their arms down her throat, absorb the blood from their bodies...

Margaret stuck her tongue to the roof of her mouth and focused on the banner above the fireplace. She wasn't there for blood. Even if she were, she was in the heart of a whitecape nest, and they were armed with practice and silver.

"Eiriksdatter, I presume?"

She pursed her lips. She supposed they didn't need to bother with "Her Royal Highness" or "Ma'am" as long as she was... what she was.

The Laird of Redcastle, Andrew Bosco, introduced himself and the other whitecapes: Thomas, Alexander, John, Mary Margaret, Hugh, Duncan, Roger, James, Isabella, Patrick, Annabelle, and Adam—too many names for Margaret to remember, even with some duplicates.

"I'm told you want to change," Andrew said.

She nodded.

"Most redcapes like the power. They embrace... the darkness."

Margaret swallowed and her eyes drifted away from him. "I can't argue either point. I do like it. But with each embrace, guilt follows... I don't want to feel that anymore." A rare moment of honesty. She didn't know where it came from, but it seemed to please them.

"It's an admirable goal," said the leader of the whitecapes, Thomas Durward. "But perhaps an impossible one, if our former sorceress is to be believed."

Anger boiled within her and she bared her teeth, regretting her brief vulnerability. "Why did you ask me here, then, if not to help me?"

"I want to help you," Malcolm interjected. His eyes, amber in the firelight, absorbed her anger like a cape drinking in blood. Another softer emotion filled its place. "I know what it's like to be a redcape slave. I want you to be free."

He was right. She was a slave. The cape had darkened her heart, made her a killer, trapped her in a world of sin. It robbed her of her throne, her humanity. Her life.

Thomas's voice tugged her attention back to him. "Most here are related, however loosely, to the illegitimate daughter of King Alexander II, Marjorie. You are King Alexander III's only scion, the last in the legitimate line of the first Scottish whitecape, William the Lion, and his mother, the witch, Ada Warenne."

Her body stilled. "What are you saying?"

"See for yourself." He gestured toward an open doorway to the right.

Margaret's neck prickled as she walked toward it, very aware of the many whitecapes trailing her.

On the other side of the doorway began a scarlet runner rug. It ran across another a third of the way into the room, forming a scarlet rood.

Margaret stopped at the rugs' intersection and regarded the raised throne, surrounded by red and white silk damask walls. Its arms were maned lions, and its back was carved with a haloed lamb in a bed of white hawthorn flowers. A slant of soft moonlight brightened a white cape that lay folded on the throne.

Beside her, Thomas said, "If ever it were possible for you to shed your cape of blood, we would offer you this. Your mother's cape."

Her eyes were fixed on it.

Margaret of Scotland, Queen Consort of Norway, her mother... was a whitecape?

"For a long while, we thought she'd lived. Like reds, white capes dissolve upon death. Hers never did. Perhaps it's waiting for you. If you're saved, and you choose to accept the cape, we will have you as grand mistress of all Scots whitecape orders."

Like the queenship, this position, Grand Mistress of Whitecapes, had once been meant for her.

She wanted to rush forward and feel the throne where her mother sat. Something solid, real, something that was hers. Since she'd lost her heart to Robin, she had nothing that belonged to her mother.

But she remembered Alice's introduction of Thomas of Erceldoune: *He was a friend of their last grand mistress.* He had been her mother's friend, and she had brought about his death.

She thought of his body falling and his eyes clouding with silver, of her mother's heart darkening, bulging, tearing between Robin's teeth, and stayed where she was.

"Orders?"

"There are members of two here today: the Order of the Hawthorn and the Order of the Thistle, currently led by Thomas and Robert Brus," Malcolm inserted. He was on her other side, a step behind. "There are others, but we are the largest in Scotland."

The moonlight moved from the cape on the throne, reminding Margaret she, too, was in darkness. She tore her eyes from it and looked through a high-up window instead, where bone-shard stars ribbed the night sky.

"Why would you show me this room if you don't believe I can be saved?"

"That's precisely why," Thomas said. "Because Malcolm here has convinced us anyone can be saved. And because I am not an expert on sorcery."

"But we know someone who is," Malcom said. "And she's requested an audience with you in England."

Chapter Twenty-One

Her mother's heart casket, now filled with earth, hung around Margaret's neck. She tucked it beneath her dress, mounted her horse, and followed the whitecaps to England.

Their party was small, consisting of five members: herself, Thomas Durward, Mary Margaret Grahame, Malcolm Elliot, and Robert Brus. They were dressed in linen undergarments and heavy wool layers, bundled to endure the wintry weather.

One of them always stayed awake—to watch for outsiders, they said, but Margaret knew it was her they watched. They didn't trust her not to kill them as they slept. She wanted to leave them behind, but they knew what to expect from London and where to go, so she waited frustratedly as they slept through each night. When Margaret did grow tired, her sleep was restless; as they didn't trust her not to kill them, she didn't trust Robert.

Over a week in, they came upon St. Alban's Abbey and Thomas gave her a bundle of cloth. A white cloak. It wasn't like her waterproof, sheepskin cloak, which wrapped around her like a blanket when she wore it, an aide to her blood-infused cape. This one felt foreign, like wearing someone else's discarded skin. As they came upon London a day later, she still wasn't used to the feeling, but she imagined her mother's would feel much the same and was glad she hadn't stolen it from its place on the throne of Redcastle.

The city burst with traffic and sound. Its streets pulsed with life and twisted like narrow veins. They joined the streets' flow to the Thames, which teemed with river vessels laden with merchandise. Robert stopped them near London Bridge and studied the sun and the shadows.

The whitecapes' mysterious former sorceress would have met them in Leeds, but Margaret insisted on going to West London. She wanted to see the sword for herself.

She pretended to watch a line of packhorses traversing the bridge, but her focus was on Robert's voice. Unfortunately, his conversation with Thomas was drowned by noise: the clacking of horse hooves, wooden rumbling of wheels, and talk of passersby.

Malcolm sidled next to her and pointed east. "There she is, now."

A covered wagon trundled over the long, stone bridge, its wheel kicking up water. It weaved between merchants, traders, and Londoners that bustled about beneath the bridge buildings and stopped to let Margaret and the whitecapes on.

"Sister Isabella Warenne," Robert addressed a woman who had made the trip from the edge of the Weald in West Sussex. "This is Margaret Eiriksdatter."

Margaret's eyes widened. Not just because the use of her true surname still felt, to her, like a not-so-well-kept secret, but because she knew who Isabella was: Alianora's sister-in-law, wife to the former King of Scots, and a relative of Margaret's.

Alianora believed her dead. Yet, here she was, eyes dancing beneath an ivory wimple, wearing a slitted, long, blue tunic and a cape white as soft snow. She ordered the driver on, and they wound over the top of the Thames.

Soon, they were on Fleet Street, then townhouses and palaces were whipping by on the Strand, and they were bracing themselves against pits and mudholes. They took the left at Charing Cross, passed the property of the Kings of Scotland and the white stone York Place, and came upon the rose-windowed Westminster Abbey.

The last English king had begun to reconstruct the abbey, but work had stalled, so the old nave clung to the new cathedral. One day, the nave would be cut off and built anew, but for now, it was a stone cape fused to the cathedral's neck, a reminder of its past and a mar to its beauty.

Isabella departed the wagon first and waved Margaret and Robert out soon after—the others stayed behind to draw less attention. A monk in a black habit was with her. He guided them through the Great West Door to another man: the Abbot of Westminster, Walter Wenlok. Margaret found herself distracted by his large ears and boyish face and didn't hear a word he said.

She stayed near the back of the group as they walked the length of the bustling nave and passed the quire. The vaulted ceiling was a giant's chest ripped open: run through with a straight spine, its naked ribs formed pointed arches with bone-bare spandrils as they reached down into Purbeck marble columns. Another skeleton in an abbey of tombs.

She held her pearly cloak close to make sure no scarlet showed beneath it, though she wasn't sure how many knew about redcapes in England. Would anyone question a red garment here? She'd seen plenty of red in the streets. Were the English whitecapes on the lookout in London, or was their base somewhere else?

Near a statue holding a gold chalice, in the heart of the abbey, was the chapel of Edward the Confessor, outside which Walter said, "Private prayers are not uncommon. Your time will be uninterrupted."

The shrine and Henry III's tomb beside it, just north, were a dazzling combination of coloured marble, semi-precious stones, porphyry and glass, and the flooring bore geometric mosaics fashioned by the Cosmati. Latin words of cobalt glass encircled the top of the shrine of St. Edward's base, and they read:

+ANNO: MILENNO: DOMINI: CVM: SEPTVAGENO: ET: BIS: /CENTENO CVM: COMPLETO: QVASI: DENO: HOC: OPVS: EST: FACTVM: QVOD: PETRVS:/ DVXIT: IN: ACTUM: RO- MANVS: CIVIS: HOMO:/ CAVSAM: NOSCERE: SI: VIS: REX: FVIT: HENRICVS: SANCTI: PRESENTIS: AMICVS

"In the thousandth year of the Lord, with the seventieth and twice the hundredth with the tenth more or less complete this work was made which Peter the Roman citizen brought to completion. O Man, if you wish to know the cause, the king was Henry, the friend of the present saint."[I]

At the centre of it, beneath a gold-coated Welsh coronet, the Sword of Living Waters was vertically displayed. Margaret's restored memory of it was accurate, but there was something she had forgotten or hadn't seen: between the lions on its silver hilt, seven runes that looked like broken *n*'s or *r*'s were etched, shining like white gold.

As if it was a babbling burn, it called to Margaret, drew her toward it. She reached her fingers out, but she didn't feel the blade. It was encased in something unseen. She couldn't touch it.

"Do you know how to break the seal?" she asked Isabella.

"I do."

Alianora said it wasn't possible, but Margaret knew it had to be. She couldn't trust a thing that vile sorceress said. "Then do it."

"I cannot. If I could, I would not."

Margaret clenched her jaw and wondered how best to threaten the woman, but she felt Robert hovering behind her, waiting for any excuse to sever her cape from her body. "Tell me how and I will do it."

"I'm aware you've practiced sorcery," Isabella said. "But you've yet to take a heart for yourself. Am I correct?"

She nodded once. What did it matter?

"Like me, you come from the longest line of sorcerers in existence, the line of Queen Grimhild of the Burgundians. I was once proud of it. I even thought it might grant me... immunity, of a kind, to the uncontrollable side of sorcery. It did not." Isabella paused for a somber moment, seeing something of the past. "Nor will it you. If you are willing to take a heart, sorcery will take you, in turn. It's a dark, addictive trade. It will sink its teeth into you and drag you into shadowy depths. I have been there.

"I'm one of the lucky few who broke free. The last was Countess Ada Warenne—she found solace at Haddington as I have at Rusper. Like her, I've devoted my life to the church and doing good works to atone for my many sins. I will never again use sorcery, and I would advise you—anyone—against it."

"You would rather I go on killing as a redcape?"

"You might kill more as a sorceress. Nevertheless, as a friend made me see... it is your birthright. The choice is yours to make." Isabella's chest filled with a slow breath, and she produced a plated box. The top was hammered to create a border around a background inlaid with garnets, turquoise, thinly slivered bone, and gold glass set with cloisons. The design was familiar—a white serpent with eyes of blood. The cloisons curled around it like gilded reptile tongues.

The serpent guarded an object: a slender metal instrument with a sharp, conical tip.

"What is it?"

"An example of the hold heart-taking has." Isabella's lips were tight, her eyes fixed on a face that wasn't there. "It's a sorcerer's trephine, used for bone extraction. Ermengarde Durward stole it from Michael Scot, and I from her. Then I stole more. She was a great whitecape and a great friend, and I killed her. I couldn't stop myself."

"What does it do?"

"It extracts bone. If you infuse a heart with your own, that heart will be yours; if you infuse one with Michael Scot's bone, the heart will be his. That is the way to unseal the sword, with his own heart, if he is the binder. His bones are out there, dead or alive, or the seal would have broken naturally." Isabella snapped the lid shut and thrust it at her. Forcefully, she said, "I won't speak more on the matter except to say again: you are not special, dear Margaret. You're no stronger than any sorceress before you. Thus, I urge you to damn sorcery, or it will damn you."

She flushed with heat, resenting the assumption. Who was she to say how strong Margaret was? Especially when Isabella herself was able to put her heart-eating ways behind her.

The hypocrite left.

"I can tell you want to use it." Robert startled her. He'd been so silent during their exchange, she'd half forgotten he was there. "So do. Save your clan."

Her clan. She hadn't thought of them.

"I'll need to find Scot before anything else."

"Yes, regarding Scot, we can't be sure—"

Movement caught her eye; he noticed and quieted. On the west side of the shrine, past the wooden coronation chair that housed the Stone of Scone and the high altar, English whitecapes approached, guided by the abbot.

Robert yanked her arm to get her moving. They bolted past an open chapel, where a simple rendering of the Sword of Living Waters being held by St. Paul hovered over the altar, but skidded to a halt around the transept arm's corner.

Men had flooded the building, slipped down the side aisles and obstructed the Great North Door. They swept Robert and Margaret through the abbey and up a spiraled wooden staircase like driftwood on a swell.

In the triforium at the top of the stairs was another Englishman. He ignored their entrance for a few long seconds while he looked down his nose at the nave, then said to Robert, "Hail, friend."

"Guy." Robert's acknowledgment was too friendly.

Guy's eyes spurned his smile. "It's been four years, hasn't it? five?"

"Come to betray us again, have you?" another whitecape muttered.

Robert said plainly, "I had the need to change friends."

Gold crosslets stitched on the man's red-dyed, fustian tunic rippled as he laughed. "You'll have the need again. Your mind was always fickle as a woman's."

Margaret glanced sideways at Robert, expecting dark anger on his face, but his eyes were light, and the corners of his mouth were lifted.

"The great take on what suits them," he said, a shrug in his voice, as if whatever betrayal occurred was a mote to be brushed off and forgotten.

"Indeed." Guy came closer, stroking his groomed, brown beard. "Why should we take you on, then? You Scots capes have grown weak."

"Some have. I haven't."

"Show me." His gaze pointedly flicked to Margaret.

The smile on Robert's wide mouth tightened.

Margaret focused on the dust that peppered the air and swirled like weightless snow. She breathed it in, swallowed hard, and tried not to feel as though she was suffocating.

Robert wouldn't kill her, even to save himself. Would he?

"I will, but not here."

He would?

Yes, he would. He said it himself: he took on what suited him. Killing her would suit him. And if he refused, they would kill her anyway.

Her heart skipped quicker, and she searched the room, but there was no way out with capes stoppering the stair and glass windows blocking the open air. The floor itself warned against running, for tips of stone vaults from below poked through it, tripping hazards, and the rest was rough stone and uneven as a handful of cloudberries.

The painted corbel heads seemed to watch her, their faces grotesquely peaceful, even jolly.

"Why not? It's God's work."

"Even so."

Guy inclined his head and considered him. "Outside, then. Before the parish church."

Margaret was forced outside. The men grabbed her arms and hair, threatened her to move, but they avoided touching her cape. In their eyes, it was unclean, evil. In her eyes, too.

Between Westminster and the parish church, St. Margaret's, they formed a ring around her and Robert, who held a blade. It wasn't unlike Ninestane. She would die in a circle of living stones, a sacrifice so someone else could live.

She looked Robert in the eye. There was no conflict there, and no apology.

He shoved her to her knees and swept her hair aside to reveal the top of her cape.

His hand gripped her shoulder hard and trembled.

Like before, she could feel it within him, pulsing through his veins like black blood—the want to kill her. And the English had given him the perfect opportunity. No one would blame him for doing it. No one else knew how much he wanted to.

Her skin prickled as the blade drew near.

This was the end.

She didn't think of Robin and vengeance lost or Alianora and stolen memories. Strangely, her last thought wasn't of herself but an image of whitecapes slaughtering reds and Alice bleeding atop a mound of corpses.

A mother stolen from her daughter.

Perhaps her last thought was of herself, after all.

She closed her eyes.

And heard a thud, a shout, metal clanging, blood gushing and splattering.

The blade wasn't at her nape anymore, and Robert was dragging her off. He wasn't against touching her cape as others were.

They were running again. Margaret had to slow to stay with him, but she was glad to be moving after feeling trapped in the triforium and escaping death once more.

Soon, the others joined them. Thomas drew up last, and Mary Margaret and Malcolm appeared around a corner. Their capes were wet and dotted with scarlet.

The pounding footsteps behind them petered out as Robert led the way forward. For fifteen minutes, he didn't give up his pace, and all but Margaret were huffing and mussed from sprinting and dodging traffic when he slowed in view of a church. It was made of Caen limestone, and its rounded nave and crenelated tower were trimmed with swirling strands of gold. A few men strolled outside, headed for surrounding buildings, their white capes stamped with red crosses. When the men were out of sight, Robert brought the group past the round temple and, beyond it, they reached their destination: a religious house owned by the Order of Carmel, just south of Fleet Street. Surrounded by a garden, the house was simple with straight, stone walls, built before a small chapel.

Robert didn't knock or announce himself but swung open a door and ushered them inside. He and Thomas went off alone down a hallway.

While they waited, Margaret leaned against a cold wall, letting the house hold her up for a moment of rest.

The place was silent, a refuge from London's din. In comparison, their comrades' returning footsteps roared in her ears long before they came into view with a woman younger than Margaret, whose steps were quieter, muffled by her hemp sandals. She wore a brown scapular beneath her white cloak and veil, and Margaret would soon come to know her as Joan Gray.

Joan showed them to a room hardly large enough for the five of them to sleep beside one another on the floor, but sleep they did. Even Margaret, who tired the least often, was exhausted from the day's events, and she was perhaps the first to fall.

Pale fabric fluttered after a knight, who turned a corner to circle the house, and Margaret ducked away from the window before he could spot her.

Supervised by Guy Beauchamp, English capes put up sentries and checkpoints leaving London in an effort to catch the Scotsmen. Naming Robert their highest priority, they swept the city and paid attention to the Carmelite house, clearly suspecting he had taken sanctuary there.

The sun rose and set once again. A week passed, and impatience trickled into Margaret's blood. She couldn't stay there forever like the others could, waiting for the English to give up on them, but she was one redcape in a city she didn't know, surrounded by whites who would murder her on sight. She could wait a few more days, even though she was, frankly, sick of the place.

The White Friars worked separately throughout most of the day, during which time they practiced silence, and their visitors were expected to be silent also. Having been left with her thoughts for days and nights on end, Margaret found her mind drifting to the bleakest parts of her life—bloody kills and dark pleasures and resounding guilt. If she stewed in her sins much longer, her thoughts might dye her cape void-black and drag them all inside it.

Frequently, she fixated on the smell of Mary Margaret's flesh or the soft running of blood in Thomas's body. She wanted to kill to escape her mind, to feel instead of think, if only for a moment. Then Malcolm's calming, russet eyes would catch hers, and she would remember they were human, and she had been human once, and she didn't want to kill them. She wanted not to.

After ten days there, when she wasn't sure she could take another night locked in the Carmelite house, their passage was arranged. They waited until sunset, and Joan released them to a man on an unlit street, closing the door fast behind them. He bore a lion rampant argent on his crimson surcoat.

Margaret's first thought was that the White Friars betrayed them, for the man was a whitecape, but her fears were quelled by Robert and Thomas, who seemed to know him. He didn't speak, and no one spoke to him, but they marched after him along the Holebourn, mimicking the movements he made—when he stopped, they stopped; when he ran, so did they.

Margaret's eyes flitted about, searching for figures hidden by night's shadows. There were humans in the dark, but no whitecapes waiting to pounce, no shouts or footsteps behind them. Above, the moon was a sliver of bone among scattered star shavings, smothered by a thick, murky sky.

They were nearly out of it when, west of the Nunnery of St. Mary Clerkenwell, a pair of whitecapes came into view. She recognized them from St. Margaret's, two of many that comprised the English wall around her and willed Robert to dissolve her body to blood. It took effort for her to hang back with the others as their whitecape guide went on to exchange quick words with the men, and the three took off running without a glance in their direction, clearing the way out of London.

A week later, about a day from the border, Robert stayed awake with Margaret while the others slept. Bundled against the cold, he stared quietly at the moon. It would be full in a few days. Thanks to the White

Friars and the man with the silver lion coat, Margaret would make it to the stone circle in time and excess lives would be spared.

"I know you want to kill me," she whispered when she was certain the others were asleep.

His eyes dropped from the moon to distant darkness.

"I'm a threat to you, aren't I? You want my throne."

"Yes." The word was a toll that clung in the air, exposing itself in the light of a pale moonbeam.

How could he, a whitecape, be honest about such a dark want?

"You could have done it. Why didn't you?"

He gestured to her blood cape. "They told me he wouldn't do this to you."

Her lips parted and she breathed, "You knew I was going to be kidnapped?"

"Not until after. It was organized by the Toom Tabard, I heard. My father said William would keep you safe."

So it was John Balliol who had carried out her kidnapping. She could see him plotting with Alianora, hiring the Soulises to abduct two children, murdering one and condemning the other to hell—all to gain the throne. She couldn't do anything about the queen dowager; she was dead already. But after Robin Elliot, perhaps Margaret would hunt down John Balliol and rip him to shreds for the part he took in ripping away her freedom.

But him and her grandmother weren't the only ones to blame. Her father knew, too, and Robert. Everyone let this happen to her—arranged for it to happen—and no one intervened. They all trusted the Soulises when only one Soulis had ever tried to save her.

"William I did. William II is the one who cursed me."

"Regardless, I didn't know you were a redcape until the night I saw you in Hermitage Castle. I thought you'd been damned. I would have killed you then if not for Thomas of Erceldoune, and I would have killed you later if not for Malcolm." He looked at her with his kind, brown eyes. "He told me you hear the water. Do you know what that means?"

She didn't.

"It means you're listening. As deer are called to water, so are you, and so am I.

"If I closed off my ears and gave in to temptation, I would be no better than a redcape, killing those with genuine hearts, those trying to be saved." He cupped his hands and breathed warmth into them. "Yes, I struggle not to kill you for the crown. It is rightly yours, if ever you become human. But you are not deserving of it as I am."

"I'll be human again. I will be Queen of Scots."

"If so, you won't reign alone. Some would have you marry Edward of Caernarvon, if England still favours the union. You would rule separately, though your children would have authority in both Scotland and England. Some don't want to unite with England. Either way, many will influence you, including myself."

She raised her chin and imagined her antler crown upon her head. It didn't make her feel in control as she'd hoped; it was as if the tines were curling into a cage around her and digging into her scalp like the crown of teeth. She shook herself to clear the image, but its essence remained.

"Then again, even if you do escape that thing, John could send an assassin for you. I've heard rumours he's on his way with a French army, and the Soulises support him. You won't be hard to take out when you're human, not for one of William's redcapes."

She was aware of that. She knew how humans felt between redcape hands, frangible and soft as newborn babes.

"That's all assuming you can get your hands on the sword. We can't be sure Scot's heart blood was used to seal it. Though I suspect Edward knows."

She turned fully toward him, begging him to go on.

"He's the one who took it from us, and it is sealed in Westminster. That was likely his idea—as far as I know, Scot has no connection to the abbey, but Edward does. Unless he was made to forget, it makes sense he would know something."

That was it, then. A place to start. She had to get to the King of England.

"You can't go back to London. They will kill you. And they'll do it quicker without us there," said Robert.

"I have to."

"My father believes Edward will defeat us in the end, and I'll be left with nothing." He scratched his large nose and tilted his head back toward the moon. "I'll go back to London. I could use him as an ally if John returns, and he'd rather have me as a friend than an enemy."

"What about the English whitecapes?"

Robert snorted and glossed over her concern. "It may take a while, but I'll find out whose bone you need. Wait for my word to use that trephine contraption, won't you?"

She agreed. Citing weary bones, she curled up next to the others and feigned sleep until morning, new thoughts of what her queenship might entail coursing through her mind.

CHAPTER TWENTY-TWO

"I marry you, my wife." Sigurd presented her with his ancestral sword, upon which a blessed, silver ring—reclaimed from Brynhild—rested.

Gudrun smiled and took it.

She kept her gaze on him when they were shrouded in a woven veil, which was meant to guard them against evil spirits. Within the sheer sanctuary, they sealed their marriage with a kiss.

The veil was removed and Gudrun felt like a new woman, hope-filled and weightless. She had Sigurd now—Sigurd, who was bright and beautiful and perfect. He would be their veil, their candle. He would protect their marriage and ward off darkness.

With him, she would be better. Happy.

Brynhild's face, puffy from crying, caught Gudrun's eye.

The light-haired woman stood with Gundaharius, whom she'd married the week before in a final effort to make Sigurd jealous, not believing his urgings for her to marry another were genuine. Now she knew Sigurd didn't want her. He didn't know he ever had.

Gudrun's smile blazed for a cruel moment before she looked back at Sigurd. Her love for him softened her heart and wiped Brynhild's mourning face from her mind.

In a blur, their post-wedding celebration commenced. Three days of feasts and joy and laughter. After those three days, she would lay with Sigurd, and he would drive out her past. They would be together for the rest of their days and dance with bare feet along the riverbanks and among the vines.

The sun would learn to love Gudrun as much as Sigurd, and she would forget what it was to be alone with herself in the dark.

CHAPTER TWENTY-THREE

Outside, the rainy sky blended with the earth, distant hills rolled in and out of blurry clouds, and rain reduced trees to murky, vague shapes in the darkening light.

Though she wanted to take a human heart, partly to spite Isabella, Margaret had choked down her pride and done what the whitecapes wanted: kept the trephine box firmly closed, resumed life as usual, and spilled only the blood necessary to survive. But, with each passing month, she felt she could be doing more.

She began to wonder if the whitecapes were trapping her, holding her back as her own cape did. She'd heard Robert married; was he working to help her, or had he said it to subdue her while he pursued his own interests? It had been six months and he hadn't sent word.

After an hour of watching, Margaret caught sight of Alice as she returned from her meeting with Malcolm, the first time she'd seen him in over two months. Small Ermengarde ran along behind Alice, blitzing through puddles, her legs covered in mud and her cape barely visible beneath her sheepskin cloak—a necessity for redcapes during the wettest seasons but a safety precaution year round.

Margaret rushed to meet them, boots squelching on saturated ground. Magnus flew above the rainclouds, visible in glimpses.

Alice grasped her forearms. "He knows who sealed it."

"Scot?"

"No, a girl. Edward arranged a marriage for one of his nephews years ago, to a young sorceress."

"What's her name? Whose bone did she use?"

Alice shook her head.

"Tell me where she is."

"A market town somewhere in England. Robert didn't tell Malcolm where. He doesn't want you going after her."

Margaret's jaw jutted out and tensed. How many nephews did Edward I have? How long would it take her to track them all down, to figure out which one had married a sorceress?

"If the English have her, they might have access to other sorcerers. They could make her forget; they may have already. Wait for Robert. He's a better chance of getting information than you do."

Probably true, but it was taking so long.

Tucked into her belt and hidden by her cape, the trephine poked at her side.

"Alice... whose heart does Alianora have? Do you know?" She could have asked Alianora, but she didn't trust her to tell the truth. Alice, on the other hand, was honest and open, and she knew a lot about Alianora, being her daughter, even though their relationship was dead.

"It's my grandad's heart. John I Balliol. It was meant to be buried in the Abbey of Dulce Cor."

Cold water pricked Margaret's skin as the weather started up again.

Alice scooped up her sodden child, and they hustled inside. "Malcolm asked me to tell you to be strong, take heart, and wait for the Lord."

For six months, she'd done what the whitecapes asked, and she had nothing to show for it. Robert wanted to decide when the trephine should be used, but it wasn't his. Shouldn't the freedom to use it belong to her?

She opened the heart casket around her neck and emptied it of Scottish earth.

She was tired of waiting; it was time to do something to protect herself against other sorcerers, especially if the English king had them waiting in the wings. And Robert would surely understand if she used the trephine to create a pure heart—even whitecapes carried those, if they could find them.

She stood alone for some time, watching long, straight lines of rain falling hard and shattering. Then she retrieved her sheepskin cloak and pulled its hood over her head.

As she stepped from Hermitage, Cecily's voice needled at her: "Wolf hunting again?"

"Evening patrol," she replied evenly, and she hurried off before the redcape could further harass her. Punishing Cecily felt a trivial thing when, after months of waiting, she'd returned to an old mission. She would create a pure heart before morning and live forevermore with an invulnerable mind and, this time, be cozened by no one, not even Robin.

"Watch the sky," Cecily called after her in a mocking tone.

Light rain wasn't dangerous, but getting full-on drenched could be deadly, and Cecily would love nothing more than for rain to beat every last ounce of blood from Margaret's cape and leave her dry. Too bad for her, it was securely tucked beneath her cloak.

As a black shroud settled overhead, Margaret moved from the castle to an umber-cast forest, a place the pockmarked quarter moon couldn't see.

A susurrant voice, a dreamlike thing only she could hear, drew her further in: "Margaret..."

She clawed into the chilled earth beneath an oak. Forest soil crumbled like velvet between her fingers, and she dug until she felt a tooth-inlaid hilt.

"Margaret..." the voice whispered as she pulled the knife from its grave. Its blade looked freshly sharpened and polished—not a seed of rust or dirt hid between its metal teeth, though, surely, it couldn't be pure gold.

"Īzeḇel," Margaret murmured in response.

Magnus swooped down and clawed her shoulder, but she didn't feel him. She stared at the knife for hours, whispering its name like a woman possessed.

In the dead of night, Margaret held Īzebel tightly as she walked, steps quickening with her heartbeat.

Should she do this? Was it right?

She'd wrung whole bodies of blood and eaten many a heart. Could taking one with a knife truly be different?

If you are willing to take a heart, sorcery will take you, in turn. It's a dark, addictive trade. It will sink its teeth into you and drag you into shadowy depths, Isabella Warenne had warned.

But Isabella had never been a redcape.

The place Margaret lived was already dark.

She found a dwelling on a remote farm, built with turf and clay walls. Its residents slept too deeply to notice Margaret, who snuck inside and watched their chests rise and fall above their hearts.

She had options: an older man and woman, two young men, and a girl.

Margaret's own chest seized when she saw her. It was like seeing a reflection of the past... she might have been the girl Bishop Narve sent back to Norway in Margaret's stead, had death and time released her.

She snatched her up and fled, listening for a commotion behind her. None came. All she could hear was a nearby burn and the sound of her own measured breath.

The girl's eyes were open wide, and her heart palpitated, but she didn't scream or struggle. She was too scared, shocked, maybe stupid.

Margaret didn't look at her again until they reached Ninestane Rig.

Blood rushing like boiled-down guilt and shame, Margaret dropped the girl in the stone circle.

"How old are you?"

The girl's hands were dirty from breaking her fall. Her eyes were fixed on Margaret, but she didn't answer her.

"Seven? Nine?"

No reply. Was she mute or frightened out of her wits?

The girl's stare didn't waver, and Margaret realized she wasn't staring at her but at the sorcerer's blade in her fist.

She grabbed the girl by the shoulder and knelt beside her on one knee.

Guilt was planted in Bergen when Margaret realized the girl she'd seen in Orkney had been murdered on her account. She'd felt it ever since, as it took root and bloomed, and there was conflict in her heart because of it. She'd killed constantly as a redcape, but that girl had been the start—the first unconfessed sin of Margaret Eiriksdatter.

She didn't save her. She should have tried to, but she didn't.

She should have understood. But she didn't.

At the same time, why should she feel guilty? She wasn't the one who committed the act, and she was only seven. She didn't know if she could have stopped it.

But she could have tried.

"Margaret..."

If she killed this girl, maybe her guilt over the other would make sense.

But did she have to take her heart?

In opposition to the goading voice, Malcolm's words, given through Alice, whispered in her mind: *Be strong, take heart, and wait for the Lord.*

Her grip loosened on the knife as doubt threaded through her fingers.

What if Isabella was right—what if there was a lower, breakable rung of darkness?

"Margaret," the voice said again. It wormed its way into her ears and called her to perform unspeakable acts.

Her fingers haltingly tightened again.

"Be strong," said the voice, twisting Malcolm's well-intentioned advice, "take hearts. The Lord calls you to act. There is no strength in waiting."

Isabella was wrong and Malcolm didn't know what strength was.

Margaret was strong enough.

She thrust Īzebel into the new girl's chest, and a scream sharp as the knife split the night.

So she wasn't mute.

Margaret began to saw with the serrated side of the knife, flinching as she remembered the feel of Īzebel buried in her own flesh, biting at her soul.

Bones cracked, tendons snapped.

The scream, and the girl, died.

She pulled the heart from her breast, and Margaret's own lurched inside her, caught on euphoric wings. The world came into stark focus as her blood pumped faster and her temperature rose. Colours became more vivid, even in the nighttime, and the fragrance of blood swelled full and rich as liquid silver.

She felt alive as she never had before.

The breeze was sharp on her skin, and her mouth watered at the sight of the girl's exposed heart. She wanted to eat it, or crush it, or put it back and cut it out all over again.

It felt good to take it. Almost... freeing.

She placed the heart in her mother's heart casket, bloodying the thing, and its silver flecked with black, like gratings from the night sky. The heart wasn't pure, but that's what the trephine was for.

Margaret lifted the girl's arm and let it flop to the ground.

Why waste good human?

She ate her remains and soaked up her blood and lay where the body had lain.

For a while, the good feeling hummed inside her. Then her cape and her stomach convulsed and, as though she was afflicted by the white curse, she rolled over and vomited up undigested flesh, muscle, bone, blood, hair, nails, and muddy swill from somewhere deep and dark inside her.

Shaded by stones from the soft summer twilight, Margaret hid the casket inside her dress, hugged her knees to her sewn-up chest, and wept.

John I Balliol's tomb broke with an echoing clatter, a sound even the deafest monk could not ignore.

Margaret let the mattock she'd stolen from a layman's barn fall from her hands. She shoved tomb fragments aside, searching, and grasped an old, dry neck bone as a monk hustled in. He would soon be followed by others.

She swept the mattock from the ground and flung it at him, knocking him down, and Īzebel arced toward his chest. His white cowl tore in a clean line to envelop a blade that would brutally shred it upon withdrawal.

Restraining her cape with her elbows to keep it from inching toward the blood, Margaret popped out the monk's heart and pressed it against the bone in her hand. She spared it a glance as she ran: a warm, bloody mass with tiny vertebra wings. And she had a quick need for it; when the way was blocked by three men, she melted the heart and skipped past them as they forgot her, giddy from the taking of a heart.

She escaped the Abbey of Dulce Cor through a garden and fled Galloway east, over flat ground and rising hills, rough grazing areas and redcape river crossings. She avoided cottar houses and hid from humans and didn't stop moving until she passed a hamlet near Hermitage.

The monk's blood on Margaret's hand and John's neck bone had dried and sloughed off in places, so its smears were grainy and striated. It continued to flake off when she used the trephine to drill a slice of bone from the atlas vertebra.

From her mother's heart casket, she took the young girl's cold heart. She pressed the bone slice inside. The heart pulsed and warmed as the bone dissolved and purified it and left her feeling calm and tense at once.

She placed it back in the casket, gnawed on the damaged, disinterred neck bone, grimaced at its stale flavour and resumed her return to Hermitage Castle—mind heavy with memories she couldn't lose, cape heavy with blood from a ghost.

CHAPTER TWENTY-FOUR

Blood spattered the crisp bracken and sank into Margaret's cape.

She slashed at her latest victim's stomach and ripped at his chest, violently murdering him and sending red crescents into the air. She was no longer careful to keep blood from her cape; instead, she drank it in hungrily and reveled in knowing she would have to kill again soon, in Ninestane, to survive and stave off hunger for another month.

But she wouldn't want to wait a month, nor did she have to.

She climbed Blackwood Hill, blood squeezing between her knuckles from the heart in her hand, and her eyes adjusted from the brightness of the autumn sun to the dark, turf-covered souterrain.

One and a half miles east of Hermitage Castle, she'd found the abandoned souterrain—a single, underground chamber with drystone sides and a flat capstone—near the deteriorating remains of a wide, low broch. She'd cleared it of various items left inside, like clay pottery, a rough quern and barrels, and she began collecting silver caskets of varying sizes, as hearts harvested correctly were smaller than those harvested clumsily.

Then she began collecting hearts to go inside them.

She placed the new one in a simple, hammered casket and watched black creep over its surface with a frown. It fell from her fingers to the floor, and she didn't give it a thought as she stumbled from the souterrain and screamed for Magnus.

The rush of taking the heart had faded.

And she already wanted another.

Chapter Twenty-Five

On a cold, cloudy day, Margaret sat against the castle's eastern outer wall beneath a tall, pointed arch. Her chilled fingers twitched in minuscule motions suggestive of heart-taking, and as she was about to get up and search for one, John III Comyn approached her. If he were a lower man, she wouldn't have let him sit beside her, but his association with Alianora—and alliances with others, now—meant he was above reproach for such a thing.

The warmth of his body made her aware of her own coolness. She didn't usually feel cold, but today her blood ran slow.

"Do you know where she's gone?" Unnecessarily, he clarified, "My mother."

Alianora had been gone for months. Lest she was dead, Margaret suspected she knew a way to take libations outside the stone circle.

"Why don't you ask Alice?"

"I have, she doesn't know." He mimicked her posture, leaning back. "From what I know, she's treated you more like her child than either of us. You're shaking."

"It's laughter," she deadpanned. She grabbed her right hand to keep it still. "You do know she tried to kill me. Not a motherly thing to do."

"If she wanted you dead, you would be."

"Still."

"I've seen her save you. In the stone circle, when that redcape stabbed you..."

With Robin? Alianora was the mysterious figure who brought her a heart?

"She concerns herself with you. Why?"

"We're both alphas."

"So is Alice."

"We're both sorceresses, then. What does it matter why?"

Shielded by a ruddy mustache and beard, his mouth turned down as he angled away from her. "She's never saved me from anything."

Is this why he became a redcape? To get her attention, or see if she would try to save him from it?

"You want her to love you." Margaret snorted. "As if she could."

His look was wintry and stiff as the air.

"Love is just another cage. You want to be strong? Be free." She unwound her hands. "I searched for freedom for years, and I finally found it. It's not love. It's not caring about people or losing your cape. It's accepting your urges. Freedom is being able to do whatever you want at any given time."

The taking of hearts. That was what freedom felt like—a rush of ecstasy, of knowing you could do or be anything you wanted. A second of life without guilt.

But for Margaret, the guilt always flowed in when the rush ebbed, in spite of her pretension that it didn't.

"It's what Alianora does. She kills and eats hearts and does what she wants. She doesn't pine after love."

John nodded and tapped his finger to his lips. "I've only taken libations with the others. I've not gone out and killed on my own as a redcape."

"We'll go together." Petting Īzeḅel beneath her cape, she stood and offered him a hand. "Let's break your cage, John."

In February, a rider found Margaret and John near Glasgow, crunching human fingers between their teeth. Margaret had to make him forget the sight before he was able to get out his news: the English had invaded, divided, and set up three camps south of Edinburgh in Rosslyn.

John teamed up with Simon Fraser of Oliver and Neidpath to hastily band together a party of mounted infantry. They marched from Biggar to Carlops, where they were fed by monks—literally, for the Red Comyn—and, in the night, a monk guided them to Rosslyn. Margaret stalked with them, unnoticed by all but John, who, knowing her hunger and ruthlessness, welcomed her support, even though she'd needed to pick off a few Scotsmen and a monk along the way.

Three thousand soldiers followed John III Comyn into the woods, and Simon Fraser led the rest of the troops, five thousand men, across the River Esk. When the river curved and Margaret passed John on the west bank, he waved her on and she caught up to Fraser's crescent of troops as they moved in on the first English camp.

Margaret held Īzebel before tents of slumbering Englishmen. The morning remained mostly dark, and the camp didn't hear her coming—the black star in the crescent's centre, the unseen heart of the ambush.

Silent as a doe, she entered a tent, slayed its occupants in their sleep, and moved on to the next.

Screams rose through flurries of blood as day began to break. Bluish-yellow light dripped through cracks in the low, dim clouds, splashed onto corpses and ruined tents, and lit the way for men who tried to flee southwest, only to find John smiling in the forest with unnaturally large teeth, waiting to inhale them as Margaret would have had they stayed.

The rush of killing consumed her.

She slurped down blood and hearts and sucked on bones.

She slashed and sawed and slaughtered.

And she laughed when a man swooned at the sight of her sorcerer's blade, its teeth threaded with stained flesh. But her laugh was empty. Her heart was empty.

She lost count of how many she killed. Hundreds. Thousands. It was a massacre.

She wasn't eating them anymore. The bodies she left behind were half drained with ripped-open chests. Sharp-scented blood soaked into ungrateful earth.

The blood tasted honey-sweet but felt bitter. Her stomach, though soured, panged with hunger or sickness; still, she wanted more. Not wanted—needed. She wanted... to stop.

Finally, she wanted to stop.

Viscid guilt washed in on a flood of gore. If she felt remorse after killing before, this was a hundredfold worse. This wasn't killing because she had to, to keep herself alive. This wasn't killing because she wanted to.

This was a need. She couldn't admit it before... but she *needed* to cut out hearts, and she had for some time.

She gave in so quickly to temptation, she always had. And she enjoyed it, even though irrevocable shame came after. But this... it wasn't enjoyment. It was a primal high caught in a bramble of thorned guilt. This was an addiction.

She ran from Rosslyn.

When she stumbled upon a bothie, she assaulted a man, hacked at him with Īzebel, and fell to her knees.

She wanted to stop, but she couldn't. Heart-taking had become a compulsion.

Her tears turned red as they poured down her bloodied face.

She'd thought doing whatever felt good in the moment, giving into cravings and temptations, was freedom. But she'd indulged herself and gotten addicted, and now she was a slave to Īzebel. She was more trapped than ever before.

Her vision swam with cold light and her brain felt like it might explode.

She remembered eating another heart. It tasted like water.

There was a blur of land, a changing sky. Mud on her hands. A golden eagle's wing. Strewn stones and caskets crusted with black. A cross on fire.

And then there was nothing.

CHAPTER TWENTY-SIX

"I won't do it." Gudrun tried to push past her mother, but Grimhild grabbed her forearm and forced a blade into her hand.

"Do it for him. For his protection."

She yanked her arm away. Her slate bracelets clinked together as the blade slipped to the floor. "You can protect him. You already have power."

"It's not enough."

Gudrun's stomach quivered. A part of her wanted to do it, but she'd resisted her urges for almost two years—or she thought she had. There were moments she knew she'd forgotten something and fleetingly worried what terrible thing Grimhild had convinced her to do, but she pushed past those moments, shoved them down, and pretended she'd imagined them. And she'd been happy.

In defense of her goodness, she weakly challenged her mother. "How can you be sure of their defeat? To take the word of a Roman prophetess—"

"She spoke the truth. I saw her eyes silver."

Gudrun breathed in through her nose, remembering the prophecy that Gundaharius would invade Belgica Prima, and he had. Sigurd had gone with him. If the prophetess's words were to be believed, the Roman general, Flavius Aetius, would defeat them, but they would not die there. They would return in peace, but it would be short-lived, for Borbetomagus and the Burgundian kings would soon fall to Hun foederati.

If Sigurd were beside her, she would press her face to his chest and lose herself in his love. But he was with Gundaharius, risking his life for the kingdom, and for her.

She could risk something for him, too, so that, someday soon, they could go on being happy.

Gudrun picked up the sorcerer's blade and held it with both hands. Even so, it felt weightier than it ever had before.

She left the longhouse with her mother, and they travelled northeast from Borbetomagus.

CHAPTER TWENTY-SEVEN

Margaret's parched cape gasped in blood like air, and her eyelids fluttered open to reveal, first, a floor littered with caskets of various sizes and levels of tarnish; second, a body with a slitted throat, its blood gushing out to revive her; and third, an alpha, stone-faced and cross-armed.

"You stole my hearts..." Margaret accused, noticing several caskets were open and empty.

"You ate them."

Had she?

"You're not well, Margaret," said Alianora. "A few more hours and you'd be dead."

"I'm fine." She crawled to the corpse and breathlessly ate. The warm meat soothed her scratchy throat. "How did you find this place?"

"Alice told me of it. Not that it's well hidden." Alianora normally towered over Margaret, but, from the floor, she had to crane her neck to look up at her. "Don't fret, I won't take your precious hearts."

She scowled at the thought of the unreformed traitor, and the memory of Alice following her to the souterrain flashed in her mind. Alice had confronted her, hadn't she?

She should have moved the hearts after that, but... she'd forgotten about it. Which was impossible, wasn't it?

She checked her mother's heart casket. The pure heart was still there.

"Go to her. You need help."

"I told you, I'm fine."

"You're not." Alianora pointed at her cape, still leeching blood from the dead human's open throat.

159

She looked away.

"There's a moment when we become lost in the darkness, when we choose to forsake the light, whether we realize we're doing it or not. Redemption comes in undoing that moment."

What do you know about redemption? she wanted to say, but the truth was, she did feel lost.

What was her moment? Was it when she took a heart? Or earlier, when she became a redcape?

Still not meeting Alianora's eyes, she confessed something: "I don't remember my attachment."

"I know."

Finally, she looked back.

Alianora's chin had dipped against her chest. Her face was red with stolen blood.

Margaret had never seen her look anything but confident. Now, she looked ashamed as she said, "Because I took it from you."

She knew Alianora had taken from her. William had, too, she was sure. But they'd never admitted it outright. Sorcery was a thing of the dark, something to be done and not spoken of.

"Where is it?"

"You think you want it, but you don't."

"You don't know what I want."

"I do," Alianora whispered, "because we want the same thing."

She went out the lintelled entryway. Margaret darted out after her, but she had disappeared.

Margaret might have been leery if her senses weren't dull from an excess of heart-taking and a lack of sleep—sleep her body desperately needed but hadn't been able to get, except when she'd passed out in her souterrain days before, but that hadn't felt like rest.

She entered Hermitage Castle in hopes that, in the safety of the hall with her clan around her, she could find a way to doze off. But her entrance had a strange effect: it silenced the redcapes, and they looked at her with harsh eyes.

"Where have you been?" Cecily, flanked by two high-ranking capes, traipsed toward her. Behind her, on her throne, sat Alice with pursed lips. "We've been waiting for you."

She narrowed her eyes and held her shoulders back. "Get out of my way."

"And Alianora, where's she?" Cecily didn't back down but stepped closer to Margaret than she'd ever dared. "We were attacked last month, and you were both gone. You weren't here to attach. Alice had to do it alone."

Alice must have hated that. She performed attachments as seldom as possible.

Margaret hadn't noticed the newcomers, hadn't missed those who'd been killed by whitecapes. She saw them now, eight new capes, and felt a pang for the eight who'd died.

As she scanned the faces around her, she realized what this was.

An insurrection.

Without her noticing, Cecily had made alliances in the castle. What lies had she spewed to forge them?

"Petronella couldn't find a libation. She dried out."

Petronella was weak and had few friends to help her hunt. More than once, Margaret had seen her libation stolen before she could spill it. She wasn't surprised she hadn't survived and, though Cecily implied it, it certainly wasn't Margaret's responsibility to keep the lesser capes alive.

"You don't care about the clan. We need an alpha who does."

Margaret gritted her teeth. She wanted to lunge forward and slice off her head, but Cecily's stance was wide and her eyes alert, and the redcapes at her side were ready to jump in. She had a few hearts strapped to her belt, but the clan had turned against her. She had no way of knowing who was truly on her side and, even if she wasn't tired, she couldn't take them all. She might not die, but she would come out of a fight worse off and alone.

So she bowed her head and took a step back, conceding her position. Her body was hot and tight, and her lungs constricted. She refused to meet the redcapes' watchful eyes but saved her angry, humiliated gaze for the throne she could no longer claim.

Cecily shifted on her toes, all but bouncing in place before turning from Margaret and striding toward the thrones. She didn't go for Margaret's but whirled toward Ermengarde, who sat at Alice's feet, and kicked the four-year-old hard in the side.

Alice snarled and lurched forward, but a redcape held her back.

Magnus swooped at Cecily from the shadows.

She tried to strike him from the air, but his wings carried him out of reach, where he circled in distress as others joined in the beating of Ermengarde.

Rooted to the spot, Margaret's heart seized as she watched.

She hated Cecily. And she hated herself—for she had done this to Cecily's sister after she'd killed her mother for the throne.

She thought she hadn't felt bad about it, but the truth was, she'd suppressed the guilt. She'd always suppressed it, but it was still inside her.

How could she let it go?

She'd beaten a little girl so violently she'd died—all to establish dominance, to solidify her position by punishing the family of the alpha she'd replaced. Cecily's mother had accepted her challenge and died as a result, but even if she'd relinquished her position, Margaret would have beaten the person she valued most, her first daughter. An alpha giving up her crown would save only her life, not her allies'. Violence proved power, and power needed to be proven. Cecily was proving hers now, punishing Ermengarde to display her dominance over Alice.

In redcape fashion, Ermengarde tried to fight back at first. Then she curled in on herself to suffer the blows, and her whimpers brought out a strength in Alice that Margaret didn't know she had.

The woman who held her back yowled when Alice bit through her arm and elbowed her in the face, and she dove toward Ermengarde.

Without a thought for her own well-being, Alice shoved her daughter aside and took the thrashing for herself.

Cecily smiled at Margaret before bringing her fist down on Alice, Margaret's closest ally in the clan.

Margaret's eyes went vacant.

Cecily punched Alice again. Ribs crunched beneath her knuckles.

Margaret closed off her ears.

They didn't kill her, perhaps because of William, but they beat Alice until she could barely move, and Cecily stepped over her barely breathing body.

Someone brought her a large, long-handled hammer. She heaved it over her head and brought it down on Alice's throne.

Teeth and dried blood shards exploded in all directions. A tooth hit Alice's cheek, but she didn't react—she wouldn't have if Cecily had hit her with the hammer. She just lay there, bleeding and bruised.

Cecily rounded on Margaret's throne and swung again.

Margaret's throat strained when the throne erupted and waves of teeth chattered on the stone floor beneath her splintered antler crown.

The hammer thudded down beside the centre throne and its handle fell against the throne's arm.

And Cecily looked straight at her as she took something that should have belonged to Margaret: the last crown and an unshared throne.

"How is she?"

Huddled beside a sleeping Ermengarde in a corner of the hall, Alice squinted at Margaret. Her eyes were too swollen to open fully, her face so bruised it was unrecognizable.

"She's alive."

"You could have warned me. About Cecily."

Alice turned fully toward her, groaning from the effort.

Her eyes seemed to say, *You could have saved me from Cecily.* But Alice would never say that, or even think it.

Īzebel called to Margaret.

Her mind ruptured with the want to take a heart. The world became fuzzy, and her emotions blurred together. She wetted her lips before she bit them.

She couldn't set things right while she was addicted. But she couldn't stop killing as a redcape, and, as long as she needed that, she would kill as a sorceress, too.

She nodded to herself and asked Alice, "Where are the whitecapes now? Where's Robert?"

"What?"

"I need to find out where that sorcerer girl is. I can't wait... I'll make her remember. I'll go back to London if I have to."

"Why would you do that?"

"I need the throne," she burst. "The sword. The bone."

"I told you whose bone you need," Alice said slowly, not only because it was difficult for her to speak but so Margaret would understand. "Robert sent word months ago, and I told you. It was the King of England's fourth son."

She shoved her against the wall and Alice held back a shriek, glancing at Ermengarde, who shifted in her sleep. "You never told me!"

"I swear I did," she rasped. "You can't go on like this. You need to stop. You need rest—"

She looked at her hands, Alice's spoiled clothes bunched between them, and released her. "I would have remembered..."

How could she not?

She racked her brain, raced through months in her mind, and she remembered—not Robert's discovery, but heart-taking. The rush of it was all-consuming. In the midst of her euphoria, Alice's words might have fizzled in her ears.

Alice reached both hands behind her back, face contorting painfully, untied something from her rope belt and offered it to Margaret.

It was the sorcerer's trephine, the one Isabella gave to her in London.

Her arms suddenly felt too heavy to take it.

"You left it in a field."

It wasn't just on Blackwood Hill. Alice had tailed her before. "You've been following me?"

"Sometimes. Sometimes Malcolm has. Sometimes Thomas Durward. Always someone, to make sure you're safe."

Her throat went dry.

She'd thought of Malcolm often, but the idea of him being there, seeing what she'd been up to...

"Shame can be a good thing. It can tell you you've done something wrong. But you don't have to carry it with you." Alice straightened her beige tunic and moved closer to Ermengarde. "You gave in. We all do it. It doesn't mean you have to be lost forever."

Margaret took the trephine.

Chapter Twenty-Eight

Margaret stepped past a smouldering campfire and searched the darkness for Edward of Caernarvon's Iberian bodyguards. Their absence was suspicious, but she could take them out inside if they were there. She entered the tent while Magnus perched on its top. It was simple enough, made of linen draped over wooden poles, but its contents were anything but. Trunks held gold-threaded gloves, leather breeches, sap green, cobalt and scarlet clothes, red-and-blue banners, assorted dice and coins, several books and expensive trinkets. Instruments lay on the tent's edge, their players gone. A falcon perched on a stand near the prince and two hunting dogs lay at his feet.

The dogs were the first to notice Margaret. When their heads lifted and growls rumbled in their bellies, Edward noticed her, too.

His laugh died when he met her eyes. A pair of bone dice slipped through his fingers, tumbled past a lit candle, and fell off the table into an open trunk of armour—jambers and cuisses, sabatons and poleyns, plate gauntlets and couters and helmets, all highlighted by golden light. When the muted clinking of bone on metal died a second later, Edward's grin returned.

Here he was, the fourth son of Edward I, the heir apparent. The man she'd been betrothed to as a child. He was conventionally handsome—he looked strong, and his hands were calloused from work—which surprised her and made her wonder if their marriage, too, would have surprised her. Would they have lived apart? Would she have grown to love him?

She saw herself in a pearl-studded, gold-trimmed, blue velvet gown in Westminster Abbey. Beside her, before the boyish Abbot Wenlock, stood Edward, cloaked in gold and grinning as he was in the tent—as if it was all some joke only he understood.

The image dripped at the corners like hot wax, Edward's face and her blue gown peeled away, and bright water brushed with colour took their place.

The water cut and wove her dress into a simpler cream kirtle, its sleeves tight and its silk edges embroidered with Celtic knots and thistles. The colours swept a mantle lined with tartan silk onto her head, painted red-and-white silk damask over the background, and sculpted her husband-to-be's face with the features of another man—a man with earthy eyes and a heavenly smile, and a cape light as hers was dark. Or should have been, but her cape was gone.

Out of nowhere, someone wrenched her arms behind her back and said, "La tiengo."[II]

Margaret could have killed him in a hundred grisly ways, or she could have grabbed a heart from her belt and made him forget he wanted to detain her, but another man held a jug of water over her cape and threatened to pour.

So the Iberians knew about redcapes; more than most if they recognized her weakness for water. But they didn't put the water to use, which meant they either wanted her for something or they knew that, if they did try to drain her, she would blindly kill to stay alive, or at least try to. She couldn't tell which, for they conversed with Edward in Aragonese and Catalan; if she'd been taught any of the Iberian languages as a child, she'd forgotten them.

They shut her in a cage of silver and wood, and someone brought Prince Edward freshly cooked, buttery salmon from the South Esk.

"You're sour," he said.

She stared.

"Don't act like this wasn't your idea."

What?

"Let me out." She consciously softened her tone and said, "If you let me out now, I'll go calmly. I won't hurt you. I won't hurt anyone."

"I hope you don't mean that," he said jovially between bites.

"I'll hurt you, then. Is that what you want?"

"Uncanny. It's just as you said." He chuckled and shook his head. "When we're done here, I think I'll take you with me to London. I'd like to see you go up against my lion. Not that I want you to win, mind you; I dare say you'd cost more to feed."

"What are you going on about? I didn't say anything." She grabbed a silver bar and it twined with black. "And I will not be going—"

"Oh, do try to stay alive. It will be far less fun for me if you die on a battlefield."

"Battlefield?"

"Now the only thing is getting you inside. Say, do you think you'd survive a great fall? Perhaps I could fling you in with my siege engine..."

Her fingers uncurled from the bar, all at once grateful they hadn't married. The man was clearly deranged.

She inspected the cage. She could break the wood, but not the silver. Even if she managed to squeeze out, which was impossible, the body-guards around her would hurl water in her direction. Most likely, she would kill them. But there was a chance that, during her moment of weakness, they might overcome her.

One of the guards from outside called, "Ell ha vingut tornam -lo veer, Sa Altesa Reial."[III]

A man was let into the tent. He raised his face to catch the candlelight, Thomas Durward.

"Release her, and the men of Brechin Castle will surrender," said he.

"I don't need them to surrender," Edward said. "She'll kill them all, and she'll win the next battle for us, too. She's said she would."

Thomas's hard glance truly made her feel like a caged dog. "Does your father know you have her?"

"I've an idea. Why don't I throw you in there with her? As a demonstration to my men, to see how fast she can eat."

Thomas didn't look afraid, but he smiled. It was the same smile Robert gave Guy in Westminster: convincing but not quite real. "If that's what you want, you have the wrong redcape. This one doesn't kill; she's rather useless. She's wants to be human."

Edward narrowed his eyes and sized her up as if he could tell by looks whether or not that was true.

"It's true," Thomas assured him. "These creatures... they're remarkably deceptive. Whatever she's told you is a lie or a trick to get something from you or lure you in. But she won't kill anyone, and she won't win you anything."

"Redcapes have to kill."

"Not necessarily. In their society, if they're high in rank, the others kill for them and pour blood on their capes. Some rarely leave the castle."

Edward looked to one of his men, who nodded and said, "Sí que ella podia ésser una alfa. Ella encara és del bando d'Escòcia i la mort."[IV]

The prince frowned, and his lower lip jutted out.

Margaret bit her own to keep from talking as he pouted, probably wondering if he should still take her home to meet his lion.

"I don't need their surrender," he finally decided. "I need a guarantee."

"Of?"

"I want my engine to take down Brechin's captain. If you can make that happen, you can have her."

Thomas didn't look at her again. He bowed and left, and Margaret was left wondering how such a thing could be guaranteed.

Night passed and the morning hours stretched long, but Thomas did return. He brought a rock for Edward's siege engine, which they departed for with all but four guards—all that was needed to watch over Margaret with her stuck in the cage.

Not long after, the Iberians fell.

Whitecapes had slipped inside the tent, silent as reds.

"Promise not to cut out my heart and I'll let you out of there." Malcolm's playful brown eyes filled her vision. A key sparkled somewhere at its edge. Edward had the key before. Had he given it to Thomas? Had they lifted it in the night?

Margaret didn't care enough to ask, and Malcolm didn't wait for her promise. He released her, seemingly unconcerned by her dark addiction, and he and the others dragged the Iberians inside the cage. He locked it, flung the key to the other side of the tent, and hugged her.

"I'm glad you're safe." His breath was hot on her cheek.

If a heart could melt inside of a chest, hers was.

He led the way out and the others followed without hesitation.

His absence was like a life snuffed out. Margaret could have escaped the opposite way, but she found herself drawn after him, craving his energy. Craving his heart.

Salivating, she purposefully slowed her steps.

She would never forgive herself if she took it. But how could she not? She'd never met anyone who made her feel so alive. The rush she would get from his heart...

Something stung her finger.

She saw herself stroking Īzeḇel, fingers striping the metal with blood.

Her hand froze and she paled. When had the knife leapt to her hand?

She took one last glance at Malcolm, who strode boldly forward, believing she would follow. Then she turned, ran the other way, and hid by the South Esk until she was sure the whitecapes were gone.

A lean greyhound moved with its nose to the ground and its tail swishing back and forth in the air. Prince Edward followed it closely.

Margaret had tempted the dog into loping after her through the woods, used him to lead the prince away from his pack of Iberians. At last, after stalking him for days and waiting for him to go out hunting, she had him alone.

The greyhound stopped before Margaret, who bared her teeth. It froze in place for a second, then whined and padded off. Noticing its abient behaviour, the prince called the dog back and searched for what had scared him.

He didn't see her rounding on him, and he didn't see anything after she whacked him on the head with a thick branch. He fell with force and lay so stiff she thought she might have accidentally killed him, but she felt for his heartbeat and found it.

She pulled up his sleeve and squeezed his forearm between her fingers, pressing hard to feel the strong, flat bone inside.

Her trephine drilled into him, sliced bone from his ulna and came out bloody.

The sight of white, gooey flesh and the rich, iron scent of his blood seemed to magnify the sound of his heart and made her water at the mouth.

She swallowed and straddled him.

She had tried not to kill him, she really had. But it was no use fighting it... she needed to take his heart.

Magnus barrelled down, alerting her.

Her ears perked.

Men were headed for them. The prince's guards.

Edward's chest rose and fell beneath her, heart tucked inside.

Not long ago, she would have taken it and gone after the guards and the nearby Englishmen too. But some capacity of self-preservation and shame and hope had returned to her, thanks to her co-alphas. Or her former co-alphas.

There was a chance she could end her addiction.

This one time, she could resist.

She wiped the trephine on the grass and left him there, alive.

CHAPTER TWENTY-NINE

The Sword of Living Waters lingered in Westminster Abbey, a frozen ray of silver among sprightly candle flames.

Before it, Margaret held a bone shard and a fresh heart. She'd made it nearly to London before she couldn't take it any longer—before she gave in and took another heart. She took another in the city not half an hour past, outside the infirmary. Her return to Scotland would be an eventful one for Īzebel if this didn't work.

Pastel shadows flickered around her, giving the illusion of life, but she was alone in the shrine of Edward the Confessor, and it had been relatively easy to get there. To occupants old and new, she hid her face, giving the appearance of a pious woman who'd come to say her prayers and go about her day. Thanks to the King of England's campaigns, whitecapes were preoccupied, and London was less supervised than it would otherwise have been; thanks to a greedy wool merchant who burgled the Pyx Chamber and brought suspicion on the whole abbey, so, too, was Westminster, as many of its monks were currently detained in the Tower of London.

Margaret undid her sheepskin cloak, exposing her red cape, and bored Edward II's bone into the heart. It fluxed, and the organ became a copy of his.

She melted it. Heart blood flowed over the sword, ate away at the seal, and dissolved before it dripped to the floor, leaving nothing behind.

The polished blade reflected her eyes. For a split second, they seemed to flash blue, but they returned to gray when she blinked, their crimson sheen apparent. She held her breath as she reached for her reflection, remembering the last time she'd done this, when the sword was impossible to touch.

She touched it now. She slid her fingers up its bevelled fuller, the metal cool and silky, then she took its hilt and lifted. It came effortlessly from its place.

She gripped it with both hands and heard the far-off sound of rushing water.

Her reflection rippled and mingled with another. She strained her eyes, caught a glimpse of fluid fur, and the blade clouded over, obscuring whatever animal lived inside and her own face.

Her heart clouded over at the same time.

For so long, she'd tried to suppress her guilt. It had frothed inside her and settled deep within, stirred up by occasional profound musings or reminders of the religion she once honoured. But she couldn't go on suppressing it, not after taking the sword. It sped up the churning process, lumped her thoughts and actions, all of her sins together.

Her guilt became shame.

Not the watered-down shame she'd felt before, scraps she could feed to the parasitic tooth inside her heart and move on from.

Real shame. The shame that came from looking back on what she'd done and not seeing her actions as outliers or murders she needed to commit at the time, something outside of her control, but seeing herself for what she was.

She had called herself a redcape, a monster, a murderer, a sorceress. But she had seen herself as the human she once had been, a little girl trying to survive. A good person searching for a way out, freedom from the darkness that trapped her.

She fell to her knees and whispered, "What have I become?"

She wasn't that little girl. She wasn't a good person. She wasn't even human. She was a horrible, shameful creature who didn't deserve to be saved.

She already knew she'd done wrong intellectually, but now she felt it. She didn't want to feel it. She wanted to release the sword, rebury her guilt and reclaim her demons, and lose herself in heart-taking. She wanted the addiction to kill her. Death would feel better than shame.

She wanted to be free. She wanted to be human.

Her lungs seized.

Claws dug inside her as some unseen force dragged a beast upward through her veins and out the nape of her neck. Her cape fell to the shrine's floor, the mass of oily, live material grotesque over the beautiful, ornate floor. It died and dried out, turned powdery like ash, and dissolved until there was nothing there, just like the heart blood.

Margaret's heart jabbed at her mother's heart casket, battering against her breastbone, and she coughed. The cough turned to a sputter, then a heave, and pain lanced through her chest. A sharp, pyramidal thing cut her throat on its way up and rolled from her tongue to the floor, coming to a stop over a brownish-red gemstone.

She held the sword with one hand, rubbed the back of her bare neck, and picked up the tooth that had plagued her for eleven years and three months. She stuffed it in her heart casket next to the pure heart.

Gold statues of long-dead kings stared down at her from the feretory. They didn't see a monster, but a woman.

In the blade, her eyes were white and light gray, rimmed with charcoal blue. The redcape sheen had cleared. Her cape was gone. She was human.

Shame overcame what happiness she felt. Again, she had been wrong. Being human didn't mean being free.

Her breaths hitched and her eyes watered from disappointment. She was supposed to feel liberated and light, but her heart, though rid of its tooth, was heavy—somehow heavier than before, like the cape had kept its weight a secret. She didn't want to bear it alone and almost wished her heart, too, would detach itself from her body.

She wrapped the sword in her sheepskin cloak and left Westminster Abbey, willing herself not to run. Though it was warm outside, she felt naked and cold. She would prefer to be alone above the city so she could don her cloak and feel less vulnerable.

On top of that, her stomach growled violently, and she desperately wanted water, but she had no idea where to get it or what to eat. The prospect of eating people was no longer appetizing, but she soon smelled something that was: the sweet, yeasty aroma of bread.

The open market on Bread Street offered superbly baked bread in every stall, and each loaf she saw tantalized her more than the last.

When she'd come to the city with the whitecapes, they'd carried thin, wide, silver English coins that were poured, hammered, and cut by the London mint workforce. She grieved not taking theirs for herself. She'd never needed to travel with money, for she could kill and eat men and take whatever she wanted, but she couldn't do that now.

Or could she? Many sorcerers were human, and she had two hearts strapped to her belt...

She eyed marked rye loaves, dusted lightly with flour, and licked her dry lips. She was used to feeling hungry all the time, but she wasn't used to her body feeling weak. She needed food.

A man squeezed beside her to purchase a loaf, and she followed him past the All Hallows parish. People passed on foot, but no one saw the heart blood spout over his head. If they had, they would have thought it an imagining, for it seeped fully into his skin in seconds, by which time Margaret had taken the bread and fled, awkwardly holding it against her bundled sword.

A street over, she devoured the loaf like a human head, biting into its crusty shell and dense crumb. She barely registered its earthy taste but immediately honed in on a sound. Water.

She could still hear it and feel it, rivers flowing in the distance.

The not-so-distant Thames was the loudest. Listening to it, she realized—she could board a foreign merchant's ship and escape to another land. She wouldn't have to return to Ninestane Rig or Hermitage or any place that had bound her.

It was tempting. Before, she would have gone, but if sorcery had taught her anything, it was that indulgence couldn't lead to freedom. Leaving would pile on more shame, and she could hardly live with herself as it was. How could she go the rest of her life knowing she could have freed Alice and Ermengarde, Alianora and John, and everyone else, but chose her own freedom instead? That wouldn't be freedom, not truly.

The bread had only heightened her thirst. She went in search of water and discovered something incredible: the Conduit. An endless spring of free drinking water built for the citizens of London, carried to a tap by a long, underground pipe.

She was allowed to draw a small amount. It didn't fully quench her thirst, and she wanted to threaten someone or use a heart to get more, but she only had one left. She would find water in the north. Three days later, she did.

Thousands of raindrops fell from the sky. Each one sparkled with a pared golden moon, courtesy of low, cloud-pressed sunlight. They fractured to pieces when they hit the ground, their crescents warping and going dark.

Wrapped in her waterproof cloak, Margaret watched them fall and break. She brought the sword up and reached it outside of the cloak. Its otherworldly blade burned cold under the rain, so the drops glowed silver beneath the gold. They splashed into the blade and sent out circular ripples as if they'd fallen into a lustrous, silvery-white pool.

Sword in hand, she swallowed hard and took off her cloak.

At first, the rain felt like so many metal shavings pricking her skin, but, after a few seconds, the shavings' edges softened. She wished they'd sharpened, peeled away her layers and left her heart open to the air, though she knew rainwater couldn't wash it clean—even now, without its tooth, it was far too impure.

She tilted her chin back, closed her eyes, and let the water stream over her eyes and her lips, drench her clothes and her hair, and relieve any doubt that she was human.

Good sense kept Margaret from Hermitage. She watched the castle from a distance, listened to the waters tumbling by, and waited.

Waiting without her cape was inconvenient to say the least. She was slow and weak and had to eat, drink and sleep far more often than she used to. Her muscles ached, and the night seemed darker than before. But she didn't have to take libations. She didn't have to go to the stone circle again, ever. She could go anywhere she wanted and not have to return, not have to kill another human, and that was worth everything else.

When the wind was blowing toward her, not behind, she would venture closer to Hermitage, where she could better see the comings and goings of capes, who were hard to spot to begin with. The winds would inevitably shift, and she would go back to her bed by the river. She felt safe there, knowing the water would give her an advantage if a redcape sniffed out her hiding place.

She wished she had Magnus to help her hunt and keep watch, but she'd left him with Ermengarde when she went to London. After hearing the English royals owned various animals—lions, leopards, elephants, lynxes, ostriches, white bears, tigers, gyrfalcons, camels, and who knew what other exotic beasts—she worried one of his cronies might spy her beautiful eagle in the sky and decide to claim him for Edward's menagerie.

One night, after what seemed like years of sleeping, hunting, watching, and waiting, but was, in reality, about a month, Cecily led the redcapes toward Ninestane.

Margaret made her way over familiar terrain and into the castle. She couldn't make much out inside, but she knew the way by heart and soon found herself alone in Lord Soulis's apartments. She leaned the Sword of Living Waters by the door, felt around for William's expensive flint to light a beeswax candle, and began her search with the desk. The howling wind outside did nothing for her nerves; she quivered with the flame.

Parchment whirled off the desk. She overturned books and unfurled scrolls, searched cases, drawers, inside chests and under furniture. She tried the walls, pulled at stones to see if they were loose, and held the candle high to inspect the bare ceiling.

Hard fingers dug into her shoulder.

She shrieked and spun, realized the fingers weren't fingers but talons, and felt embarrassed that she'd shrieked. She'd never done that as a cape.

"Magnus." Her rough breath broke up his name as she laid a hand on his back and tried to relax. It helped to have him there, unchanged, not caring that she was.

She resumed rifling through papers, squinting as she scanned for her name in the dark. Next to writings on mantel makers, in a copied codex, tucked in the pages of a poem entitled *The Dream of the Rood*, she found them: the papers from her father that proved who she was.

Magnus didn't warn her of incoming intruders as he usually would have because they were redcapes, ones he trusted, but a warning was unnecessary—Alice screeched as she reached for her daughter, a sound that overpowered the wind.

Ermengarde was too fast for her.

She'd grasped the sword and stood, frozen, in place. The sword looked weightless, even held by her little arms.

As if she were made of water or foxglove bells, Alice recoiled, nearly falling over to avoid touching the sword.

"You brought it here." Alice's tone was harsh in a new way, almost disgusted.

Ermengarde's cape didn't fall away, writhe and shrivel, like Margaret's had. Something different happened to her.

She wept and her tears were red.

Black bile and a heart tooth hurled from her mouth. Margaret picked it up, a redcape habit, and kept it without realizing.

A roar sounded, and blood washed from Ermengarde's cape in a stream, flooding into the hall and down the steps.

Her cape detached from her neck, but it didn't let go. Bloodless, it flowed off her neck like white moonlight, fastened by a silver, hawthorn flower fibula that had emerged from some unseen river.

"Is it a cape?" she asked with innocence, twirling cheerfully.

"Ermengarde," said Alice stonily. "Drop the sword."

"Take it," Margaret urged her.

"You think we want that? That we want to be weak, like you?"

"What's wrong with you?"

Ermengarde stepped toward her mother, who backed frantically away and yelped, "Drop it!"

She didn't.

"Get out!" Alice was screaming now. "Get out!"

A maternal instinct Margaret didn't know she had kicked in. She picked up Ermengarde and the sword and ran. She didn't slow down until her lungs were splitting and Hermitage Castle had sunk behind a wee hill, and she could no longer hear Alice's screams.

On the ground, trying to catch her breath, Margaret clutched her identification papers and wondered what to do about Ermengarde. Should she return her and hope Alice would regain her senses, or bring her to Malcolm, her brother?

Ermengarde held the Sword of Living Waters in one hand while she plucked berries from nearby brambles. It was an impossible sight, a sword in a child's hands, but what Margaret couldn't stop staring at was Ermengarde's white cape. It was like the one she'd seen in Redcastle, the cape that belonged to her mother.

Hate welled in a corner of Margaret's heart. Why hadn't her cape turned white?

And a familiar, silken voice said her name—it was Īzebel.

The knife hadn't called to her since... when? Westminster Abbey?

"Look at this!" The tiny new whitecape held up an ordinary berry, half squished between her small fingers. "Come look!"

Whatever instinct had made her protect Ermengarde died out. She left the girl and the sword in the brambles. Magnus ignored her call and stayed with Ermengarde, and his sad, weak whistle, like a coronach, rang in her mind long after the sound had faded.

Chapter Thirty

Margaret wanted to declare her queenship, but to whom?

Should she tell anyone who would listen who she was?

Anyone could want her dead. Who could she trust?

Last she'd heard, John Soulis, William's non-sorcerer brother, was the sole Guardian of Scotland. But hadn't he gone to Paris? And wasn't he appointed by John Balliol, who might still return with his French army? He wasn't a safe option.

She could tell the whitecaps, but then Robert would know. She hadn't been a true threat to him before, but now that she was human, had her papers, and was actively seeking to rule, he would see her that way. He'd admitted he wanted to murder her. Perhaps now he would.

And Malcolm... how could she face him after leaving his sister in the wild? She could tell him it was safer for the four-year-old to be alone than with her. She could say that guilt had brought her back to the brambles, where she'd called for Magnus and Ermengarde, searched the skies and land for days, but they had gone. If Ermengarde wasn't found, or if something happened to her, would he forgive her?

She would steer clear of the whitecaps for now.

But there was someone else she could try. Her uncle.

She was the rightful heir. She didn't need the King of England to instate her as queen. But if she went to him, if he backed her, he might leave Scotland in peace after all these years and wars. He might set aside his ego and uphold the Treaty drafted at Birgham. He might want her to marry his son—who, as far as she knew, remained unengaged—as a way for him to have a hand in Scottish affairs without losing more men. And hadn't he favoured her mother?

The meeting of Edward II in Brechin prodded her brain, along with chopped scenes from Rosslyn. The prince's eyes, delighting in the idea of a lion eating her alive. Bodies with gaping chests, blood rain and intestines squelching beneath her feet. She imagined battles she hadn't seen, English knights hammering Scotsmen to mush. She was as bad as them, but she didn't need to be anymore. She could stop the violence.

She would do it, a marriage of state. Reprieve from England would be worth the sacrifice of marrying that deranged prince. They could rule their kingdoms apart as separate entities, take their own lovers and see each other little.

The more she thought about it, it seemed the obvious course of action—the possibility that Edward I might reject the idea seemed less likely by the minute. He would read her papers and recognize their validity, for he had written King Eirik many times. War would cease. Scotland would be free as it should have been thirteen years ago. And Margaret would be powerful and free.

Wouldn't she be?

"I am Queen of Scots," she breathed. Louder: "I am. Queen. Of Scots."

Under Edward I, had John Balliol been free?

Had any queen? Any king?

"I'm human. I'm queen. I'm free."

How could she convince Edward when she couldn't convince herself?

CHAPTER THIRTY-ONE

Margaret's teeth chattered. Her frosted fingers were clamped around folds of sheepskin and her toes felt numb in her boots.

Had Scotland always been so cold? It almost made her miss her blood cape, but only almost. She would rather freeze to death in the rain than take it back.

She was more comfortable talking to people now. They'd helped her on the way: a hospitable few had given her free meals, some food, and even lodging in exchange for work; others provided information and gossip. She'd learned Edward I and his army had travelled north in September, marched through Aberdeen, Banff, and Cullen. They'd stayed in Moray a while and departed in October. His plan was to winter in Dunfermline, she'd heard.

She was close—she intended to cross the Firth of Forth at Queensferry but was currently approaching Edinburgh. Getting there, in many ways, was more difficult without her cape. The temperature reached her; she had a new need for food and water, she felt slow and inefficient. But there were upsides, too. She could travel freely through rain or winter's dwies, cross bridges or wade through streams without fear. And she could approach anyone now, though judging the untrustworthy was a task: one man had beaten her, stolen coins from her, and might have tried more if she hadn't slashed at him with Īzebel and scared him off.

Sunset coloured the towers of Holyrood Abbey in a hazy gradient of iced yellow and blue lavender. Margaret entered through a Gothic Romanesque door and passed columns beneath high arches. Holyrood wasn't as fine as Westminster, but it had something about it, a lingering magic, perhaps seeded by the rood once housed in a silver casket within a gold reliquary at the abbey's heart. The Black Rood of Scotland, carried to the country by King David I's mother, Margaret of Wessex, brought multitudes of pilgrims there in warmer months before Edward I stole it away in 1296. Today, the nave's eight bays were fairly empty.

For the first time since she was a child, Margaret was able to seek out a man of the cloth. He didn't see a demon sheen in her eye and cast her out, alert others, seal his own death.

On edge, she knelt before him and wetted her lips. With her head down, her neck felt too exposed, though her skin was concealed beneath her hair and cloak.

She wanted to confess everything. She needed to separate from her shame. But how would he react? What if her penance was so severe it interfered with her queenship?

"When have you last confessed?" he asked.

"I was seven."

He waited, and she murmured, "There isn't a sin I haven't committed."

He seemed neither skeptical nor believing but said flatly, "Your transgressions are indeed grave."

She nodded, eyes downcast.

"However, there is no sin too great to be forgiven. There is only the matter of penance, then I may absolve you."

She'd been waiting for this.

"As a supplier of redemption, I am equipped to grant you an indulgence and give unto you Christ and the Saints' merits, if you choose to recite prayers and perform a good work. Your cloak, for instance, in the form of a donation to the Church. That and other finery might be enough."

He wanted her cloak?

"I have no other finery."

He stared pointedly at her throat.

No, not after everything she went through to get it...

But wasn't it worth it to be free?

She gave him her cloak, shifting her belt so he wouldn't see her knife or trephine, and removed the casket from its place over her sternum.

He gave her a prayer outlining her sorrow and regret. "I absolve you from your sins in the name of the Father, and of the Son, and of the Holy Spirit."

She repeated the prayer for hours in the abbey before the place the Holy Rood once lay. They didn't ask her to leave, so she fell asleep with the prayer on her lips and woke early with a stony heart.

She could feel it: she wasn't absolved. Her heart was the same. Her shame lived on.

Heinous man, a voice perturbed her.

Was it her thought or Īzeḇel's?

The layout of Holyrood Abbey was typical; it wasn't difficult to locate the dormitory on the upper floor. When its occupants rose and left for the chapter house, Margaret searched the room and found her cloak folded beneath a desk.

"Committing another sin?" The priest.

She didn't hear anyone coming anymore.

Swindler. Fraud.

Morning light poured through windows, flowed through partitions, and bathed her silver heart casket in gold.

She'd watched him leave the dormitory and hadn't seen it. He must have hidden it under his clothes and pulled it out to taunt her. Surely he planned to keep the cloak for himself, as well.

He's evil.

Īzeḇel was right. She grabbed her by the hand, by the hilt.

This man wasn't godly, or God wasn't who she thought He was.

The priest's face knotted with fear.

He blocked her forearm, shoved her back. Opened his mouth to yell or scream.

She jerked forward and closed up his throat with a blade.

Her own closed up with rocks. The priest was larger than her, but only just, and his arms weren't thick with muscle. Overcoming him shouldn't have been a laborious task, but everything was laborious now.

Īzebel's exit kindled an eruption of hot blood. Odd to see it spatter on the floor, useless, with no cape to drink it up.

She blinked, and she was on a ferry hours from Holyrood, drifting off from shore.

Her silver casket was back where it belonged. Her cape was wrapped around her neck. Īzebel was clean. And the priest's heart was in her hand. She didn't remember cutting it out, but she could feel the effects. She could feel herself relapsing.

Chapter Thirty-Two

Inside a stone circle, Gudrun opened the silver casket and her mother dug through the animal teeth inside, selecting the largest one she could find. She watched as Grimhild swallowed and seemed to relish the tooth, and she set the casket at her feet.

She'd been to this circle years before and since, but the first time was the one she remembered.

"Coven of old," Grimhild had addressed the standing stones, a circle of ancient sorceresses, "grant me strength and power. Grant me a weapon to spill blood and break bodies." She wanted such a weapon for the protection of Burgundy, back then, and for the same reason now: so they might triumph over Rome and defeat the Huns.

Gudrun had repeated her words, and she'd felt the teeth of beasts buried deep within the earth, preserved by olden witches.

Grimhild couldn't ascertain how to use them, so the burden was heaved on Gudrun. Her witching prowess was unmatched, but her heart was weak. She could handle the killing but not its aftermath; it sometimes made her useless, so Grimhild made her forget. But the lack of memory made the process of discovery slower; thus, years passed, their weapon lay idle in a casket, and the decline of Burgundy loomed ever nearer.

The Alamanni woman they'd acquired and bound on the way writhed and squealed when Gudrun cut her. The sorceress knife jerked in her hands, almost of its own accord, and the murder was done.

Blood left her body and sprawled on the ground. Gudrun felt it. She urged it toward Grimhild, whose grin was wide and feral, and tied it around her neck. It bit down and wriggled inside her, gushed down her back in the form of a cape.

Grimhild's grin was still there. Her panted words made it eerie: "I hunger for bone... and my helper needs blood."

Gudrun's heart skipped. Her mother's eyes were red and fixed on her. She didn't like their look.

The casket tipped, spilling out teeth. It tempered and burned under an invisible flame, so blackened silver drops rolled off it like wax. Teeth rolled and welded together, silver winding around their cracks and grooves, until it was built and embellished: a diadem fit for an angel of death.

Grimhild and she glanced at each other, but Gudrun hadn't shaped the diadem. It was the work of the stone sorceresses, and it was clearly meant for her. Before her mother could stop her, she placed it atop her head.

The teeth pierced her skin.

Need, want; thirst, hunger. Survival instinct. Predatory spirit, the breath of beasts.

Pain and images flashed with each incise. Long-dead animals in caves of bones, their thick coats stained with blood, grinding hominin and red deer remains between their teeth. Competing with humans for food and shelter. An eventual battle for survival. Women riding them with hearts in their hands. The women turned to stone. The animals were killed and set on fire, but their teeth didn't break down. They were pulled under, buried in the earth.

The crown of teeth settled and Gudrun quaked with cold spasms. She croaked, "Let's get you something to eat."

Chapter Thirty-Three

Margaret's stomach was fine on the ferry, her head steady and her temperature normal. She was sure now that she wasn't prone to seasickness—not as a redcape or a human, not as a little girl. John Balliol had had her poisoned. Others had seen her sick, so her death story was believable, even to those closest to her.

She stepped off the ferry onto the northern side of the strait and stumbled over her feet.

Malcolm was there, leaning against a wooden house in the small settlement, waiting for her. He burst forward when he saw her and hugged her without reservation.

"Thank you," he said, lifting her off the ground.

She felt dizzy. He shouldn't be thanking her. "How did you find me?"

"When Thomas told me he lost you in England, I went back to Hermitage Castle to wait for your return. I missed you somehow, but your bird led me to Ermengarde. She had the sword. I can't believe you got it. Anyway, Robert guessed you'd be coming this way. Thank the Lord he was right."

Her chest hurt and she stuttered, "I... I left her there... left her for... for dead... how could you—"

"She's fine. Better than fine. I hoped for it, but... you made it happen. You saved her."

"I left her."

"Come inside."

The house he'd been leaning on was small, but it was cozy and warm, though it smelled of livestock; there were currently three sheep and some chickens in the corner, but no one else was inside.

Malcolm gave her some stodgy oat bread and they sat together on a wooden bench next to a crackling fireplace.

"I'm not a sorcerer. Never have been, never will be, but I know what sorcery does to people. To you. I've been there for some of it. I've seen what you've done."

The bread was hard to swallow.

"I forgive you for it. And I owe you for Ermengarde." He took her hand, the one not holding bread.

She swallowed.

"I like your eyes this way." His voice was low but assured. "Margaret, I like you."

He kissed her.

Stars burst inside her and left glittering ash clouds swirling in her stomach like a starling murmuration. Her heart had never raced so fast, not when shedding her cape or taking hearts or almost losing her own to Robin.

Malcolm pulled away just an inch, and she closed the space again. This was more intoxicating than heart-taking, a greater rush than killing. She wanted to kiss him forever.

She was human now... did that mean she deserved love?

She wanted it. She wanted to lose her heart the right way.

"I didn't come here just to thank you." His face was flushed, his breathing hard, his pupils large.

She didn't care why he'd come, she just wanted him closer.

"I need you to come back with me."

"Why?"

"We brought the sword back to Hermitage Castle. It isn't releasing the other redcapes. They can't touch it—it's like it's still sealed. But when you were there, Ermengarde was saved. Thomas thinks you might be the key. He wants you—us—to go back inside the castle. We had to leave the sword there, in the hall. We barely escaped with our lives."

The kiss had stifled the livestock odour but it returned in full force when she took a deep breath. She coughed lightly.

"Will you help us, and them?"

"I'm on my way to Dunfermline, but..." Her hand went to the nape of her neck. "Yes. After Dunfermline, yes."

She couldn't help but smile when he did. They kissed once more before they agreed to meet in Hawick, and Margaret left, heading for Dunfermline.

Two hours after leaving Malcolm, in the late afternoon, Margaret was near the burgh when a southward Englishman approached her.

"Travelling alone, are you?" His eyebrows curved like dirty earth-worms.

She should have asked Malcolm to come with her.

She walked past him, but he followed her.

"You're in need of a companion."

"I'm not."

"For the night, then." He gripped her shoulders from behind. Not hard, but she stopped, and her hand flew to the knife beneath her cloak.

Not again... please let go, she thought, but she licked her lips and whispered, "Don't let go."

He forced her down suddenly and grabbed at her clothes.

Margaret closed her eyes and let Īzebel have him.

She didn't black out this time. She cut his heart out and ate it, and her tears fell into the gaping wound in his chest.

She wasn't supposed to need this anymore. So why did she need to do it?

She waited to feel sick from eating the chewy heart, like many normal people would. But she didn't. She looked human now, but she was still a sorceress; she no longer craved blood and bones, but she still itched to take hearts.

She had the horrifying thought that Malcolm might have followed her, might be watching her murder, so she glanced around and listened for footsteps. But he wasn't there; of course he wasn't. He would have intervened when the man took hold of her.

Did he know she was still killing when he kissed her, or did he think she was saved now that she was capeless?

She tried to drag the body into the trees, but it was too heavy, so she left it and ran toward Dunfermline, uphill.

After a dry day, the overcast sky let out its rain and she used it to clean the heart blood from her face.

"Why bother?"

"John?" she asked.

Had everyone followed her here?

When she had a cape, the Red Comyn was hardly a threat; now, he seemed menacing, and his silent approach was beyond unsettling, even in winter when the growth was thin—maybe especially then, when it was easier to see through the forests.

"I say leave the blood. You're a monster, why hide it?"

He was too close.

Would Īzebel stand a chance against him?

"I've never seen you like this." He smiled, relishing the fear she tried to hide.

"Why are you here?"

"For these." He held her identification papers, their edges aflame. She hadn't felt him swipe them.

She reached for them and he danced away. Her heart clenched as the papers curled and crinkled to ash, her father's words dissolving to nothing: "Margrete Dei gratia Regina Scottorum."

Margaret, by the Grace of God, Queen of the Scots.

Queen of the Ashes.

Queen of Nothing.

"Now for your life."

"We were friends. I helped you."

"Awfully emotional for an alpha," said John. He moved forward and she backed away until she was up against a tree with whorled branches.

"I thought you wanted that—emotion in an alpha." Her hand moved slowly to Īzebel. "Isn't she the reason you're here—your mother? You're still pining for her and jealous of me."

"I don't pine." His voice wobbled. "She may not have killed you, but she got you out of the way for Balliol. So too would she move you for me. She'd approve of this."

Was he trying to convince himself?

Margaret whipped Īzebel toward him.

He was faster than her now.

He cranked her wrist sideways and the knife dropped harmlessly to the ground, soundless against her cry.

"You're wrong... Alianora... wouldn't approve," she choked. "And you... do only what she wants... don't you... John?"

The pulse in her throat beat fast against his hands.

He squeezed.

She gagged and coughed. The air smelled like drying rain. Pain wrapped her throat and throbbed in her cheek, their swelling soothed by cold grass and soft mud.

She tried to force her eyes open, glimpsing shapes through her lashes. Her eyelids kept closing, so she lay there a moment until they obliged.

She moaned as her neck twisted to look up—from John's legs to his torso to his downturned face.

"We brought this for you." He dropped a knotted prayer rope and she looked at it with apprehension.

Its blood-splotched knots spun like whirlpools.

As had the effigy in Hermitage Castle, the rope unlocked for her a memory.

Shadows like demons danced around Eirik II Magnusson. He lowered a heart into her tiny hands. Īzebel stuck out of it, shredded muscle stretched over the blade's teeth.

Margaret cried and turned her face away but obediently kept her hands around the mutilated heart. Eirik laughed darkly.

He suddenly recoiled, pulled at his ears, and swept his head back and forth.

He was afraid. Of what? Of her?

"Narve!" he shouted, shaking. "Narve!"

Eirik had Īzebel? Margaret's eyes moved to the next closest knot.

She threw heart after heart into the sea and watched it swallow them down so she couldn't. She was still small, still in Bergen. A sorceress before she knew she was one.

Another knot.

She melted a heart and her father nodded. She didn't want to melt another, but he used lies to convince her. He would hit her, he said. He would die if she didn't. The heart would turn into a snake and eat her up if she didn't kill it first.

The next memory was blurry, like a curtain of water surrounded the scene, but she made herself out.

Eight-year-old Margaret stabbed a redcape with Īzebel. She sawed off his cape and took his heart tooth. She swallowed it, killed a girl her own age, fashioned a cape for herself from heated blood, and begged Alianora to make her forget...

John snatched the prayer rope away.

"This is my mother's. Did you steal it?" he accused.

She opened her mouth to argue and demand he let her see the rest, but he knelt next to her, firmly clutching the rope.

"Did she give this to you?"

You did, she wanted to say. What came out was, "Have you gone mad?"

Disgust scrunched his face.

"You've been dead for too long. Even with your papers, you think the king would believe you? Do you think anyone would?" He placed his hand back on her throat, his touch disturbingly gentle.

Gruffly, she said, "Times are uncertain... Scots need certainty and relief... from the English. My... odds are good."

"You won't be queen, Margaret. If you try to reach him again, if you try to rally support, then I *will* hunt you. And I will kill you."

She gathered the ashes of her papers when he left, scooping what she could into an empty heart casket.

Those memories: sorcery, Īzebel, her cape attachment...

She closed her eyes, remembering the day as she always had.

The nape of her neck tingled; something new was fixed there. A cape.

She gingerly touched it, trying to place its soft material. Was it silk? No, it was thick as wool with the velvetiness of oiled leather but more malleable, almost liquidlike. And it smelled of sharp iron.

She released it in shock.

Blood. It was made of blood.

It wasn't fastened in the front. She reached back to undo it but couldn't find a pin or a clasp.

It wasn't just fixed to her skin. It had fingers that reached inside her, fused with her veins, twined around her heart.

Though she could never remember the actual attachment, she'd blamed William. But it wasn't his fault. It was hers.

She'd done it to herself.

Why?

Why would she choose to be a redcape?

"Because he's right. We're a monster." It was her voice, but she hadn't said it.

Her fingers flew to her mouth. She tried to pull down her smile, but it was plastered there. Something was terribly wrong with her. With them.

"Who are we?" she asked.

"We are Abaddon."

Her heart trembled.

"Get out!"

She remembered Alice saying the same thing, how she'd screamed it over and over again, how unlike herself she'd been.

"Get out!" she wailed.

"For now."

Her smile fell as the demon left her.

The lost time, even after she had a pure heart... How long had he been possessing her? How could she make him stop?

A sorcerer could tell her.

William performed his duty as Lord Soulis but did seemingly little else, and Alianora was missing. Hermitage Castle held books on sorcery, but she was meant to go there with Malcolm, who was rounding up the whitecapes now...

What if she blacked out with him near and woke up to his heartless corpse, her kiss still warm on his lips?

No. She couldn't meet him. Until she dealt with this, she couldn't risk it.

She paced back and forth, staring north, the direction John had gone.

There was someone else who might be able to teach her: the wizard who had mastered sorcery, made nearly every breakthrough on the subject, taught the Soulis line everything they knew, and had extensive experience with demons—if the legends were to be believed.

She couldn't properly look for Michael Scot before, with a cape holding her back.

Now she could.

The rumours of his whereabouts were stale, but she would sniff out new ones in Europe. If he'd somehow defied time and lived, she would find him; if not, she would find his books and hope he'd written one on demons.

CHAPTER THIRTY-FOUR

Gudrun woke in the night and edged closer to her sleeping husband.

She pressed herself against him, wrapped an arm around his side, and shivered. He was usually so hot when he slept. Had the Burgundian defeat chilled him?

He had, after all, lost his shining silver sword in Belgica Prima to the barbarian devils—Attila had wielded it when the Romans' Huns attacked. Grimhild had been there, the Burgundian weapon, and she'd eaten her fill. Still, they had lost. But they hadn't lost everything. They were allowed to keep their city, to live in peace on the Rhine. She could only hope the Roman prophetess had been wrong—that their peace would go on. Or that her mother was right, and they had changed the future together.

"Sigurd?" she whispered.

His chest, where her hand rested, was wet. Iron coated her nostrils.

She jolted up, tense and awake.

Sigurd had been stabbed.

She shook him, yelled for help, begged him to breathe.

He wouldn't.

They came too late. She'd awakened too late.

How could she have slept through her husband's murder?

Gundaharius and Brynhild were the first to arrive, as their bed was nearest, and their son, Gondioc, followed.

Brynhild half collapsed against the wall when she saw him.

"What have you done?" Brynhild choked. "What have you done?"

Gudrun looked down at herself. She was covered in blood.

"He never slept with me. I said that to punish you," she admitted in a defeated voice. "If I knew you would do this, I—"

"I would never hurt him!"

"Cruel, cruel!" sobbed Brynhild as she fled the room, colliding with Grimhild on the way out. Others came behind her, but Gundaharius ordered privacy before going after his wife with his son.

Gudrun crumpled next to Sigurd and caressed his face.

She'd thought him immune to the evils of this world. Her sun, her guiding light, had been stamped out in the dark and left her with nothing to orbit. How could she go on without him?

"Who would do this?" she asked herself, Grimhild, God.

Her mother picked at a bloodstained nail.

No... Grimhild knew Sigurd was everything to her. Not even she would go that far. Would she?

"Tell me you didn't do this."

"I did not. I do know who did."

Gudrun's tongue felt waxy and thick. A sour taste, like the bitter skin of a grape, trickled across it. "Who?"

"Brynhild."

She shook her head slowly, trying to understand. Brynhild's despair seemed genuine. There was real hatred in her words. *You're a monster.*

"Why do you think she told you she lay with Sigurd?"

Weeks ago, Brynhild had approached her with the news. She and Sigurd were together long before Gudrun married him—it wasn't Gundaharius who took her virginity, it was Sigurd. She didn't know why he didn't remember, but their affair resumed after his marriage.

"She wanted you to do it. When you didn't, she took matters into her own hands."

"She didn't want him dead..."

"On the contrary. You had him in life. In death alone could she be with him."

"She plans to take her own life?"

Grimhild nodded.

Gudrun turned back to Sigurd, soaked lashes quivering. "Please, let me alone to be with him."

Sigurd's funeral pyre blazed strong and bright, a reflection of his soul. Its flames reached for the heavens.

Gudrun hardly blinked when Brynhild leapt into the fire as Sigurd had once done for her. The ustor tried to get her out but failed; the fire was too hot.

She solemnly watched her rival scream and burn alive. Her body dried and shrank, and her bones fused with Sigurd's riches, the jewelry that hadn't burned to ash. When the fire was put out with water, the star-crossed lovers' bones sizzling and cooling, Gudrun left to bury his horse.

A silver heart casket glistened on her chest.

Brynhild had stolen Sigurd's body.

But Gudrun had won his heart.

CHAPTER THIRTY-FIVE

Toledo was dry and gray, sown with dusty green trees, and suffused with the faint aroma of sweet olives undercut by the brine of fresh, oily mackerel and tuna.

Before leaving Scotland, Margaret had retrieved two more fist-sized heart caskets from her souterrain vault, so she now had four strapped at her waist, along with Īzebel and the sorcerer's trephine. They were pushed to the sides and back of her belt, hidden beneath her sheepskin cloak.

She held the cloak's edges to keep it from shifting when she met with an astronomer and precentor, Isaac Ibn Sid, at the Church of St. Mary of Toledo. It was built in a Gothic style over an old mosque and far taller than the abbeys she'd visited in Scotland. Inside were glittering treasures: serpents' tongues and eagles' talons, ampullae ornamented with enamel, ivory caskets and crosses of cut rock crystal, scattered gems, sculptures of the Virgin Mary, copper lions, gazelles and doves, and paintings of scenes from the Book of Kings. Gilded reliquaries held thorns from Christ's crown, Bibles, cross fragments, and assorted fabrics.

"You want to read the books of Michael Scot?" Isaac had tried Arabic first, then Castilian, before settling on French. His accent was difficult to parse, but Margaret was thankful she found someone she could, with effort, understand.

She remembered the last time she'd met a man in a church—and murdered him. She ached to do the same to Isaac and twined her fingers to keep them from Īzebel. "Yes. Can you tell me if he's been here?"

Unfinished, stained-glass windows poured and fitted by Netherlandish glaziers filtered coloured light onto his long, whitish beard and thin lips. "Hm... eighty years ago or more. I have read certain studies and translations. Très bien."

"But not recently?"

"He is dead, do not you think?"

The question was in her eyes, reflecting the triforia that arched overhead.

His shoulders raised. "Rabbi Zag is the person to ask. He knows a man."

She walked with him from the sanctuary, past elaborate tombs and naves and cream, bricked columns, to the cathedral's library—the location of the School of Translators, where Michael Scot had worked. Its collection was broad and arranged on Mudéjar constructed brick shelves decorated with yesería.

Rabbi Sujurmenza Zag was in conversation with a group of philosophers, physicians, or scientists at a table stacked with books, papers, pens of reed and metal, and alchemical and astronomical instruments. He was bearded with an intellectual gleam in his eyes; like Isaac, he looked the part of a scholar, but they were both too aged to endure the work of translators.

Isaac spoke with the group in a southern dialect of Castilian and the words flowed over Margaret's ears. When Sujurmenza said something she could comprehend, it took her a minute to realize.

"The books," he said again, gesturing to the table. "After you study will I answer your questions."

The scholars resumed their discussion, sending occasional glances her way.

She examined the books, loose parchment, and rag paper. There was a letter to Scot from a Moorish astronomer on Ptolemaic theories being taught in the school systems, another from a man named Petroches who spoke of a sphere, one from an Arabian naturalist on wild lupine flowers and carob leaves. There were star charts, drawings of earth and the human body, occult studies and diagrams.

She picked up the *Abbreviatio Avicennae* and read its full title inside, "Avicenna de Animalibus per Magistrum Michaelem Scotum de Arabico in Latinum translatus."

Liber Quatuor Distinctionum, Liber Particularis, De Causis, De Coelo et Mundo, De Partibus Animalium, De Perfecto Magisterio, Liber Luminis, De Sphaera, Timaeus, Parva Naturalia, Liber Abaci, Physica, Metaphysica, Meteora, Nova Ethica, Secreta Secretorum, De Substantia Orbis... works Michael Scot had either translated or written, writings on astronomy, astrology, chiromancy, geography, psychology, anatomy, medicine, ethics, mathematics, alchemy, meteorology, logic, et cetera, in Arabic, Latin, even Greek.

On several, names were printed in handwriting that wasn't Scot's: Averroës, Gerard, Proclus, Philip, Aristotle, Polemon, Hermannus Alemannus, Maimonides, Zetzner, Plato, Alpetrongi...

Flipping through manuscripts, she found an original treatise, the *De Animalibus Sanguinum*, written in Latin.

Neither when she'd gone through William's books and scrolls at Hermitage, nor when he'd read scholarly articles to her when they were children, had she come across an exposition on redcapes.

It began with predators, animals, and humans who lived thousands of years ago. There wasn't enough space for both groups to survive, so they warred. Six sorcerers turned. They shed their clothes and humanity, took the beasts' side, and fought against their own. In a final stand, a lion covered them with stone, like a cathedral erected over a mosque.

"Magnis maleficis: hyaenae dentes veneficiis imbuti."

Hyena teeth imbued with magic.

That was what lay beside her pure heart in its casket, a hyena's ancient tooth laced with those dying sorcerers' curse.

Scot wrote of Grimhild of Burgundy, the first redcape and most powerful sorceress to date. She was gifted as a child, a brilliant student, adept at wielding a sorcerer's knife. She had unheard-of abilities—namely, the ability to feel magic-leavened teeth in the depths of the earth and pull them to the surface. She explored how hearts were purified, had theories about trials by fire or fire-laced love, but was never able to cleanse one on her own. She did, however, find silver could reveal a heart's purity, and she invented the silver heart casket, at which point she no longer had to make do with fresh hearts but could preserve and carry them within caskets. And she discovered tar could turn any heart black as sin and nullify pure heart properties.

Later in life, she owned an enchanted, garnet-inlaid ring named And-varanaut that could locate sources of silver for casket-making. The ring had once been guarded by a dragon, who was slain by a hero, Sigurd, but it was unclear when Grimhild acquired it. She'd had four children of note: three Burgundian kings and an unremarkable, unnamed daughter, who either died or was captured when Hunnic troops attacked Burgundy—the writing was vague on the point. Grimhild became a red-cape and died a valiant death fighting to protect her children and her kingdom. Her found hyena teeth resurfaced decades later in Vienne, and Michael Scot excavated more centuries on for Ada Warenne.

The *De Animalibus Sanguinum* overlapped with Aristotle's *Secreta Secretorum and* Scot's *Physiognomia,* even some of the books on psychology, in that it discussed the birth and death of redcapes, their humanity, and the relationship between redcapes' physical features and the way they moved to their behaviour, their souls and their destinies. Compared to humans, redcapes had disfigured-looking, wide jaws, more muscular necks and shoulders, eyes haunted by blood, cape fingers shifting beneath their skin, slightly ruddier complexions, and thicker hair. Most could pass as human but none were quite, and the book also called them blood animals or bone crushers. According to Scot, they still had souls, lest they were created from hearts and not living beings, but their souls were blackened like silver tarnished.

He reviewed redcape strength and longevity based on the temperature of their blood, the size of their hearts, the state of their sacrifices' hearts, and the light conditions during their cape attachments. It was necessary to create them at night, otherwise their capes would suffocate them. They could be created under any moon or weather condition, but the strongest seemed to be made with black hearts beneath a new moon when clouds concealed the stars. He'd graphed maps of the stars for varying attachments, researched their survival rates and how high they rose in the redcape ranks.

There were studies on their slow aging process, on alphas, how capes killed, cape material, redcape sodomy and the sterility of red males—the reason females mated with human men, often before taking them as libations. And a surgical analysis: he'd somehow captured a living red-cape and cut them open. He detailed cape fingers like tendons wound through their veins before the cape died. There was a following ex-periment on the heart tooth left behind, and Scot determined it was indestructible.

A section on stone circles succeeded an illustration comparing the physiognomy of a hyena and a redcape who looked strangely like Aliano-ra. There was a note that said Aristotle's belief that hyenas' manes ran the length of their spines was not incorrect, but that his hyenas differed in this way and others from the extinct species Scot studied, which had once occupied Europe.

Margaret gasped when she read: "They can take libations at any circle or gathering of stone sorcerers, including the one in which they were created."

She ground her teeth and skimmed sentences, barely catching words. *Tide, moon, Guadalperal.*

The next section, an essay that examined the redcape existence in regards to religion, blurred under her view. She closed the book, unable to focus.

That was how Alianora had disappeared and why Robin never re-turned to Ninestane Rig. They knew. They knew they could survive anywhere as long as they could find a circle to sacrifice in, and there were many in Scotland.

"Finished?" Rabbi Zag gave her a start.

The men and women he'd been conversing with had left or moved on to other things. Isaac, too, was immersed in some book at a desk on the other side of the room. How long had she been reading?

She nodded. She was finished, for now.

He had an expectant look, forehead down and eyebrows raised.

"I'm told you know a man... one who can tell me about Michael Scot?"

"Yes, yes, Dante. He lives in exile. Look here." He moved in front of his astronomical instruments, things like candle and quicksilver clocks, astrolabes, a kamal, sundials, sky discs, a dioptra, a triquetrum, an armillary sphere, equatorial rings, a scaphe. He picked up a flat astrolabe, which previously held down writings on a spherical one. "This man is an astronomer. He has this in silver and gold. His is no common astrolabe, no. No, he uses it to see death. He will know if Scot had his."

He seemed to wink, as if it were all a game, as if Scot were dead and he was joking with her. Maybe that was just his face, the wrinkles permanently fixed to the corners of his lively eyes.

"How can a man see death?"

"With the stars." He smiled. "There is magic to science, or science is magic. This man knows science and silver and stars."

Dante had joined L'Arte dei Medici e Speziali, the Guild of Doctors and Apothecaries, before taking office as one of the six priors of Florence for the typical two months. He was exiled a few years past for holding position and opposing outside interference in the city's affairs.

"You are in luck," Sujurmenza said, "for he sent me a letter. He writes of woeful events in the Florentine Republic, a Romanesque basilica in Verona, our shared scholarly pursuits... He waits for a saviour to welcome him back to her, his city." Sujurmenza sighed sympathetically. "But it seems his Florence has been corrupted... he will never return, even if he does."

He waved the letter. "From Verona this was sent, from the house of Bartolomeo I della Scala. For you to go there is a small gamble; if Dante has left, I know neither how to find him nor where he will go next. But this Bartolomeo he writes of is his benefactor—he gives him board and bread and a space to think and write. He will remain there a while, my belief is that."

He gave her a copied paper map and indicated the Scala house. She asked him one more question: if there was a way, with science or magic, to restore her identity papers. There was not.

She eyed the *De Animalibus Sanguinum* and considered swiping it but decided not to jilt Sujurmenza's generosity. Someday, she could return and finish reading it. Or maybe she wouldn't want to learn more about redcapes; maybe, one day, she could leave all thought of them behind.

When Sujurmenza took up with someone else, she left Toledo northeast for Verona.

CHAPTER THIRTY-SIX

Shrieks and howls cut the air. The sounds of horse hooves, lives being taken, and buildings being razed rang through trampled vineyards and dove through sagging willow branches to drown in the Rhine.

The scar-faced Huns had returned to Borbetomagus, come to finish Rome's work.

A female savage brutally murdered a Burgundian woman with a mace, then fixed her eyes on Gudrun, who swallowed hard. It was fitting for her to die like the grape-laden, twisted vines, to be crushed before veraison as her marriage with Sigurd had been.

Grimhild swept over her like a cloud shadow.

The Hun fell. Glass and lapis lazuli beads flew free from her embroidered leather tunic and skipped over blood like insects over water. Her bones cracked between durable teeth.

Someone tripped and Gudrun and Grimhild's heads snapped toward the door.

It was Gundaharius. He was fixated on Grimhild, scrambling back against the wall.

"Are you... eating her?" His throat was dry. His eyes raced back and forth, tracing connections in his brain. "You've done this before, haven't you? Last year... last month. And Sigurd... What have you become, Mother? What has done this to you?"

"She didn't kill him. It was Brynhild."

"I heard something that night. I saw her"—he marked Grimhild—"in the hallway before you screamed."

"No... it was Brynhild," Gudrun reiterated. "Tell him."

Red saliva dripped from Grimhild's mouth. "Brynhild didn't kill Sigurd. We never said that."

"What?" The word left her on a drained breath.

She moved closer to Gundaharius, distancing herself from her mother. Her hands closed to fists, and she grabbed her brother's weapon—a sword modelled after the one Sigurd lost, the same length and shape, but without its light.

Her eyes blurred. The man she loved, her sun and stars, her everything. With murder and lies, her mother had darkened her sky and her life.

"You took him from me!" she yelled. She raised the sword and thrust it toward Grimhild, who stood still before her.

The tip stopped an inch from her throat.

"She's not our mother," said Gundaharius. "Kill the monster."

The blade shook.

Queerly, Grimhild revealed, "You have to cut off our cape."

Did she think she wouldn't do it?

Gudrun's heart skittered like the Hun's beads. Her hands gripped the hilt so hard they hurt.

"Go on. Kill us," taunted Grimhild.

Gundaharius jerked the sword from her and sliced the cape in a quick motion.

Grimhild's face changed, her expression shocked, as if she hadn't truly seen them there until that moment. And her body became blood, dissolved to nothing but a heart.

Before it, too, could burst and leave only the tooth, Gudrun placed it in a casket, preserving it for later. Her crown of teeth broke and dropped to the floor in pieces, dying alongside the last and only redcape.

Gundaharius's lips and eyebrows were pinched. He turned his back on her and the fallen teeth, and Gudrun realized she'd given away her sorcerous nature.

It might have been the feel of Grimhild's heart, the sight of tremendous gore and death, but Gudrun was suddenly overcome with a dark need.

She couldn't stop herself. She drew her sorcerer's knife and plunged it into Gundaharius's back.

"I'm sorry, brother," she cried as she sawed out his heart. "I'm sorry."

She didn't blame her mother anymore for killing Sigurd. It was the retribution she deserved, the penance Grimhild had circumvented for her for so long. She would serve it, endure miserable, lonely, painful self-punishment, and then she would rectify his murder.

She would find a way to bring him back, and they would be happy. Finally, she would be happy.

Chapter Thirty-Seven

The ground floor of the Scala house was rather public as it was made up of shops that faced the square—the centre of Verona, once a Roman forum. By way of an alley in the back, Margaret made her way to the second floor, where the family's apartments began, and she was welcomed inside after explaining who she was—a lie that she was under Rabbi Zag's tutelage—and whom she'd come to find.

Bartolomeo I della Scala, Lord of Verona, was a decade or so older than her, as was his wife, Costanza. His was a full house, bursting with chatter from the upper rooms and lower shops. She met numerous Scaligeri members, children, and guests: Alboino, Verde, Can Francesco, Caterina, and others. One boy in particular had warm brown eyes that made her think of Malcolm. She forced down all thoughts of him and the hurt or worry he must have felt when she failed to meet him at Hermitage.

Wealth was apparent in the glittering Scala house; there was no sign it had previously been used as a granary. It was colourful with exquisite tilework, its ceilings ornate, and its walls painted. The walls held oil paintings with gold-leaf backgrounds and reflected warm-hued light on bronze sculptures and gilt candlesticks. Tapestries and banners displayed woven scenes and metal-threaded ladders over luxurious, padded, carved, and traceried walnut furniture inlaid with tortoiseshell, marble, and bone.

Margaret was led to the third floor, which was raised over half the building, and the man, the astronomer she'd come so far to meet, looked up from his writing, the beginnings of the *Convivio*, and smiled at Bartolomeo. His nose was long, his lips naturally downturned, his eyes stern—the eyes of a man who knew too much or of things too dark, but his smile lightened his face and softened the angle of his eyebrows, an expression of genuine joy, made stark by his underlying air of perpetual misery.

He rose and introduced himself to her as Dante Alighieri. She didn't waste time in bringing up the astrolabe and Sujurmenza's claim that he could see Michael Scot's death, and he sneered at the mention of Scot.

"Ah, you should have said! I might have saved you the trouble." Bartolomeo frowned. "He does not have it!"

"My Lord speaks the truth." Dante sighed and returned to his seat. "In poor Florence it remains."

If he went back, the Republic would burn him alive.

The false Margaret's screams echoed in her mind when he said it. She saw Dante, with his short frame and lean figure, being strapped to a post, flames distorting his face and wrenching enraged screams from his small mouth.

"A misery for my friend, but fortune brought him here to us. We must leave him to his work," Bartolomeo said. "Come down and eat before you return to your School of Translators!"

She chewed on her cheek and stared out the nearest window. It was cool now, but in months the market across the square would feature onions and carrots, kale and cabbage. Sage, bay leaf, parsley, thyme, and rosemary scents would waft into the Scala house windows and people would flood the view.

On the journey there, she'd caught on a bit to Italian. Perhaps she'd learned words when she was young, or it was easier after having learned several other languages; still, she knew little to nothing of Florence, its politics, its culture. But she'd spent her life in the shadows, blending in. Surviving.

"I could get it for you," she proposed.

Dante's hands were flat on the table. They pushed him partway back up. "If you can, I will show you more than his death. I will show you his life."

Chapter Thirty-Eight

For years after her brother slayed Grimhild and she took his heart, Gudrun was anguished, then depressed. She was numb, enjoyed nothing, slept through her days, and ate too many hearts.

She still had Sigurd and Gundaharius's hearts, but her mother's had gone missing that day in Borbetomagus after she'd preserved it in a casket. She couldn't help but wonder if she'd eaten it by mistake. If so, where had Grimhild's heart tooth gone? Had she swallowed that too?

She watched the Huns and the Romans from afar and haunted Borbetomagus as a ghost. Her nephew, Gondioc, had taken his father's place as king.

When the Burgundians were relocated, she went a different way—to Thoricus by the Aegean Sea, where veins of silver pulsed strong. There, she woke up. She felt the sunshine on her face, the gentle breeze in her hair, ambition in her heart. She was thirty, then, and energized for the first time in years.

She set up base in Attica, travelled and returned. Went to work gathering materials and information, performing experiments and using natives as fodder, exerting herself until she reached exhaustion and made herself sick, resting to heal only to the point she could continue.

A decade passed, and she was older than Sigurd ever was.

In her workshop outside the dense city of Thoricus, a small, hidden mud house, she drew a square around a stemmed bowl decorated with eleven six-petalled palmettes. Three hearts turned to liquid and splashed in the bowl, three more after she drew a triangle. Earth soaked in the

215

blood. A pure heart, found northwest in Aegilia or Anagyrus, the only suitable vessel, drank it all in.

Gudrun brought the bulging heart to her lips.

A heart to pause aging, an elixir of life.

After ten years, she'd succeeded, as she would succeed in resurrecting her husband—or never die trying.

Gondioc had watched his father's murder, the loud breaking and shearing of his chest.

It wasn't hard to do what Grimhild said, to melt a heart over Gudrun's eyes and take his heart casket from her grasp.

"Leave her alive," Grimhild had been firm. "It's important that she lives."

He almost hadn't listened to her then, but he was a boy and frightened of her. He was grateful, now, that he hadn't killed Gudrun, though he wished he could be the one who would.

Now, he was a man, a king, and a sorcerer. Grimhild was dead, Gudrun was gone, and he was left without a family—his uncles had died on the same day as Gundaharius, and he suspected Gudrun had killed them, too. But, thanks to Grimhild's foresight, he wouldn't be fatherless much longer.

His spies informed him Gudrun was close to unsealing the gate between death and life. When she prevailed, his men would bring her findings home, and she would let them. Grimhild had said she would.

Until then, he would prepare: he would take a wife, for Gundaharius would want a body of his own blood.

CHAPTER THIRTY-NINE

People flooded the torch-studded banks of the Arno River to see the festival boats on which artisans had constructed massive, intricate scenes from hell. Faux fires burned, sunlight hot on their tongues; amidst them, devils and souls of the dead gyrated and screamed absurdly and elicited laughs from the multitudes.

Florence burst with flowers, greenery, and the saccharine aromas of acacia and chestnut honey, roses and violets, poppies and honeysuckle blooms. Brightly clothed dancers paraded through the alleys and flags twirled overhead. Instruments sounded from various places and their music rippled out and overlapped, mingling to create unique, compound songs. Young lovers sang ballads of spring and romance, alms-givers went door to door, and the piazza before the unfinished Palazzo della Signoria was overcrowded.

Margaret dashed beneath hanging cages and square-crenellated buildings, clutching a wooden bucket that contained jars of oils and loose pigment, perfume, spices, green leaves, and borax. Outside of the bucket, away from liquids, she held a copy of *Questiones Disputate de Veritate*, written by Thomas Aquinas, which she'd barely been trusted to carry.

She had been there, in Florence, for over a month. Bartolomeo had funded the journey and provided her a change of clothes—a linen dress and wool socks—and Dante had given her information on the city, a rushed course on the Florentine vernacular, instruction on how to act, and where to begin her search.

He'd left the astrolabe, which he called Bella and described as being shaped like a noose, in his family houses near the small church where he'd been married, San Martino al Vescovo. She'd gone there. His family had moved out, and she could only assume they'd taken the astrolabe with them. So she'd begun working for a man from Dante's guild, an apothecary, and used the opportunity to expand her knowledge of the language and Florence's occupants. She'd recently learned Dante's wife, Gemma, was a Donati, and she was living with her father in Dante's absence.

Margaret made deliveries to a Dominican friar, an upper-middle-class lady, and another L'Arte dei Medici e Speziali member, a painter. The latter two were out, but she dropped things off where she was told—with the lady's servant, who answered in livery, and inside the painter's door behind a homemade easel. Margaret walked a winding alley that separated the Cerchi and Donati properties and knocked on the door of a pear-coloured house, complete with hanging flowers and painted golden rain trees.

No one answered. She tried to push and pull the door, but the wood was reinforced, and it was locked from the inside with a series of metal bars. The windows had glass panes in bronze frames behind closed shutters.

There had to be a way in. Or would it be easier to wait for Dante's family to return from the festival and ask directly for the astrolabe?

Unexpectedly, the scratchy sound of metal on metal ran the length of the door and it opened. A fat old man with white hair and a beard demanded to know who she was.

"Margaret, Dante sent me—"

"Do not speak his name so loud." He yanked her inside. "Another loan, is that what he wants?"

"No, I'm here for Bella."

"She died many years ago."

"Died? What? How could..." She blinked. "Are you Manetto? Is your daughter living here?"

His eyes narrowed, and his hand reached for the door—likely to open it and shove her out. But a woman's voice stopped him. She wasn't out celebrating spring, after all.

"Yes. I live here." Gemma wore a red dress with a square neckline. Her face was naturally stern like Dante's but slightly softer. Her tone was less abrasive, and her features were more attractive. "You say my husband sent you. How can I know?"

She described Dante, said where she'd found him, the things he'd told her of his family and who his friends were, his thoughts on Florence's forthcoming ruin.

That convinced Gemma, but she asked frankly, with no emotion, "And have you been with him?"

"No! I never—no!"

"Our marriage was not altogether unhappy. He wasn't easy to live with, but I desired him. I was kind to him." Gemma sighed. "I know he wants to return, but not to me. In Florence, Verona, wherever he goes, the distance between us remains the same. There is a part of his heart I could never reach. I made peace with that long ago. Now I must make peace with this, the ending of my marriage."

She retrieved a chamois leather scarsella embellished with silvered stars and feathered wings.

"My son found it the day Dante left," she said. "Take it. To him, the Arno, I won't care."

Margaret opened the leather flap. Like Sujurmenza said, Dante's astrolabe was made of silver and gold—a gold rim, silver disk, gold plates, and silver points.

Manetto peeked out the door, eyes flicking left and right, and bade her to go.

She hesitated and glanced back at Gemma. "Is there anything you want me to tell him?"

"There is nothing left."

Margaret hurried from the house with the scarsella at her belt.

And straight into the arms of two waiting Neri.

The Black Guelphs covered her mouth with their hands and grabbed at her arms and legs.

"What have you gotten into with Manetto?" one queried with suspicion.

Another suggestively asked, "Here for the day?" The implication was clear: he thought she was a festival prostitute.

The second man tugged at her clothes, but the first hit him in the arm. "I heard her say 'Dante'," he said. "Corso will want to interrogate her. You can enjoy her after."

Margaret's eyes bulged. Their hands smothered her yells and contained her struggling body. Less than a mile away, through alleys and up a back entrance, they tied her up on the top floor of a granary.

"Corso won't need this..." The first man ripped the scarsella from her belt, then saw the caskets behind it and opened one. He dropped it and the scarscella in horror when a heart fell out and thudded beside her.

She grasped it with both hands, tied as they were, and sprayed heart blood over the men. She willed them to forget her and what they were doing in the granary, catching their memories in the casket, and she dragged the sarscella with two fingers alongside her as she inch-crawled to hide.

Between the wall and a grain bin, she waited while they looked around in a daze and joked about drinking too much wine.

She squirmed and fought her bindings and managed to get hold of Īzeḇel. It took some time to finagle the blade between her wrists and to saw her way out, but the ankle bindings were effortless.

You can enjoy her after, he'd said.

Her chest heaved.

If not her, it would be someone. Those men had freedom here, strength and opportunity. It wasn't meant to be used that way, to take freedom from someone else.

These were demons she knew how to be free of.

She recovered her casket and stumbled down the stairs to the ground floor. She walked past people in the loggia, jubilant festival goers all around, drinking and playing games. As shadows lengthened, she went court to court, dance to dance, to scan faces, searching for harsh eyes and waiting for her heart to seize with sickness.

"Tell me where to find him."

Margaret had stalked the Black Guelphs for weeks before she found the first man, following him down an alley in the dark, climbed into his home through a window while he slept.

"Who?"

He didn't recognize her, but he would remember his friend from the festival.

Īzebel kissed a line of beaded blood from his clammy neck and opened his mouth like a sluice gate. Information spewed forth—the second man was from Lucca, and he wasn't a Black Guelph as she'd thought, but a Ghibelline, and currently staying with a White Guelph who, thanks to the Pope, had been recently allowed to return.

The man's eyes darted around for a weapon or a way out from under the sorcerer's knife. She almost let him go but felt the pulsing artery in his neck and shoved Īzebel into it, covering his mouth with her hand as he had covered hers.

She left him heartless in his bed, jogged from the house to the time of her own fast-beating heart, and located the White Guelph's residence based on the man's description. It didn't have unfastened windows or doors, but she didn't need to get inside. The door opened, and her mark emerged.

She hid around the corner, trailed him to a granary, and crept after him up familiar stairs.

Where she'd been tied up weeks before, a new woman was tied up now, struggling in vain to free herself. This woman was younger than her and black-haired, with a length of cloth dampening her voice.

The man unhooked his belt.

Margaret surged from the stairs and drove her knife into his back, well below his heart. She promptly tore it out.

He screamed and flailed, struck her in the face and wrestled Īzebel from her. But when he took hold of the knife, lightning branched from nowhere and struck him and the granary.

His body spasmed, and the air filled with a scorched smell. Flesh sizzled and blood burned. Fragments of his clothes were blown off—ragged and frayed, it looked like they'd been half eaten by Īzeḅel.

The black-haired woman's scream strained at her gag as flames lapped at the walls and reached to melt the pre-charred corpse.

Between the flames, Margaret saw a face beneath a crown of white and pale-yellow holly flowers.

"Robin?" she whispered.

He held something.

Her hand flew to her belt. The trephine—he'd taken it.

Like the flash of lightning, he zapped out of existence.

Margaret tentatively touched Īzeḅel, expecting more lightning or heat, but the handle was cool. She cut the hysterical woman's bindings and they ran down the stairs.

Chased by heat, they escaped, and Margaret abandoned the woman and Florence. Behind her, the great fire stained the sky with orange blood like a hellish sunrise that wouldn't set; even when morning came, she could see its pillars of smoke in the sky—ash-gray ghosts of another man murdered and countless buildings burned to cinders.

CHAPTER FORTY

Among stone sorcerers by the sea, Gudrun sunk a tooth into her lover's heart and set it gently in the grass.

Before it, she killed a man. His body fell apart and reconstructed around the heart. Bone sloshed upward on a wave of blood, tendons attached them to muscle, and skin solidified over it all.

Fuzzy light billowed through Gudrun and tears welled in her eyes.

The body had his face. Sigurd's beautiful, perfect face.

Her knife found the next sacrifice.

Blood erupted and flew to Sigurd, cascaded down his back like silk and wormed its way inside him.

He opened his eyes and her hopes broke; he came at her and they blew away on salty winds.

It had his face, but this monster wasn't him.

She slashed the cape from his neck and scrambled to collect his heart in a casket, clinging to it as she rocked herself, chilled by the winds and the relived loss of Sigurd, and looked over the harbour.

She could create the body but not the soul.

She would need to trade for it. A soul for a soul, a heart for a heart.

That was it, the missing ingredient. A heart from the person who connected him to the land of the living, the last person to touch him before death—his murderer, her mother.

To bring him back, she needed her mother's heart, but Gondioc had taken it—a fact she'd discovered after Gondioc had sent her Gundaharius's sword, the weapon that had killed Grimhild. Why he wanted her to remember had but one explanation: he must have wanted to ressurect

223

Grimhild and assumed Gudrun did too and that she was working toward that end. What she couldn't fathom was why he would want to bring back Grimhild instead of his father; why he hadn't taken Gundaharius's heart. He would need it either way, but he wouldn't have known that back then—or now, without her insight.

She walked through Thoricus, past houses, smithies, towers, stairs and gateways in the walls, Doric stoas, a temple and a theatre, and returned to her workshop to record the resurrection formula, scanning all the while for Gondioc's desultory spies. Gudrun didn't want her mother to be resurrected, but she couldn't get to her heart unless she was—Gondioc had it too well guarded. He would only release it from his hand to place it in a new body.

Trusting her judgement of him was correct, she placed a tooth and Gundaharius's heart casket in a gold larnax and watched from afar as the spies stole it away.

Chapter Forty-One

"Keep still, Gundobad. Swallow."

In mountainous Sapaudia, the four-year-old boy choked on a tooth. He managed to get it down, lowered his eyes and stilled, and Gondioc opened one of two silver heart caskets, the one marked as his father's.

Gudrun's formula required two hearts and two sacrifices: the heart to be revived, one to be traded for a soul, and a sacrifice each for the body and cape. But, before her death, Grimhild had been working on her own formula. She said he would need one less sacrifice if he already had a body, and that would give the resurrected a longer life; however, she couldn't place the final ingredient, couldn't figure out how to bring back a soul.

Gudrun had.

Now, he could merge their formulas as Grimhild wanted and resurrect his father using Gundobad's body.

"Still," he said again, noticing the boy's restlessness. "Eat this."

Gundobad's nose scrunched, and he recoiled. "I want cheese and milk."

"Eat it." His tone mimicked the snowcapped mountains, cold and sharp, immovable.

He cowered and tried to bite into the heart, but the muscle was too thick and tough for him to break. Gondioc diced the heart, and he reluctantly downed the cubes, gagging after every few bites.

Gondioc sliced the sacrifice's neck and blood attacked Gundobad's nape.

He screamed in pain.

A heart melted and his screams stopped, for his soul had gone, replaced by an old, once-dead breath.

"Gundaharius?" Gondioc knelt before him. "Father?"

"Gondioc, my son." The boy placed a firm hand on his shoulder, arm angled up. "You have done well."

That night, the boy smiled a frightening smile and opened his mouth to an invisible serpent—the demon who'd been in Borbetomagus seventeen years ago, who'd made sure Gondioc took Grimhild's heart instead of Gundaharius's. Who made Gondioc believe his spies had killed Gudrun and brought back her heart when that heart had truly been the heart of Grimhild's murderer, his father's heart, the only one that could bring her back.

As he had when he'd been Grimhild, Gundobad welcomed in Abaddon.

Chapter Forty-Two

Upon her return to Verona, she learned Bartolomeo had died. In the week following his death, his brother, Alboino, was appointed Captain General and Scaliger Podestà of the Merchants, and Dante had moved on; rather than joining the Florentine exiles who'd recently attempted and failed to return to Florence, Dante rejected their ideals and formed a party of one.

He'd left a note for Margaret saying he was travelling to Lucca, where she learned from a Madame Gentucca that he'd gone on to visit Ravenna. She caught up with him there, praying in the Basilica di San Francesco, and waited for him on the mosaicked pavement outside. He was surprised to see her—more so to see Bella, but he was delighted at that—and, as promised, said he would use the astrolabe for her, but he needed a clear night to do so.

She agreed to accompany him to Bologna, for he'd prepared to leave Ravenna, and his hosts, the Scarabigoli family, provided them provisions to last a few days. Despite his spasmodic, tempestuous humours, Dante seemed to have patrons and accommodations wherever he went. He even had a room to study in at the Bologna Studium as an artist, as opposed to a jurist or doctor, and he stored his books and writings there.

A recent drawing showed Michael Scot beside Amphiaraus, Tiresias, Manto, and other men and women. Their necks were twisted, and they walked backwards, beards fell down their backs and hair tumbled over their naked chests.

"What does this mean?" She traced Scot's name under the drawing, pointed to the man she thought was him.

"Contrapasso. Those are the charlatans, soothsayers, fortune-tellers. False prophets possessed by silver-tongued demons. Their punishment is eternity gazing at a past they cannot see."

She flinched, envisioning herself among them, eyes blurred and body distorted.

"Is it not similar, what you're to do with the astrolabe?"

"Bella is not a product of magic, but science."

"Rabbi Sujurmenza said science is magic."

He scowled and said brashly, "Science is science, and astronomy is not astrology. The past is recorded, not divined. I do not involve myself with demons and their magical arts."

She watched him write a couple of lines, "Tant' è amara che poco è più morte; ma per trattar del ben ch'i' vi trovai, dirò de l'altre cose ch'i' v'ho scorte," and took up reading a book already in the study while they waited for the day's final rays to fade.

Written by Dionysius the Areopagite, one section resonated with her: "...the brilliant likeness of the Divine Goodness, this our great sun, wholly bright and ever luminous, as a most distant echo of the Good, both enlightens whatever is capable of participating in it, and possesses the light in the highest degree of purity, unfolding to the visible universe, above and beneath, splendours of its own rays, and if anything does not participate in them, this is not owing to the inertness or deficiency of its distribution of light, but is owing to the inaptitude for light-reception of the things which do not unfold themselves for the participation of light."

She was skimming Thomas Aquinas's *De Operationibus Occultis Naturae* when Dante snuffed out his candle.

On a terrace laden with nightshade and violets that overlooked Bologna, Dante cradled Bella and contemplated the sky. He lined up the vanes with stars, used the alidade to take measurements, and jotted down numbers.

When he had the proper values, he moved Margaret to stand where he had been, slid the astrolabe's top ring over her thumb, told her to hold it at a certain angle, and rotated the star-webbed, silver rete and the gold dial.

Starlight glinted in her eyes.

Michael Scot was not born when he should have been—he was a full-grown man at the time of his birth, for he had been someone else before Michael Scot and the name was stolen. Was he immortal? Had the demon kept him alive?

He looked familiar, his dark eyebrows and wide forehead, but Margaret couldn't quite place him. His life flashed in bursts—he lost weight, his face reduced to skin and bones—and she could. Michael Scot was Robin; rather, Robin was Michael Scot, or an emaciated version of him.

Scot manipulated sorcerers into using trephines, creating potions and casting foreign spells, and ate their hearts when they were done. It became clear: he was half a sorcerer. He used hearts to make others forget, but that was the extent of his power and explained why he'd used her the way he had.

He held up a mirror and spoke with Abaddon. He hunted Alianora, coveted her heart, but, like Margaret, he wasn't strong enough to fight her and win, and she saw through any trap he set.

He *had* been there in Florence when the granary burned. He slipped the trephine from Margaret's belt and walked through fire like he couldn't feel the heat.

The astrolabe reached the current day. Scot was alive and in the German Kingdom, holding a bag of teeth over a line of corpses beside a kidnapped German sorceress.

Scot had never expelled the demon. He never even tried.

"Show me Margaret of Scotland in Norway. June 1, 1282." She clamped her teeth together. That was her voice, but the words were Abaddon's.

Dante's eyes narrowed. She thought he might have one of his angry bouts, but he obliged. With a pre-determined date, the astrolabe was easy to alter.

Margaret's mother scribbled furiously in the library where Bishop Narve had schooled Margaret herself. She flipped pages, opened books, and sat down to stare at a page filled with her own writing, glancing over her shoulder at intervals in a paranoid fashion—was she searching the darkness for the queen mother, who would plot her death in less than a year?

Before she burned the page, Margaret, watching from Bologna, was able to read it. It was a sorcerer's discovery, one that could have terrible consequences and, strangely enough, one made by her mother, an intellectual whitecape who, as far as Margaret knew, had never practiced sorcery. She didn't belong in Bergen with Eirik. She should have been in Toledo or Bologna, among teachers and scholars.

A young Narve surged into the library and tried to save the fiery page. He screamed at her to rewrite it, but the Queen of Norway said it was too late. She would never reveal what was on the page.

"You destroyed it, but you can't unwrite it," Narve hissed. "Your daughter will read your words in the stars."

"If I have a daughter, you won't be able to touch her. She won't listen to your lies."

Margaret, in Italy, realized the second Narve opened his mouth that it wasn't Narve with whom her mother spoke: "It's you we can't touch. She is lost."

That was her answer.

Abaddon couldn't inhabit a whitecape, but Margaret was lost. He could possess the unsaved—coil like a snake around their hearts to constrict and enslave.

Was that why he'd asked Dante to show her the scene—to take away her hope? She'd failed to become a whitecape, so she couldn't drive out the demon.

The night sky, clear and deep, reappeared before Margaret.

"No! I want to see her life. I want to see more."

"A selfish ethos." Dante's eyes flared. "You've done me a service, I've done you two. Do not let indulgence blacken your heart. Set your course and leave me."

The astrolabe's metal points dug into her skin and drew blood that shimmered like mercury.

She could draw Īzebel and force him to show her the entire world's history if she wanted to. But what would Margaret's mother have done?

She'd burned her own research, research that had the potential to bring her anything she wanted, wealth or glory or knowledge. She'd destroyed it for the good of humanity.

She had been selfless. She wouldn't threaten or harm Dante.

Margaret loosened her grip and let him take the astrolabe.

Dante adjusted it again, but for himself, and she heard him say, "Sweet and precious Beatrice," as she left the terrace.

CHAPTER FORTY-THREE

After leaking the formula to Gondioc's spies and following them to Sapaudia, Gudrun had been evaded. Gondioc was always guarded, always with his sons. She got close to him thrice over the years and his eldest son drove her away each time. She'd scoured the city for her mother's face, left Burgundy to expand her search, returned to try again, but Grimhild was nowhere to be found.

Using heart magic, Gudrun had manipulated her way back into the family. She became Chroma, daughter of Chilperic II, and began to lose hope. She wondered if Gondioc failed to resurrect Grimhild, or if she'd died a second time, but a sign of her mother's presence surfaced in the city of Valentia; after spending decades with her new family, she almost wished it hadn't.

Her substitute mother, Caretene, had been turned into a redcape, had stones tied around her neck, and was now drowning in the Rhine. A man stood at the water's edge with a cape of his own, flowing and glistening like the river. It was Gundobad.

Gudrun hadn't seen him since her final attempt to reach his father approximately twenty years ago.

He walked away from the Rhine and picked something out of the darkness. A human leg and foot.

She squinted at the dark mass and recognized the gold torc around the corpse's neck. It belonged to Chilperic II.

Gundobad had murdered, and was eating, his own brother.

"I can make you forget." Gundobad looked straight at her. Anyone but a redcape wouldn't have seen her in the dark.

233

She ran.

She hadn't dealt with a redcape since her mother.

Grimhild had talked of seeding redcape nests, even said they would be her legacy. But Gudrun couldn't fathom anyone but her becoming one. Had she turned only Gundobad or his other brothers too?

Hiding beneath Roman ramparts, Gundobad found her. He was a shadow with sharp teeth, but a weakness Gudrun knew.

"I could make you forget," he said. "But with this new body... that's the extent of my sorcery."

New body... he couldn't be...

"I need you to create another formula, one to restore my magic."

"Mother?" choked Gudrun.

Gundobad smiled.

Her mind raced with calculations.

Grimhild resurrected into someone else's body... why hadn't she thought of it? This whole time, she'd been looking for a face when she should have been looking for a soul.

"You didn't want your old self back?" she squeaked, unsure what to ask, how to react. She'd expected her mother, not her mother dressed in a man's skin.

"Gondioc presumed he brought back his father. I let him think that. He died believing he'd done it."

That's why Gundobad kept her from seeing Gondioc. He must have thought Gundaharius's heart, the heart she'd left in her Thoricus work-shop, was hers. He'd thought her dead.

"Why did you kill..." She almost added *my mother*, for that was how she'd come to think of Caretene, but it was too strange a thing to say to her real mother. Nevertheless, Grimhild—

Gundobad—knew who she meant.

"She was an experiment. Water washed out her cape and she died of exsanguination." Gundobad seized her forearms and pulled her up. "Always know your weaknesses, Gudrun. Or should I call you Chroma?"

As her mother spoke and her shock subsided, Gudrun remembered she'd needed this. Her mother was back. The new shell didn't matter; her murderous heart beat inside it.

Quick as a viper's strike, Gudrun snapped her sorcerer's knife into Gundobad's chest, just right of his heart, and yanked it out to slice at his nape, now bent toward her.

But he was fast. His hand was at her throat, his thumb and middle finger pressed against the angles of her mandible.

He pushed his palm against the front bones of her throat and her head turned against the hard ramparts.

Would her mother kill her?

After everything, she might.

"You don't need a formula." The pressure from Gundobad squeezed high, whistly notes from her throat. "Just a heart."

He released her and she wheezed. The warm night air scratched her throat.

"Whose heart?"

Something knocked Gundobad to the ground. A long spear stuck out of his stomach.

"Chroma!" a woman's voice called.

She sprinted after Clothilde, her sister and saviour, and her escorts.

Surely Clothilde was also a target, someone Gundobad would trap with a cape and maybe perform deadly experiments on, maybe use as a weapon in some army. So Gudrun told her everything, or everything from this life: Gundobad had killed their parents, he might come for them next, he was a redcape. But Clothilde already knew, because he'd already made her a redcape.

She showed her cape to Gudrun. She'd stashed it by a tomb—a cape as bright as Sigurd's smile. There was a way for redcapes to be human again, but, for the life of her, Gudrun couldn't understand how she'd done it.

Together, they fled Valentia to seek shelter from their uncle, and Gudrun plotted how to poach Gundobad's heart when he inevitably came for hers.

CHAPTER FORTY-FOUR

Light snow swirled within the stone circle where, late at night, Margaret huddled in her sheepskin cloak and stared at her old heart tooth.

"We'll always be with you," the demon used her mouth to say.

She didn't have the energy to shout or to beg for him to leave. Defeatedly, she asked, "Why?"

"Because you're a monster. You always were and you always will be."

She thought back to John III and the prayer rope, her younger self killing and creating her own cape.

Abaddon was right: she was a monster, then.

Malcolm believed she was savable, but she'd chosen to be a redcape. She chose to kill and eat hearts. Even when she wanted not to, she killed. She couldn't break the addiction.

William once said it, too. *Even if I lose this crown, even if you lose your cape... we're unreachable. Lost in darkness, forsaken. We can never be free.*

She deserved darkness. She deserved to be lost. She didn't deserve a white cape or love or freedom.

She swallowed the tooth.

Abaddon laughed.

"No..." She gagged.

What was she doing? She didn't want it back inside her. It was poison, like the demon.

She doubled over and rammed her fingers up her throat. Could she vomit it up, or was it already boring its way into her heart?

Abaddon took control before she could find out.

Blue morning shadows spiked from the standing stones like the fangs of a crown.

Īzebel lay next to Margaret, blood fresh on her blade.

There was a heaviness in her body and her heart. Something was wrong, very wrong. Familiarly wrong.

The land rocked.

As if she lost her sea legs, sickness rolled through her, and bile smouldered in her throat. She touched the front of her neck, and her cold fingers wound around it.

It was back.

She screamed.

Fell forward and pounded the earth with a fist.

Tears mixed with snot, ran down her face, dripped over her trembling lips.

And her cape cried out for blood.

"Help me," she pleaded hoarsely, but the stones were still.

Her jaw ached. The cape's hooks twisted inside her, webbed through her veins and latched onto her heart. Had it hurt so much before?

How had she lived with this feeling—an unwanted thing within, scratching and wailing, ripping at her soul?

"Please..."

Take hearts...

Her head raised, eyes fixed on the tallest stone.

Use them.

Was that the stone sorceresses? Was Michael Scot lurking nearby, speaking for them? Or was it Abaddon, his words dragging through her brain like black slugs?

Her cheeks were cooling, her tears drying, her mind working.

She shouldn't take hearts. She shouldn't use them. She should find Malcolm and try the sword again. If it still wouldn't work for her, she could try to save the others. She needn't fear John III Comyn if she had the sword to save him. She could go to Edward I as she'd planned, make him see who she was.

Remember your mother's work... you can control the redcapes. With them, you can control the lords. Forget the king and take what's yours.

She'd been mulling over whether or not to utilize the discovery for two months. If she could control others, could she learn to control herself?

Her mother had destroyed it for a reason. She didn't want Margaret, or anyone, to have it. But, unquestionably, she hadn't wanted her to have a cape or a demonic passenger, either.

And if she could control the lords... if she could have the life she was meant to, the one her mother meant for her, maybe she wouldn't be lost. The sword wouldn't work for Margaret, Maid of Norway, but would it work for Margaret, Queen of Scots?

Not to mention, if she could control capes, getting back into the castle and retrieving the Sword of Living Waters would be far easier. Her mother would want that, wouldn't she?

Using the circle she was in, Michael Scot had planted another redcape clan; she'd seen it with the astrolabe. For a year, Margaret practiced the art of control with their teeth. She hunted, killed, and created new capes.

When she was confident in her skill, she ate the pure heart she'd made, for it was a useless thing and she needed an empty casket. She gathered soil from the circle into the casket, replacing the pure heart with dirt, and began the journey back to Hermitage Castle.

Chapter Forty-Five

Īzebel wrenched a cape from a woman's neck and she died in a field of delicate bluebells, listening to the rippling whistles of a plump crossbill and the scampering of fluffy red squirrels.

Margaret added the woman's heart tooth to a bag tied to her belt. She hadn't known the redcape in her time at Hermitage, nor the others she'd recently hunted. Had Cecily replaced those who'd been her allies at one time or another? Was William still protecting Alice, or had she, too, fallen to Cecily?

She wondered at the goings on within Hermitage Castle as she now had two-thirds of Clan Elliot's heart teeth. The redcapes were likely in a frenzy, perhaps scheming against Thomas Durward, not knowing it was Margaret who stole from them and not the whitecapes. It was possible Cecily had been supplanted, having lost so many teeth. She would find out soon.

She corralled sacrifices in the night. Hunting on her old grounds, in territories she knew well, was comforting and depressing. Becoming human had raised her hopes, but Abaddon had eaten those hopes like hearts and left her as a cape. A small one remained, beating weakly deep within, and that was what kept her from slicing Īzebel through her own nape and dissolving to nothing.

During the night of the new moon, beneath a starless sky, with heaps of sacrifices at the ready, Margaret raised a redcape army from hearts and teeth and bodies.

She inserted cave hyena teeth into the hearts, yanked bloody human teeth from the bodies and downed them herself, and killed countless unconscious, but breathing, people.

As the muted, gray sun rose, she took a libation with her twenty-two redcapes and led them in a march toward Hermitage Castle.

The southeast tower's postern was closed, its portcullis down and its wood door locked with a sliding bar. Margaret's eyes climbed the sheer walls but, even with redcape strength, her body couldn't. She ordered capes to an outbuilding for axes, and they took them to the lower half of the door, riving the wood. Margaret commanded, "Raise it."

Most of the redcapes positioned themselves before the portcullis, took hold and lifted. It raised slowly. Margaret ducked under and opened it fully from the other side.

As they made their way to the central courtyard, the corner of a red cape flitted into the darkness like a red wing, an Elliot off to warn their alpha. She soon arrived wearing her antler crown.

Cecily's mouth was a line, her eyes dull. Her place as an alpha had worn her.

Behind her, the remaining redcapes, Alice among them, appraised the new ones on Margaret's side.

"Your clan looks weak, Margaret. Like you."

"You're outnumbered," said Alice. Not "we're" but "you're." She had never affiliated herself with Cecily, though her wounds from her beating had healed.

"We'll fight." Cecily snarled through gritted teeth.

Margaret walked toward her alone.

Cecily assumed she'd maintained her alpha status, but the clan wouldn't fight for her. She'd already lost them.

Alice was the first. She knelt, exposing her nape, and Margaret passed her. One by one, the redcapes knelt, rose, and joined the new capes, until the only one standing was Cecily.

Margaret punched her in the stomach.

Cecily swung back, clawed at her skin, and Margaret beat her down like she'd beaten Ermengarde and Alice in front of everyone.

She kicked her in the leg and hit her in the jaw, delivered blow after blow until Cecily was in so much pain she forgot her pride, removed her crown, begged for her life, and rolled over to bare the cap of her cape.

Margaret glanced at Alice. "Bring me her hammer."

"No."

She narrowed her eyes. She could tear out one of her teeth, then Alice would do anything she wanted. But it was Alice.

"You do it," she said to a different redcape, who sprinted to the hall and returned with the long-handled hammer, the one Cecily had used to destroy the thrones.

She swung it up and over and brought it down on Cecily's head. Her skull cracked and released her brains.

Margaret stepped on her cape and ripped it from her neck. Cecily, brains and all, melted away; seconds later, her heart did the same, leaving her tooth on the cobbles.

"Have you learned nothing?" Alice whispered to her.

There was a gnawing in her heart, the biting of too many guilt-enamelled teeth. She wished she could take it back, the beating and the killing. Cecily may have deserved it, but if that was true, so did she, and everyone.

She placed the antler crown on her head and fronted a procession to the southwest hall.

The sword was there. It lay on the stone floor before the throne. The redcapes gave it a wide berth, forming a crescent around it.

"Where are the children?" she asked Alice.

Alice said they had touched the sword and turned to humans or whitecapes. She'd smuggled most of them from the castle before they could be eaten.

Margaret could command the older redcapes to pick up the sword as the children had and save themselves, but then she would lose her army. She would use them to threaten the lords first and free all of them when she was Queen of Scots.

She lowered herself onto the throne.

After years, she was the sole alpha of Clan Elliot.

It didn't feel at all how she'd hoped it would. With so many teeth stuffed in her heart, she felt heavier than ever before.

Chapter Forty-Six

Roman mosaics flared around a figure as lightning flickered outside.

Beside Gudrun, Clothilde called out.

"They won't come," Gundobad said. Blood dripped from his hands, its sound drowned out by rain showers outside.

Lightning's glow showed him rounding on Gudrun's bed. There was no sign he'd been injured the month before. He'd no doubt been eating hearts, hoping he would gain his powers back, and realized he needed the heart of a sorcerer. The most powerful sorcerer in existence.

Another flash, another figure.

The stone points of a mace caught the light like wave crests or stars and violently punctured Gundobad's arm.

Their uncle, Godegisel, shone in bronze lamellar armour, a gold-hilted spatha strapped to his side. Warriors trickled in behind him.

A heart melted over Gudrun.

She blinked at Gundobad, registering his cape for a second time.

Grimhild had turned Gundobad into a redcape. She was out there, somewhere, and Gudrun would find her.

But what was Gundobad doing here, in Geneva, at her uncle's house?

"I'll return for you."

She couldn't tell if he was talking to her or Godegisel.

Gundobad leapt out the open, third-floor window—a shame it wasn't on the other side, where he would have plunged into the Rhine.

Gudrun and Clothilde rushed to the ledge and searched the darkness while the warriors exited the fortified house and fanned out, but he'd escaped them.

"Chroma, that man is a demon." Clothilde gulped. "I'll make Clovis believe me. He'll defeat Gundobad and you won't have to be afraid anymore."

Clovis I, King of the Franks, had requested Clothilde's hand. To reign over Christian Gaul, he needed the clergy on his side; to win over the clergy, he needed a Nicene Christian wife, as he himself was born a pagan but had converted, as many pagans had, to Arian Christianity. For political reasons, Gundobad, back in Lugdunum, agreed Clothilde should marry Clovis.

Gudrun returned her tight hug, blinking back tears. Clothilde's bravery in the face of redcapes reminded her of Gundaharius. Though she wasn't her real sister, and would never know she wasn't, Gudrun felt a real bond with her.

It was hard to say goodbye, but she knew Clothilde, with her white cape, was better off with Clovis, where Gudrun couldn't tarnish her with sorcery and sin.

She and Godegisel watched Clothilde leave with her escorts for Parision. There, she would work to convert Clovis to Nicene Christianity and would eventually convince him Gundobad was a demon who should be vanquished. Clovis's counselor, Aridius, would persuade him Gundobad wasn't a demon, just possessed by one, at times, but he was working to rid himself of it. So Clovis and Clothilde, King and Queen of All the Franks, would live apart from Gundobad and pray for his soul, and Gudrun would never see Clothilde again.

Soon after her departure, in case Gundobad returned to Geneva to look for Gudrun, she too would leave her uncle, take refuge in a nunnery, and continue her hunt for Grimhild's heart.

CHAPTER FORTY-SEVEN

Margaret approached Greyfriars church in Dumfries alone to meet with the greatest contenders for the throne, John Comyn and Robert Brus, along with various other nobles. She was fairly sure Robert would support her, but if the meeting went awry, she had the means to right it—a third of Clan Elliot waited, crouched in shadows about the friary.

They'd each brought men—Malcolm was among Robert's, but she couldn't get a word to him lest she shouted. The men were arguing in the garden. It had been clear for some time John Balliol wouldn't return; Robert didn't want a Comyn on the throne; yes, Eirik II's daughter was alive; no, he wasn't mad; John had supporters; Brus had supporters. Each thought their claim was more credible than the others' if Margaret weren't a factor, and neither would settle for another succeeding the throne.

"Where are her papers, then?" John III demanded, pointing accusatorily at Margaret on the edge of the fray. "The Maid of Norway died in the Orkneys, King Eirik confirmed it himself. This woman is an imposter at worst, delusional at best."

She stamped out the image of the imposter burning in Bergen. Any attempt to burn her would be the last attempt they made at anything.

"You know well enough what happened to my papers, Sir Comyn." She spat his name, his destruction of them implied. "I am Margaret Eiriksdatter. I'm the only legitimate heir. It is my right to inherit the crown."

They continued to argue.

"We'll settle this the two of us," Robert eventually asserted.

He and John entered the friary and Margaret strode after them. The men would have reached out to stop her, but her look frightened even them—they could sense something dangerous about her, whether or not they perceived the red in her eyes and the strange look of her jaw. A Comyn blocked Malcolm from following her, though he tried.

In the Minorite chapel, Robert was saying, "We had an agreement, in good faith, and you betrayed me to Edward." His tone was composed, but his eyes were hard.

Margaret slipped closer, noting two redcapes positioned near the altar who watched her closely.

"I swore to him to uphold homage and fealty," John then retorted. "And what does it matter if she's your horse?"

"The matter has nothing to do with her but your betrayal. We could have had peace, you and I."

"There will never be peace in my life as long as that girl breathes. I'll put her down and be done with the both of you."

So fast Margaret hardly saw it, Robert stabbed John in the gut.

On her order, the two redcapes leapt forth and held John back from retaliating. He looked up at her and said, "She told me not to harm you, but I hate you so. How can there be room in her heart for you and none for me? If you are to kill me"—to Robert—"do it quickly, before she can, and let my soul into the world."

"He's not a man to be trusted," said Robert to Margaret, "but I won't kill him today."

He left the chapel to tell his men what he'd done.

John's death was quick. Margaret severed the cape from his neck; at that minute, two of Robert's men dashed inside, perhaps to finish the job of killing, but they were too late if that was their cause.

John III Comyn's body bled to a heart before the altar.

Painful sadness pulsed through her, the same feeling as with Cecily.

Alice said she'd learned nothing, but that wasn't true. She felt and knew she did wrong; she'd simply been unable to change. She acted on her impulses and let regret build into bars around her, a sin-black cage she strengthened at every turn. With a crown of teeth locked in her heart, she could command the capes, but she was still rash.

Her two redcapes stealthily moved from the friary. Margaret took John's heart tooth and sprayed a heart over the men on her way out to make them forget. They would think John had lived and escaped, that they'd killed him, or that Brus had, maybe, but not her.

"Where's John?!" Sir Robert Comyn and others rushed past her.

Robert Comyn fell to Robert Brus's brother-in-law, Christopher Seton.

Men's voices and swords clashed; Comyn's supporters declined and eventually fled on horseback.

"You murdered him," Robert stated upon their exit.

She lowered her eyes.

His face hadn't changed when she'd arrived, and he'd seen her cape. He'd surely heard she'd lost it but perhaps hadn't believed or wasn't surprised at her regression—if it was that, for she'd never felt a progression. As a human, she'd kept killing. Though the pain and weight of the cape had lifted, the weight of guilt had doubled. Now that the cape was back, the guilt hadn't muted as before but boiled hot beneath her skin.

"You might have. You stabbed him."

"If he were human, that might have been enough, but he's a redcape. He would have lived."

"Would you have let your men kill him?"

"I do my best, but I don't pretend to be God. My friends have minds of their own. Walk with me."

She glanced at Malcolm and quickly looked away when his longing eyes met hers.

She wanted to talk with him and get away from him at the same time. So much had happened. What if he couldn't forgive her for abandoning him? What if he hated her for becoming a redcape again?

Her wish to get away was granted: Robert motioned for Malcolm to stay behind, and they walked north to the River Nith.

When they'd first met, Margaret never would have imagined herself on a stroll with Robert, much less feeling safe with him; after all, he'd nearly severed her cape in Hermitage Castle and had admitted on the way back from England that he struggled not to kill her.

She'd worried he might do it in the past, but now understood he never would. He could have let someone else hurt her—John, namely, or the whitecapes in England—but he'd always protected her, never left her to die, because it was the right thing to do, even though she stood between him and the thing he wanted most.

A redcape would never put another's life before their own desires. Was that what it meant to be a whitecape?

She voiced the question.

"All whitecapes face temptation, as do redcapes; the difference is the act."

She wondered if her clan were listening to his words. She could feel them all around, their thirst and hunger, but he was safe with her.

"Faith is forged in fire. If a heart was never tempted, its true nature would never be revealed. Victory over temptation refines a heart like silver in a furnace; one day, I hope mine will shine pure, that the fire will consume all darkness, and I will be able to resist all temptation," said he, though he resisted the killing of John, he had stabbed him out of anger. "Yes, I am tempted as anyone is. I still give in, like you do. Each failure brings shame, and that shame is a path toward good. I bring it to light, and it burns away, for I am already forgiven. Again, I am tempted; again, I try to resist. Today, I might fail; tomorrow, I will succeed. Each day must be faced anew.

"You give in easily to temptation, more easily than any whitecape. You've let the darkness take you and own you, but there is One greater who will buy and free you if you choose to be a slave no longer."

His speech was like the dawn: it cast light on her shadowed heart and made her think she wasn't so lowly, so lost, that she couldn't be found again. She took Īzebel by its toothy hilt.

"If your hand offends you," Robert said knowingly, "cut it off."

Just holding the knife made her hands moisten and twitch. She'd given in to it countless times, killed more to feel less.

His heart would taste divine, Īzebel urged. *You would relish the cutting. Think of the sounds... the feel of his ribs breaking. Think of the taste.*

Her mouth watered.

What had Robert thought of when he felt tempted to kill her: the weight of the crown, his own gold temptation? The sound of men chanting his name, the taste of glory?

He might have salivated then, and how would he have forborne his desire?

There is One greater, she inveighed against the knife, sharply repeating the phrase in her head.

There is no one greater than you, replied Īzebel, building bars with smooth words.

Giving in would reinforce them; each time she did, she held herself in bondage. There was no one else to blame.

"Stop it!" Margaret shouted. "Stop lying to me!"

On her own, she would give in easily as Robert said. But she wasn't alone. There was One greater, One who could go to war in her place, One who could fortify her weak resolve and overcome Īzebel's cold-metal lies.

She screamed and cut off the source of temptation—she hurled the knife into the Nith.

The river swallowed it with a gurgling sound and ripples, and she stared at the place it vanished, reflections of blue sky and tan, skeletal trees.

She hadn't given in easily to temptation today, but how much harder would it be when her foe couldn't be seen?

Robert was strong, dignified, steadfast. He wasn't fickle as Guy Beauchamp believed, but calculated—since their run-in at Westminster, she'd learned that Robert shifted sides to protect his friends, family, and tenants from the war's violent waves.

She was the rightful Queen of Scots, but he was best for Scotland. Better for it than her. He would fight to liberate the land and never abandon it, as faithful as he was, and she could put a life, the life of her country, before her desire. She could do the queenly thing. She could be the woman her mother had believed she would be, the woman Alice once saw buried inside her.

She bowed her head softly to him, conceded her right to the throne, and left Margaret Eiriksdatter behind in favour of Margaret Elliot.

He would be crowned King of Scots; she would be remembered as a seven-year-old monarch doomed never to set foot in her land. Robert knew her full story, but his teeth were sealed against it—her secret would live deep within his heart, to be guarded in a casket of silver even after his death. She would make his men forget her, and Comyn's already thought she was mad.

They walked back toward Greyfriars, on alert in case Comyn's men hadn't all gone, and she clasped his arm and blest his future kingship. He and his allies made for Dumfries Castle, but Malcolm stayed to face her a ways from the chaos of the friary.

"Where were you?"

He had every reason to be angry or hurt. She'd abandoned him without word and left his mother trapped in Hermitage.

"When did you retake the cape? Were you forced?"

She looked down.

"Then why?"

She had no answer.

"I thought we... Why didn't you meet me?"

"Because I don't deserve you, Malcolm!" she divulged. "My heart is black and full of teeth. I've been a sorceress and a murderer all my life. And I'm possessed! It's dangerous for you to be near me. He could take over at any time and—"

He cut her off with a kiss.

She was aware of her teeth and jaw, enlarged by her cape and the cursed tooth in her heart. It felt different than kissing him as a human. She was less comfortable and more self-conscious, but she still wished he would kiss her again when he stopped.

"Did you hear what I said? Don't you see what I am?"

"I see who you will be after the fire," he said. "None of us are perfect; it's the surrendering that matters—letting the lion swallow the wolves inside us and break our chains, realizing the battle's already been won."

She didn't understand, or he didn't, but they hugged each other, and he didn't shy away from her cape.

Over his shoulder, she met the red eyes of a man in the shade of a leafless oak.

Like Robert said, they weren't gods. She shouldn't have the power to control others. She should have listened to Isabella Warenne's warning and kept away from the dark waters of sorcery so it never would have pulled her under—but she'd yet to drown.

"I release you," she said to the redcapes. She still had their teeth, but she would command them no longer. She couldn't let herself go on like the Soulis lords, using others to kill or threaten. She was sure he'd done it with her and made her forget—though she didn't want to remember or know for certain, not knowing was almost worse. "I implore you to return to Hermitage and be saved by the sword, but you have the choice."

As they scattered like snakes through grass, she closed her eyes, listened for the waters, and prayed for them to guide her home.

CHAPTER FORTY-EIGHT

Anyone could have walked into Hermitage as its doors and portcullises were open. When Margaret and Malcolm did, they found the redcapes holed up in the castle's hall like snakes in a pit. They snarled and growled. They could see Margaret was weak—today was the day she needed to take a libation and she had, so far, refused to take one—but they didn't attack. They feared the teeth within her heart; they didn't know she wouldn't use her power of control, and she didn't tell them for the sake of herself and Malcolm.

He helped her to the throne, where her antler crown sat upright, its tines rising from each side like twisted teeth from two jagged knives. She threw it aside and sat down, parched and breathing hard, and Malcolm retrieved the sword, which hadn't been moved from its place on the floor. He offered it to a redcape man, but the man shied away and curled up in a corner to escape it.

Malcolm went around the room, but each cape retreated, even ran, to put as much distance between themselves and the sword as they could, as if touching it meant death instead of freedom.

At last, he brought it to Margaret.

She blinked and she was straddling Malcolm, choking him. He was turning purple.

She flung herself off him and stared at her mottled, traitorous hands.

"Malcolm, I—I—"

"It wasn't you," he uttered.

No, it wasn't. It was the demon. He'd kept her, all of them, from the sword.

She tried again to reach it, for it lay close by, but someone reached quicker for her.

Michael Scot—Robin—stood over her.

She didn't have the strength to fight him. She rolled her eyes to beg Malcolm's aid, but he and Alice were nowhere to be seen.

Around her, Clan Elliot watched. Unless she ordered them to, they wouldn't help her. They weren't really her clan anymore; she wasn't really their alpha. Should she lapse on the decision not to control them? How far would she go for that judgment? Scot could kill her, they could stop him, and what would they lose—a moment of choice?

She inhaled through her nose, surrendered the breath and the impulse. Demons and sorcerers were time thieves, and she'd renounced her sorcerous ways with the dumping of Īzebel. She would no sooner be a demon than cut out her own heart, though Scot might soon do that for her; after all, he'd tried once before at Ninestane.

Long fingers wrapped around her jaw and forced open her mouth, and something hard hit one of her teeth. Pain like thick needles shot through her gums and into her skull. Blood coated her tongue.

"A beautiful discovery you have made." Michael Scot removed a red tooth from her mouth and popped it into his own. "You won't mind if I make it mine."

Her eyes flicked back and forth, searching again for Malcolm, Alice, and William. But there were only redcapes in the room, red shadows pinned against stone walls.

"You're going to do something for me," he said, and she felt in her heart she would, for he had stolen what she'd returned to Clan Elliot—the power to decide.

He leaned down and she smelt his sickening breath, the breath of a scavenger. Up close, his eyes were the colour of burnt, blood-flecked bone. He took pleasure in his next words as if the very idea was a thrill: "And then you are going to die, and I will eat your heart and take that precious tooth inside it."

Chapter Forty-Nine

A Breton vicar met Gudrun in the woods above the south coast of Brittany, near her dolmen heart vault and mounds of buried teeth, on her six hundred and sixteenth year of life. She knelt before him to beg forgiveness for acts she wanted to forget and waited to accept her penance.

"We absolve you from your sins." He laid a hand on her shoulder and said, "You must first cast yourself down with the sinners, for you have transgressed the law of God."

He gestured to the right, where mossy menhirs stood.

She shuddered. "You cannot mean for me to..."

"Yes." He gave her an ancient tooth, stolen from those she buried. "Use our body, for we are committed to saving your soul."

She went with him between the stones, lagging behind. The tooth was pressed between her fingers, and a terrible feeling distended her chest, as if she were about to throw herself off a cliff. She didn't want to swallow the tooth; she didn't want to be like her mother. But it was what she deserved, the price she had to pay.

"This is your penance: avenge the murders of your husband and brothers, punish the sinner, overcome evil with good. Do as we say, and you will be at peace."

That, at least, she wanted to hear—a thing she was already working toward. She'd long since avenged her brothers' murders; she had conspired to marry Attila the Hun centuries past, and he had died at her hand. And if she had doubts about cutting out her mother's heart, those were gone now, too, for the vicar confirmed it: her vengeance was lawful.

She swallowed the tooth, killed the vicar, made from him a cape of blood, and left the menhirs and the woods, past pines and eucalyptus and narrow oak trees, blooming heather and fields of furzy, sedges and ryegrass, to find a libation from a nearby coastal settlement, though she already had a taste in her mouth like soured blood.

CHAPTER FIFTY

Drifting hills caught clouds in dark-forest webs beneath a heather sky. Small animals cocooned themselves in burrows or nests while red deer continued grazing, partly sheltered by trees, and an eldern oak stood tall and lonely against the rain. Its leaves dropped fast, weighed down by water, onto and around a pair of recently cast-off antlers between its exposed roots. They lay odd angles to each other, like a crooked alpha crown that had been snapped in half and discarded.

At the base of the oak, Margaret lifted the door to Thomas of Erceldoune's cavern, as she had with Robin six years past, and let it fall back into place above her, shutting out the sounds of increasing rain outside. Her breathing came easy even after the trek, for her strength was back—Scot had made her take a libation at Ninestane on her way to the Eildon Hills.

Water dripped off her sheepskin cloak onto the stone steps; a raincloud in itself, at first, but the drops slowed as she spiralled down into the earth. The stair torches weren't lit this time, but the cavern glowed ahead near the end of the case.

Alianora was there, as Scot had said she would be, sorting through books.

Margaret clenched her fists and took a step back on the wide stairs, around the corner from the cavern.

She'd wanted Alianora dead not so long ago but had come to see her differently. The woman had spared her life several times. When she'd made herself a redcape and wanted to forget, Alianora had taken her memories. But she remembered now how she hadn't wanted to.

"It's better to remember," Alianora had said, "even the terrible things. It's better to trust your mind than wonder."

She couldn't trust her mind or body now. Even as she stood there, remembering, dreading, it fought to move forth and complete the task Scot set for her. She entered the cavern.

"Margaret?"

"You should run," she said. "I'm here to kill you for Robin, but he was never Robin. He's Michael Scot, the wizard."

"He's more than that," Alianora said. "He's a man I've hunted eight hundred years. I unmasked him at Luce Abbey with you. Of course you don't remember—he made us both forget. I came here and Thomas of Erceldoune showed me the truth."

She showed Margaret a triptych carved in ivory. It displayed three painted scenes.

First, a woman with chiselled features in purple garb and a black wimple, with a young Alianora looking up at her.

Second, a Burgundian king leading a siege on Vienne.

And third, Michael Scot before Thomas of Aquinas, wearing a skull-cap and tearing a page from a Bible. His cape was swept behind him, barely visible between his waist and left arm.

"He goes by many names—Robin, Michael Scot, Gundobad. But he is truly Grimhild of Burgundy, a sorceress reborn. My mother."

"Your *mother*?"

She'd once thought Michael Scot would be her saviour, the man who could release the Sword of Living Waters or expel the demon from her mind. But he was demon-possessed himself, and he wasn't her saviour; he was the one scheming to grow redcape nests like mushroom clusters in the dark, to ensure Hermitage seeped scarlet decay forever. The wizard who controlled her now, her slaver.

"Yes. My first name was Gudrun. I've now gone by many, not all in Scotland. Gundred Warenne was the last here—though I suppose I masqueraded, for a time, as my daughter, Gundred Beaumont, before later becoming Alianora Balliol. Alianora Comyn. She's dead now... they all are. But I hope, as I have hoped, that I can soon return to Gudrun."

Margaret searched her face, unchanged for centuries. "How…" She felt foolish as she asked, for the answer was obvious. "You took the elixir of life."

"I created the elixir of life. Gundobad claimed it as his as he's claimed many sorcerous discoveries after killing their discoverers. To return his own power, he needs the heart of the most powerful sorcerer or sorceress. No one has surpassed me, and no one will as long as I live, though he hopes. He's lost the courage to face me himself since he's tried and nearly been killed more than once; surely he believes you can get the better of me, as I've shown favour toward you."

It was like Īzebel was with her again. She didn't want to do it, but the order, the need, couldn't be ignored.

"Kill me," Margaret pleaded.

"You know I won't."

Desperately, she said, "I murdered John. I murdered your son."

"We've both done regrettable things."

"You truly never cared about him." How could she expect her to care about any one person after living such a long life? Then again, "Why do you care what happens to me?"

"We share blood. I see myself in you, a girl made into a monster, longing for redemption… we didn't deserve to become what we are."

"I made myself a cape."

"You think so, but if you were another girl, born in another place, you wouldn't have done it. It was your upbringing that made you thirsty for something poorer than water. It was Abaddon. He did the same to me. Him and my mother made me want blood when—"

She couldn't hold back any longer. She dove for Alianora, hands out to wring her neck, and the fires in the cavern died.

She opened her eyes, and the torches were lit again. The feeling was familiar.

"We will not kill her," the demon said with Margaret's voice.

She almost yelled for him to leave her—but he had kept her from murder. He'd made her kill in the past, why stop her now?

"So he possesses you, too. I suppose, in our line, he's inescapable," Alianora lamented. "If he wants me to live, it's because I kill and create chaos."

"Then don't. Help me get to the Sword of Living Waters. We can both be saved—"

"I will be saved when I right my wrong."

"Right it, and come with me."

"It's been too long since I acted as a whitecape would, but there's something about you that reminds me of him, or myself when we were together..." Her eyes were faraway and reflected a star lost. "Come look."

Margaret followed her, grimacing. She could feel them inside her like two black wolves, Scot's order and the demon's.

Alianora stopped at a shelf. On a plush cushion were two silver orbs. "Thomas of Erceldoune's left and right eye. The tongue has gone missing. They are his prophecies left behind, like memories, but different."

Margaret picked up the right eye and gazed into it, imagining it gazing back at her. The prophecy appeared to her in silvered images and etched words:

Old prophecies foretell to thee,
A warlike heir she's born,
Who shall recover new your right,
Advance this kingdom's horn.
Then shall fair Scotland be advanc'd,
Above her enemies power;
Her cruel foes shall be dispers'd,
And scatter'd from her bower.
And after enemies thrown down,
And master'd in war,
Then Scotland in peace and quietness,
Pass joyful days for ever.
The left eye was next, its silver tarnished:
In former age the Scots renown,
Did flourish goodly gay:
But yet alas! will be overcome,

With a great dark decay.
Then mark and see what is the cause
Of this so wond'rous fall!
Contempt of faith, falsehood, deceit,
The wrath of God withal.
Unsatiable greed of worldy gain,
Oppression, cries of the poor;
A perpetual and slanderous race,
No justice put in ure.

The eyes were two futures. In one, Scotland flourished; in the other, she was overcome by a great, dark decay, a decay of the worst kind, the redcapes.

"Do you see what Gundobad plans? He wants to scrape more teeth from the earth's bowels and seed redcape nests in every nation. They are his prize, his legacy. And Scotland, first, will fall."

"You created the elixir so Gundobad, Grimhild—this *evil* could abide. Is that the wrong you have to right? If so, it's also my wrong. He was dying when he used me to create more elixir. I saved his life. I will help you defeat him, and we can take the sword together."

Margaret couldn't judge her expression—relief, strife, contempt?—but Alianora clasped her hands, and they left the cavern in the Eildons for the castle, where Gundobad waited for Gudrun's heart.

CHAPTER FIFTY-ONE

Blood lifted from Gudrun's eyes, and she was with a spindly man behind a wide standing stone. Gundobad whispered, "Teeth."

The world and its dark stars spun. She felt she was a child again, weak-willed and afraid of Grimhild, and she did what she was asked as she would have done then—she called teeth from the earth. They surfaced before the trembling sorceress Ada Warenne.

Gudrun blinked hard at the man. She'd forgotten things she wasn't supposed to forget, but her bones remembered, for they ached at the sight of him, and her wits began to trickle back.

"You're her." Her voice rattled like the teeth in the stone circle as they came together and formed a crown. "Mother. You live."

Some part of her felt it, or suspected it due to memory loss, but now she knew. She wasn't searching for a dead thing or a heart kept in a casket, but one beating in a chest of flesh. And it was here, asking to be harvested. If only she could remember—where was her knife? She reached to unclasp a heart casket strapped at her waist.

"Let us kill her," said Gundobad.

"And end the butchery? We will not," he argued with himself. "If she is to be a victim, let her be her own."

A sorcerer's trephine bored into her arm.

Gundobad extracted more bone to make her forget a thing remembered as she had many times before. He'd made her forget he lived and who she was, manipulated and tortured her into committing for him sorcerous acts. It had become difficult for him over the years as Gudrun noticed she was forgetting, refusing to help him and placing him quicker.

It was dangerous to use her now and would perhaps be impossible soon, but there were others to be used, fallible sorceresses like Ada.

Gudrun's mind was muddled. Her body felt weak, but she sprayed a heart at Gundobad and made him forget the recipe for the elixir of life. The book was sealed against him and all the males in her line; to read it, he would have to find her again and, next time, she would be ready for him.

Gundobad pressed her bone into an organ, and Gudrun desperately tried to hold on to the man's face as heart blood streamed over hers. Its features scrambled and vanished from her mind, but she remembered the fact: her mother lived. Sigurd, too, would soon breathe in Scottish air, for she would not fail to avenge his death, no matter what she was forced to forget.

Chapter Fifty-Two

Alianora tried to give Margaret a heart casket, tarnished and decorated with pearls and amethysts, before they entered Hermitage Castle. *What harm could melting a single heart do?* a voice inside her had asked, but she knew the harm. Even flirting with the idea of sorcery could be dangerous, so she'd refused the casket before she could dwell too much on the matter, and they went in through the main door, the one that opened directly to the courtyard. Margaret searched the open windows above but saw no one. She followed Alianora to the hall.

Gundobad waited there with the redcapes. He touched his throat with a dark expression.

"Why did you not kill her?" he asked. With her tooth in his heart, he'd no reason to think Margaret wouldn't complete his murderous task and was clearly unaware of Abaddon's intervention. "Why do you wait? I've told you to do it, so do."

The order was back in her mind, the need back in her heart.

"I shouldn't have come," she apologized to Alianora and turned to attack—but slowly, so Alianora had time to stab her or escape.

"All of you, kill her. Take care to leave the heart intact. No—" Gundobad stood from his place on the throne of human teeth. "Hold her down. I will cut it out myself."

The capes circled and converged, a red whirlpool with the sorceress at its centre.

Blood splashed, and Margaret forgot Gundobad's order. The man himself was blinking dumbly before the throne, heart blood seeping into his skin.

And Alianora was behind him, a sorcerer's knife at his nape. "You'll stay dead this time, Mother."

The knife slit the edge of Gundobad's cape.

Sweat beaded on his forehead and upper lip, which he pressed to his lower as he held something up to Alianora's eyeline. A silver Arverni coin, one of many lost to time.

Alianora didn't slice the rest of the way through the cape; she froze and witnessed her own terrible memory.

"No," she whispered. She took the coin, which was just a coin, threw it down and screamed: "No! It isn't true! It can't be true. My Sigurd..."

"It was you, not Brynhild. Not us. You. You are his murderer."

"What did you remember?" Margaret stumbled toward her and tripped over the sword, which hadn't been moved. "Alianora—Gudrun—"

"Stay back," said Gundobad, trapping her in an invisible cage.

"It was the adder," Alianora cried. "It dripped venom into my veins. It was the adder who killed him, not I—the adder!"

She plunged her knife into her chest, cracked her own bones and sawed away at her own body. Gundobad reached to stop her but held back, for he saw she wouldn't harm the heart.

Finally, after so many years, Alianora, Gudrun, had cut out the adder. She'd cut out her own heart. She'd avenged Sigurd's death.

Her rose gold hair tumbled over her shoulders like a golden waterfall poisoned with blood. Impossibly, she raised her heart and her heart casket necklace toward Margaret and said, "Resurrect him and save my soul."

But Gundobad took her fresh heart and ate it. She'd caused the deaths of tens of thousands—Alianora, bright lady—before she died.

Her heart tooth joined Margaret's and the two Gundobad had been reborn with in his chest. Spiked with so many teeth, his heart must have resembled a morning star.

Gundobad closed his eyes and licked blood from his lips as his sorcerous powers returned. Smiling a satanic smile, Abaddon said, "We were a good mother. We did what she asked and made her forget she walked in darkness. She said it is better to believe the lie than know the truth when you are one who can't be saved. Would you like to believe you're worthy? You aren't. Do you want us to make you forget?"

He didn't stop her when she ran for Alianora's casket, which didn't hold the heart of John I Balliol as she'd thought, but Sigurd's, and looped it around her head.

"Pure hearts have their uses, but protection is not one," said Gundobad, and Margaret remembered the granary in Florence, where he'd stolen her trephine. He chuckled, "All in jest, I won't make you forget with a heart. I will make you forget with death. I made you a deal, do you remember? You mayn't have held up your side, but I have no qualms about mine. You wanted death, Abaddon knows; I'll heartily give it, for the tooth you carry is worth more than your life. I'm sure you won't argue over that."

He took Alianora's knife, dirty with her blood, and took steps toward her.

She remembered tripping over the sword and crawled backward on the ground. She reached for it, and the demon entered to arrest her.

If hearts were like silver, Abaddon was the lead glance, heavy and dark as teeth in a chest. She wished him thrown on bone ash in a furnace and consumed.

"Abaddon." Her head whirled toward William II Soulis, out of his apartments for the first time in who knew how long. He clutched a terrified, human girl against his chest. His body was starved—he was smaller than he'd ever been—but his voice was a clap of lightning when again he spoke the demon's name.

"Abaddon!" he said a third time, and he slit the girl's neck. Her blood flowed forth, a scarlet cataract.

A hateful groan began in Margaret's throat and ceased abruptly.

William had ripped the demon from her, if for a moment—she seized it and took the sword's silver hilt. It wasn't like the last time she'd done it, when her cape unlatched and left her human. She was transported.

The floor became a coaly lake and a current towed her under. She tried to swim against it, but the current was stronger than her.

She spun in a maelstrom of gold-veined gloom, whipping back and forth and gasping in blackened silver. It funnelled her onto a floor without temperature. Lying there, dizziness rotated the gold veins around her, so it took a while for her to feel she'd stopped moving and stand, though she swayed.

"I tried to warn you. You are not worthy," drawled a man of seraphic beauty; his face was perfect, his skin flawless, and his eyes the colour of sunlit bluebells. He was Abaddon in the flesh, wearing his golden crown. "You are forsaken."

She turned from him, ran into the darkness, and came upon a child she knew too well and didn't know at all, a young version of herself.

"Let's forget," said the child. Blood streaked on her skin. Tears were in her eyes, and a heart was in her hands. "I want to forget."

Her heart ached. She was so small. She should have been innocent and protected, but her protectors had failed. She'd become a sorceress and a murderer.

She wanted to make the young Margaret forget, to take away the pain and give herself back her childhood, but that was already gone. Her wrongs couldn't be undone, her past couldn't be changed. She couldn't go back; she could only go forward.

"We've forgotten too much. It's better to remember than to wonder," she replied, using Alianora's words, and left the girl to cry.

The dark world tipped and she fell over. When she righted herself, she was before a dead girl. Margaret stood over her with a fresh cape, the one she'd fashioned for herself when she chose to be a redcape.

"I don't want this," she shouted. "I want to be free! Let me be free!"

"We all want to be free, Margaret," said Alice sadly before the door to Lord Soulis's apartments. Behind her, crowned with teeth, William said, "Go inside." But it wasn't William who said it. It was Abaddon possessing him, Abaddon who would rape Alice and father a new redcape child.

Her throat was thick as clotted blood and her face hot. She'd once supposed Alice a harlot. She was ashamed of that now.

Warm blood rained from shadows above. It ran down Margaret's face, stained her dress and sunk into her cape. Carcasses rose and fell in mounds on either side of the path she walked, where gore squelched beneath her feet, and white serpents slithered between and through bodies. The sickly smell of bodily fluids and decay was absent; only the sweet, intoxicating scent of iron blood weighed the air.

With Abaddon, a naked woman waited at the end of the path, young and vibrant with golden hair and desert skin. She wore gold jewelry, plated armlets and sweeping chains, and a vulture headdress with hanging wings. Teeth dug into her skin, lining her arms and legs, and an impossibly long adder wrapped around her body. Its head rested on her chest, between her breasts, reminiscent of a uraeus.

Beside her, Margaret felt plain and ugly.

"You have killed all these people. See them and tell me, what god would love you after that?" The woman's words were syrupy and purled from her mouth like sugared venom. "We will love you as you are and accept you without condition. We will be your home."

Margaret didn't remember kneeling, but she was, and a whitecape, Isabella MacDuff, Countess of Buchan, was crowning her Queen of Scots, while, at Scone, the real Isabella crowned Robert Brus king.

The ground shook and the earth crumbled into a cliff. Margaret was at its peak, bearing a duplicate of the gold circlet of Scotland, with Abaddon and the woman on her either side.

A red waterfall spilled over the cliff and, above, the eastern moon was a crescent stained red, a fingernail oozing blood.

"This will be yours if you will worship me," said Abaddon. "You can be a slave to God, or you can follow me and be free. You don't need to hide in the shadows and feel ashamed of what you are. You can live in the light of day as sorceress and redcape. You will be more than home and more than Queen of Scots. You will be Queen of All the Peoples."

Scotland was laid out before her, oceans and islands and continents after it. Redcapes emerged from the blood waterfall to join an army of millions. They bowed to her from below, ready to do her bidding, waiting between sea stacks and crags teeming with shadowy, carnivorous seabirds.

"Take back Īzeḅel and fall at my feet."

The auric woman became a sorcerer's knife. Margaret saw herself taking it, going out into the world with Abaddon, summoning armies and demons and gorging herself on hearts and power. She saw Gundobad as Robin at her feet in Ninestane Rig, the knife sticking out of his half-sawed chest as she took the revenge she'd once craved, killed him for trying to kill her.

She unfurled her fingers to take Īzebel.

A woman with a whitecape hovered before her. She'd seen her before in Dante's astrolabe: the mother she'd never known, Margaret, Queen of Norway.

The former queen shook her head and, as if her soft, loving, ghostly eyes held Margaret's memories, she remembered Robert's words. *Shame is a path toward good. I bring it to light, and it burns away, for I am already forgiven. Again, I am tempted; again, I try to resist. Today, I might fail; tomorrow, I will succeed. Each day must be faced anew.*

This was her new day. She'd given in time and time again, when she had to and when she didn't; as a princess in Norway, a redcape in Hermitage, a human, an alpha, she had given in. She'd let herself sink into darkness and follow her whims, but she had never been free.

Abaddon's way was not the way to freedom but a trap.

She closed her hand and drew back from Īzebel.

The demon growled and lightning flashed.

Her crown and her armies vanished, and they were in Hermitage Castle's courtyard with tens of gold statues sculpted in her likeness.

Abaddon stretched out her arms and nailed her to a rood with nails made of excruciating lightning.

"Abaddon, release me," she spluttered, unable to breathe in enough air to fully yell, but he'd abandoned her.

A thing fell from the open sky, sharp with many points. She squeezed her eyes shut and ducked her head, but its points fell around her and dug into the ground. It was her alpha antler crown, turned upside down, made into a cage with alternating tines and black-silver bars. The white serpents from before snaked around the bars and, between them, the forest of false Margarets stared at her with unforgiving eyes.

She couldn't move her hands, and her arms and lungs screamed from the weight of her body. She wanted to scream, too, but had no air.

She strained her muscles against the nails, pushed herself up with her legs, and breathed in. But, already, she was losing strength.

On her own, there would be no escape.

"It's too late."

She raised her head.

William II Soulis hung from his own rood inside the same cage, his legs broken and eight-inch nails in his hands. "We're already dead."

"It is never too late." Alianora, alive again, stood outside the cage. "Repent now, sin later, repent again. Contrition, imperfect or not, can save you with the right penance. Mine is undoing what I did to Sigurd. Resurrecting him will free me. You can also free yourself, Margaret. Confess and take your penance."

"How could she bear freedom when he is caught? It would be sinful to leave him there. The guilt would consume her soul." Alice looked sadly at William as her cape spread from her nape to her throat and began to strangle her. "Suffer with him and feel no regret."

"Sinful, sinful," jeered Michael Scot. "What is sin? It differs across times and cultures; morals shift as tides. You feel shame now when, in a century, you would be praised for committing the same acts. If there is no wrong and no right, and sin cannot be defined from beginning to end, why, then, should you feel shame? It's a thing used by the religious sort to control, not a thing that can stain your soul, for how could we stain our souls when they are manifestations of the Divine? Souls' imperfections are inconsequential. They will be reabsorbed once our bodies die; as the Divine is perfect, so too will our souls be."

"Sin separates you from God..." William took his last breath. His body hung limp, and Margaret saw her future.

"Alianora, Alice, help me."

They walked past the false Margarets, away from her. Alice glanced back with sad eyes, and they disappeared inside the shadowy castle. Even if they'd tried, she knew, deep down, they couldn't get her off the cross.

She hauled herself up for breaths again and again, her lungs on the verge of caving. She was sure her weight would pull her hands down from the nails and leave them halved and useless. It seemed hours passed, but the dim light never changed, her lungs held out, her hands stayed in place. Her legs lost all strength, and a heavy weight pressed her chest. Life was a heart being slowly, torturously crushed.

Lukewarm, old blood pricked her skin.

Bloody water and red hawthorn blooms rained down and built rippling reflections of men and women in rising and falling kingdoms. Some took capes and killed, some ate and melted hearts. They engaged in occult rituals and every kind of sin and desecrated lands in blood. One of them, a Scotsman, whispered, "When the heart's past hope, the face is past shame."

The dark rain turned to clear, cool water and came down heavy. It half filled the courtyard, which now had no openings, and brushed at Margaret's cape. If she didn't suffocate by hanging first, her cape would soon be leached of blood and she would suffocate by water. And the serpents sneaked toward her through the water; they, too, could wrap around her chest and constrict her lungs—so many ways to die trapped and strangled.

One by one, the men and women fell to their knees and welcomed the water. The hawthorns' petals grew and descended into white capes, and the sorcerers, humans, and redcapes took them and changed their lives. Some held the Sword of Living Waters, some didn't; it wasn't the sword that changed them, though it was a guide that helped them see. She recognized quite a few of them: her mother, Malcolm, Robert, Ermengarde, people she'd met in her travels. People who were lost, many who'd committed acts as horrific as hers. They all deserved to be damned, yet not a one was beyond redemption.

She heard whispers in the water.

"They shed innocent blood..."

"Sacrifice to idols..."

"Tormented by the guilt of murder..."

"Seek refuge in the grave... let no one hold them back..."

"Wages of sin..."

"Wage war against their minds... prisoner... slaves to the law of sin..."

"They do not understand what they do... deliver them... forgive their wickedness..."

"Eternal life..."

"Cleanse with the shedding of blood... righteous acts of the saints..."

"Guard your heart..."

A voice from above said sweetly, as if to calm a panicked child, "Bloodshed follows bloodshed." Abaddon perched on top of her rood, a giant over her head. "You've shed much. There is no repenting. There will be no salvation. You are forever lost. And forever mine."

Margaret wept with the skies.

Abaddon lied.

She wasn't his. She didn't have to be.

She'd seen it in the rain and the flowers, people like her who chose to do wrong switching sides and letting in love. Not escaping the darkness, but overcoming it.

All this time, she'd been searching for a thing outside to save her: her queenship, her old life, humanity, the sword. The waters called to her, but she'd never truly listened. They told her the thing that could save her had been there all along. She only needed to let it in. She was already forgiven, she only needed to accept it. Freedom wasn't what she thought it was; it wasn't power or control, giving in to every desire or having the highest position in the clan or the country, not having to answer to anyone else. Freedom was redemption.

As William had mustered a last breath, final words, so did Margaret.

"I am not yours," she said to Abaddon. "God save me."

The deafening sound of rushing water filled the world.

Below her, in the courtyard lake, a watery lion swiped his paw across the bone and silver cage, and its tarnish vanished. It shone purer than any earthly silver could. The cage flew to pieces, and the pieces disintegrated.

The lion opened his mouth and roared.

The sound shook the universe.

And Abaddon, scared, fled to the other side of the earth on the back of a bestial cape, a hyena of discoloured blood, followed by a tangle of serpents.

The water rose until it covered Margaret's head.

Red swirled around her like smoke as it drained from her cape. She didn't fight the water and try to keep it out. She let it wash over her.

Underwater, she opened her eyes. The lion was there. He stared back at her, and she was afraid, but, even if she could have, she wouldn't have moved, wouldn't have wanted to be anywhere but before him.

The water left the courtyard, an eagre reversed, and she dropped onto the cobbles where fires sprouted. They flourished and reached for the rood, where another Margaret with a blanched cape was still pinned, the Margaret she had been.

As that Margaret and the thing that clawed into her neck perished, the new Margaret lurched with violent sickness and began to vomit. She regurgitated tooth by human tooth until, finally, her cursed heart tooth, an upper premolar, made its way up her throat and out of her mouth. She no longer had a hyena's heart, twice the weight of a lion's. She picked it up, held it between her thumb and forefinger, and threw it at the rood—into the fire. As if it were a leaf instead of a tooth, it shrivelled to ash and crumbled to nothing.

Lapped at by the fire, the impure, soft statues in the courtyard melted, and purple, gold, and black dross rolled off Margaret's slaggy body. The flames retreated and a flurry of white petals fashioned her a new cape, one of flaxen moonlight.

The ashlar walls collapsed with the rood and revealed, again, the lion made of water. Margaret's mother stood beside him, her hand on his glittering mane. It withdrew as her form rippled and gave up its human shape for that of a deer. In the throne room at Redcastle, her white cape dissolved as her soul, having helped her daughter through her trial, left the world. And Margaret knelt before the lion and gave thanks, for someone greater had restored her blood and teeth, taken up her yoke, and redeemed her by love, and she was free at last.

CHAPTER FIFTY-THREE

Hermitage Castle's walls rebuilt, and Margaret surfaced in the hall as if she'd dived into a lake and emerged clean. A pile of teeth was beside her, but her own heart tooth was missing, destroyed by sun-hot flames.

Though the castle's walls had returned, the walls around her heart had been demolished. She now knew freedom wasn't a prideful thing used to indulge desires but a thing of peace and serving others; it was walking in the light. And as long as she did, walls raised by the world were meaningless.

Time had stopped when Margaret took the sword.

William, now purged of Abaddon, was withdrawing to his apartments and Gundobad was before her, knife in hand, glowering at her new cape. He ordered, "Release the sword."

The order didn't clutch her heart or seize her mind. Her tongue prodded where the gap in her teeth should have been, but it wasn't there. The tooth he'd taken from her was back in her mouth.

Margaret brandished the Sword of Living Waters and Gundobad ran after William, retreating to the upper floor. She lowered the sword.

She emptied her mother's heart casket of the German soil and replaced it with Sigurd's pure heart from Alianora's casket, then called out, "Alice? Malcolm?"

She looked at the shadowed faces encircling her and scanned the floor for bodies. There weren't any. "Where have they gone?"

The redcapes gave perturbed, intermittent stares to the sword, rubbed at their faces, and shifted uncomfortably on their feet.

"Where have they gone?!" she shouted.

"The whitecape went to William's apartments," a redcape finally disclosed in a quiet, trailing voice. "We were ordered to throw him in the prison."

Malcolm had left her in the hall and gone to William's apartments, and Margaret now understood why. There was only one logical reason: he'd wanted revenge for his mother's rape. But he'd been captured and hadn't gotten it.

She rushed to the castle's opposite tower, where the pit prison dug into the ground. The Elliots had heaved a great rock slab over it; Alice was desperately trying, and failing, to budge it.

"Your cape!" exclaimed Alice. She protested, "Abaddon," when offered the sword.

"He won't stop you. He's gone."

Alice reached for it, and her fingers curled back. She reached again with trembling hands and, at last, took the hilt.

Margaret didn't know what Alice saw, whether she visited a demon's home or stayed aloft in the world, but, a second later, she coughed up her molar heart tooth and her cape was washed clean. Her hand was pressed to her heart and her head bowed, eyes glistening. She gave the sword back to Margaret and, together, they did their best to free Malcolm from his prison.

"Why did Robin keep him?" She used the name Alice knew.

"Leverage against you? Or me? I can't say."

They shoved at the stone slab, pushed and lifted for several minutes.

"We can't—move this—alone." Margaret huffed, and they gave up. How long had he been in the prison? five days? six? How likely was it that he lived? Not very. "Did they—give him water?"

"I did for several days. I tried to pull him out yesterday when I thought I was alone. That's when Robin ordered this put on. He's alive, I'm sure of it."

"He is." She hoped so, and couldn't entertain the idea he might not be. "We'll need help to get him out."

"When he was first captured, Malcolm sent Ermengarde's—I mean, your—golden eagle to alert Thomas Durward."

"Magnus? He didn't come with us—"

"He's been flying off from Ermengarde since he led her to the white-capes; everyone knew it was to you he flew."

Her heart swelled. Magnus's loss had been a hard one to bear. To know he'd been there, watching over her... and to think she'd been jealous of Ermengarde. That was Gudrun's way, but there was room in Margaret's heart for love—it wasn't about deserving as she'd once believed, for she would never deserve it. No one would. She had been loved without deserving it; she could love herself and Ermengarde, Alice and Malcolm, even William and Robert, without begrudging Magnus for doing the same.

"We still don't know when, or if, they'll arrive." Margaret turned from the prison and picked the sword back up. "We should save the redcapes. There are enough of them. We can move it together."

As they crept from the northeast tower, Margaret wondered if Alice understood what had happened to her mother. She hadn't been there in the hall when Alianora had been called Gudrun and wailed over Sigurd. Did Alice know her mother was over eight hundred years old? Did she even know she'd died? Now wasn't the time to tell her. After they'd rescued the redcapes and Malcolm and had no other worries, that would be the time.

They checked the entire floor and found not one redcape; in the short time since she'd left the hall, they'd disappeared. So Margaret climbed the spiral stair to William's apartments—she didn't want to force Alice back to that place, so she had her wait below as a sentry.

The door was cracked. She swung it open and found William staring out a window, searching the skies for starry night pools between thick clouds, the cadaverous crown of teeth on his head.

"They went to Ninestane," said William. "Robin had his own hearts, and he took one of mine. The second Lord of Liddesdale's, rather. It belonged to a Warenne."

"What's he to do?"

"Kill you, I think, and create redcape clans across Scotland."

"He's to spread decay... We have to stop him."

His eyes dropped from the sky.

"You saved me from the demon and Robin. Don't you want to save them, too?"

"What would it matter if I did? You think saving their souls will redeem mine?"

"No. But God can. Take the sword and see."

He sulked.

"You thought I was beyond saving, and you were wrong. Can't you see you're wrong about yourself? No one is beyond saving, not you or I or any of the capes."

His eyes drifted away, and he looked at anything but the glimmering metal.

"You once said you loved me like a sister. I loved you in the same way." She was on her knees beside his chair. He loved her still, didn't he? Some part of him must have believed. Why else would he save her from Abaddon? "You're forgiven for what you've done. You only need to accept love. Take the sword. Be my brother."

"You don't understand. No one does," he said bitterly, rejecting the sword and her and embracing himself.

Margaret cried as she left him there, and the sword vibrated low as the lion wept with her.

In the night, Thomas Durward arrived with what whitecapes he'd been able to gather. A small army. They dragged Malcolm, who was dirty and weak from hunger, from the pit and gave him food and water. Despite his pitiful state, he was as overjoyed to see Margaret's new cape as Margaret was to be reunited with both him and Magnus.

When Malcolm heard that William was still there from a whitecape, Margaret expected the news to send him into a rampage; she endeavored to prevent that by telling him it was Abaddon who'd subdued Alice, not William. She didn't know Alice was within earshot.

"He suspected as much when he went after him the first time," Alice said quietly.

So he knew, but he'd been so angry he didn't care who paid the price as long as someone did.

But he didn't seem angry anymore, and not just because he lacked energy. He had become meek.

Malcolm started to say something, coughed, and drank more water. It took him some effort to talk. "Yes. She said, 'Forgive him. He's lost.' But I couldn't forgive that."

"I did," said Alice. He rested his hand on her arm and nodded.

"I imagined it—killing him—while I was in the prison. I watched myself do it a hundred times, and I prayed a thousand times after. And I remembered a proverb." His voice was warm and easy as he recited, "'There is more glory in forgiving an injury, than there is pleasure in revenging it.' And how can I expect forgiveness if I can't forgive him? You were right, Mother. He's lost. I hope he can find his way as I continue to."

He spent the night recovering. In the morning, they rode and marched toward Ninestane—Malcolm took Thomas's horse, for the prison had weakened him somewhat, though he was quickly gaining back his strength, and Margaret headed the march.

From atop Hermitage Castle, William watched them advance like sunlit frost with a silent, frozen heart.

CHAPTER FIFTY-FOUR

Ada Warenne grieved her son on his deathbed in the royal castle. He drew his last breath. She kissed him and her tears clung to his hair.

The stone sorceresses were liars. They hadn't blessed him with the longest, most prosperous reign of any Alban king to outlast even Constantine II, the son of Áed; they'd enlarged his bones and cursed him with a premature death.

Her other son, William, would now be crowned King of Scots. She prayed they hadn't cursed him, too, for she couldn't bear to be responsible for more death, not after she'd repented for the first six. Seven, if she included her child, whose death was the most painful by far, or seven that she knew of. She'd created those terrible, red-caped goblins, who might have killed hundreds, thousands, in a quarter century. It was a ceremony she regretted with her whole heart, trading death for death, and would spend the rest of her life atoning for.

The door to her son's chambers opened. She didn't turn, thinking it was a monk returning, but her second son's voice met her ears.

"William! Where have you been?" When she did turn, her scolds melted on her tongue.

William, a man in his twenties now, stood before her wearing a new cape.

"I was at a small stone circle, Ninestane Rig. A place you know well—they spoke of you, but a lady I do not know. They called you 'Cape Mother' and cheered your corruption."

"You were with the redcapes?" she choked.

"I *was* a redcape. I met with Grandfather's magnate, the Lord of Liddesdale, one Ranulph Soulis. He deals in souls and hearts, and he...." He couldn't bring himself to go on. He raised a celestial sword. Its hilt crawled with lions. "This was my saving grace."

"Oh, William, William! It must be from God. He has spared you the consequences of my sins. Let us go to the chapel and I will tell you everything. You will see I'm at fault for it all, and I will beg your forgiveness. Please, my beloved son, you must gather an army and conquer those ghastly creatures with your sword."

She could never bring back her first son, but her second, a whitecape, was strong of heart and mind, and he could face the evils that lurked in Scotland's corners.

He forgave his flawed mother and did as she asked. He founded the Order of the Thistle and slayed the redcapes.

Ada retired to Haddington and her crown of teeth crumbled, and she never knew it was Abaddon who spoke to her in the stone circle and not the sorceresses, Abaddon who stole away the hyena teeth and brought them back to Hermitage.

And William didn't tell her when the redcapes returned. He fought them with his wife, who became Grand Mistress of the Order when he grew too old and trained their children to combat reds. Thus, the Scottish whitecapes originated and spread and fought the darkness on behalf of Ada Warenne.

CHAPTER FIFTY-FIVE

Morning mist concealed much of the landscape, including the nine standing stones, of which Margaret could see but a few vague shapes. As she and the whitecapes neared the stone circle, three soulless goblins crawled from it. Mist clung to their capes as wispy fingers trying to restrain them.

"Elliots, go forth! Giselher. Gundomar. William. Slaughter," said Gundobad as if he gave the command to wolves and not men, and Margaret supposed it held; these redcapes were more hyena than human, creatures the likes of which she'd never created or seen, the kind built from bodiless hearts.

Giselher and Gundomar shared features with Gundobad: their hair colour, the shape of their foreheads, and the wideness of their faces. William was the Warenne stolen from Lord Soulis, William Warenne, Ada Warenne's father. His heart had been used before; someone had cut it out and preserved it again.

Alianora had wanted her to revive Sigurd, though Margaret didn't know how that was possible. Now she wondered, as the three redcapes surged toward her, whether revivification was another avenue to immortality. Gundobad drank the elixir at intervals to stay alive, as had Alianora. Could he be resurrected into a new body and resurrected again and live forever that way? Would his heart eventually give out, or would his soul be called back to the Divine as Scot said, or to Dante's hell?

Giselher's arm swung toward Margaret and petrified all thought. She cleaved it with the sharp edge of the impossibly light sword. The sound he made was high and brutish, the scream of a beast.

Clan Elliot, controlled by the teeth inside Gundobad's heart, flooded to battle the whitecapes while Margaret avoided a second attack from Giselher.

He landed the third. His knife-like fingernails sliced into her leg. A shallow wound.

She ignored the pain, pivoted, and rent his cape from his body. When his borrowed bones and flesh trickled to a heart, she stomped it to dust. Giselher, an old Burgundian king, would never walk the earth again.

Beside her, William Warenne murdered a whitecape, Hugh Rose. William lifted his corpse and tore off chunks with his teeth while his cape inhaled streams of blood.

The whitecapes' goal was to impede, not kill, and they were suffering for it. The reds would soon suffer, too, once the white curse took hold. They would be retching and feverish and dry, they would struggle to breathe, and blood would leak from their eyes. But the curse wouldn't come on soon enough to end their attack.

Margaret beheaded the former Earl of Surrey and separated him from his cape in the same stroke. She crushed his heart. Its blood dripped hot through her fingers, dissolving before it reached the dewy grass, and its tooth stabbed her palm. She dropped it and wiped her hand on her sleeve.

Most of the reds were engaged with whitecapes—Thomas Durward cut down Gundomar I—but a few fell beneath her sword as she fought her way toward Gundobad. His low rank in Clan Elliot might not have been a guise, a way to hide his identity from Alianora, but his lot; or, if it was, he hadn't recovered from the effort. He was as gaunt as he ever had been, which was perhaps why he held back at the circle while he sent the redcapes forward. Killing him, weak as he was, wouldn't be a difficult task if that was the route Margaret chose to take.

Heart blood splashed her face as she reached the first of the nine stones. Thanks to Sigurd's pure heart, it didn't sink in.

Gundobad's tendons were taut. His eyes shot from stone to stone as he backed away from her and called shrilly, "To me!"

The capes ebbed in retreat as a red spate, but not fast enough for their leader.

Margaret's hand pressed against his throat, pinned him hard against a stone taller than them both and topped with moist, green moss. The redcapes watched from outside the circle. They wouldn't risk themselves to save him without an order, and they soon had to return to their fight, for the whitecapes caught up to them.

Margaret couldn't bring herself to rip off his cape without giving him a chance. He had done terrible things, but so had she.

She eased back a bit, and he took the opportunity to rasp, "Kill me and you doom Scotland."

"How's that?"

It was a struggle for him to speak, his voice a scratched whisper, "The redcapes are Scotland's best weapon, and I control them. An army of one mind—think of the possibilities. With a steady supply of libations, we can protect against England's forces and bring peace. You remember Rosslyn with the redcape Comyn, you remember what you did, and there were two of you then. Imagine what an army could accomplish. What they could guard against."

The blood, the death, the massacre. She would never forget.

"I was a weapon for Burgundy," Gundobad went on. "I thought I could protect against Rome and save my children. If I had a clan like the Elliots, we would have won. My children would not have turned on me, and I would never have been forced to hunt my own daughter. Would you take the ultimate weapon from Scotland and have her be overcome by the English? Think of the tragedies such a loss might beget, the families you will destroy because of—what? misguided righteousness?"

He had a point. Human forces couldn't match a redcape army.

She tried to recall the images in Thomas of Erceldoune's silver eyes. The decay was made up of faces and capes... had they been those of redcapes or Englishmen?

She glanced down at her wavy reflection in the Sword of Living Waters, stared into her own clear, cool gray eyes.

"You summoned demons. You corrupted Alianora and schemed with Abaddon for her to take her own life—I saw your terrible smile. *You* destroyed your family with sin and bloodshed. You're not a victim, or not just, like I am not. That's the difference between us: I want to end the carnage, and you would have it go on forevermore."

"How was I to know she would leave her heart unscathed? It was Abaddon who showed the coin. I would never risk that."

"So you say. Does it matter? You admit you hunted her. The murder was already done in your heart."

"Did you not hear me? I want peace for Scotland."

"Peace with libations for the Elliots, and how many new clans—how many Scots would you sacrifice each month? How much blood would you pay for freedom when true freedom has already been paid for? Your peace, with its endless killing, would be a plague and bring no peace at all. It would rot Scotland from the inside and rot the world after."

"Kih..." Gundobad's voice ground against the stones. He worked to yell, scraped the words from his throat, "Kill her!"

Some redcapes managed to evade the whites and infiltrate the circle. Margaret felt them closing in, intent on killing.

"Listen for the water," she said. "If you listen, you will hear it and understand—even you can be saved. Take the sword, Gundobad. Grimhild. Leave the darkness behind and you'll never be thirsty again."

"Kill her," he wheezed once more.

A redcape woman's sharp nails clawed into Margaret's shoulder. Before she could dig too deep and tear it off, Alice tackled her. They tumbled down, white on red, red on white.

More came for Margaret, more reached and stretched their necks to catch her with their teeth.

She forced the sword's hilt into Gundobad's hand, hoping it would set his heart on fire as it had hers and guard it thereafter. But he promptly dropped it after it wrung the cape from his body and the teeth from his heart—redcapes were released as tooth after tooth left his mouth on strings of pitchy bile, Alianora's carnassial was last. Many capes fled into the burning mists, but a few stayed, grouped a ways away, wary of the whitecapes.

It was the same as when Margaret had first taken the sword; it banished the cape but left Gundobad untried. She picked it off the ground, offered it again, but he wouldn't take it of his own will. Maybe his heart wasn't ready. Maybe it never would be.

Thomas Durward, who had minor injuries, watched Gundobad while Margaret flew to Malcolm's side. He knelt beside Alice. She lay broken and bleeding, with his hand in hers. She took Margaret's as well.

Magnus landed on Margaret's shoulder as if to console her, and her eyes searched Alice's weeping body. There were too many wounds to stop. She was losing blood fast. If she were a sorceress, she could eat a heart and live. But she wasn't, and she wouldn't. And she knew it.

"Watch over Ermengarde," said Alice. She died trying to repeat it; they clutched her fingers tightly as they went limp and laid them to rest at her sides.

The time for mourning was short, for a whitecape asked, "What are we to do about Gundobad?"

Margaret ran her thumb over gashes on Alice's face, scratches from the redcape woman, then stood and walked to Thomas and let Malcolm say his goodbyes alone.

"He's still a sorcerer. If we let him live, he'll retake his cape or steal teeth for control, or both," Thomas said. "We have to execute him. It's the only way to stop his bloodbaths."

She'd given him a chance and he'd refused forgiveness. But how could she execute him when she, too, had lived and breathed in darkness yet been rescued?

On his knees, Gundobad said, "That sword won't save you, but I could. You'll fall to England without me."

As orange rays burned through the mist, Margaret raised the silver sword.

And slowly lowered it.

"It's not our place to judge his soul. We'll throw him in the prison at Hermitage," she said, and Thomas and the whitecapes were satisfied with the conclusion. "There, he'll live the rest of his days cut off from sorcery, left alone to consider what he's done, and perhaps time will chasten his heart."

Quick as lightning, Gundobad severed his own cape with an ancient seax—a weapon that held memories Gudrun would never remember of the brothers she had loved and murdered and died believing the Huns had slain.

Having lived almost a millennium, the resurrected Burgundian king, once queen, died.

Chapter Fifty-Six

Thirteen-year-old Grimhild ran through a riparian forest with cold, wet feet and a broken spear. Her face was dirtied, her clothes torn. Prickly shrubs and branches cut her flesh and she tripped over dead wood, clawed at the ground, and pushed herself back up. Her captors were getting closer, barrelling through the forest behind her.

She'd escaped them with luck, but they'd chased her too long. Her legs and lungs were tired, and the world was growing dark. She couldn't outrun them.

She dove behind an old tree, pressed her back against it, clutched the spear shaft and tried to quiet her crashing breaths.

The older man approached first.

Her heart beat louder with each step he took toward her tree. It pounded in her ears and drowned out the sounds of nesting jackdaws and rooks in the wicker along the riverbanks.

He passed her tree and she lunged.

The spearhead dug into his back. It found its way through his ribs and into his heart and he jolted violently.

She scrambled back.

He fell, and the fall seemed surreal. It took ages.

She waited for him to get up and reach for her. Was he breathing still, or did she imagine he was?

She scooted forward and kicked his arm. He didn't move.

He was dead. She'd killed him.

Something vile bubbled inside her heart.

She pulled on the short spear, but it didn't slide from his back. It was stuck. She didn't want to pull harder, didn't want to feel it come back out. So she took a weapon from him instead, a small, single-edged knife.

The boy was upon her.

Grimhild backed away from him and brandished the knife, but he was at the man's side, checking for life, shouting, trying to save the unsavable.

Voices wound through the forest, and Grimhild looked behind her.

She could run, but where? They would find her, like they'd found her settlement. They would keep her, rape her or kill her, use her as a slave.

But her parents were coming, weren't they?

"They will save me." The words were a murmur in her throat, stifled by a thick tongue and netted by quaking teeth.

"They did not save you before," whispered the wind.

Blue eyes shimmered in the air.

It wasn't the wind but something in its shadow, a man beautiful and beguiling.

His slender fingers dragged across the boy's throat, passed through falling tears, and a perfect mouth formed lengthened words, "They will not come to save you. But you need not be afraid. If you trust in me, I will remain with you and guard your heart. I will do whatever you ask."

Grimhild's knife followed the fingers' path, sliced through skin and cartilage. The boy's blood spilled over the dead man, dribbled onto the splintered end of the spear.

She was the spear. Broken, half buried. Useless against the oncoming men.

She said, "Demon, I invite you in. Make me into a weapon."

He entered her and they reaped hearts, and Grimhild believed she'd evaded rape and slavery and death.

Epilogue

For the second time, Margaret walked the scarlet runner rug in Redcastle, this time clothed in a queenly mantle and bright, fine linen. Midday sun rays unfolded through the windows and made her brilliant.

Her mother's heart casket sparkled like a silvered star at her breast, a reliquary for Sigurd's heart, and men and women in white capes stood on her either side, blocking the silk damask walls. They nodded as she passed. Malcolm, who'd been declared chief of the new Clan Elliot, was one of the last to salute her, as he was near the front beside Ermengarde. Her small smile pierced Margaret's heart.

The throne was empty, her mother's cape gone. She stood before it and bowed her head softly to Marie, the laird of the castle's daughter and wife of the slain Hugh Rose, whose capeless body had been taken back to Kilravock to be buried. Marie crowned her Grand Mistress of All the Whitecapes with a circlet of hawthorn flowers, and John Seton of Parbroath knelt before her with the Sword of Living Waters. It felt as light as the heart in her chest.

Margaret, the twenty-three-year-old Grand Mistress, seated herself on the throne beneath a new banner of a lion rampant and a unicorn ringed by red and white flowers and curled her right hand, the one not holding the sword, over one of the throne's lion-carved arms.

Cheers went up, calls for good health and victory over the sorcerers and redcapes, and a feast in the hall followed her coronation. Rich venison and beef, wild boar meat, lamb, and herring seasoned with salt, garlic, and honey were merrily devoured, and imported wine, goat milk, and laughter flowed liberally. The whitecapes basked in the victory over

Gundobad and the crowning of Margaret and Brus, knowing more battles were soon to come but suspending, for the night, the worry of them.

An hour into the feast, Margaret spotted Malcolm slipping away. He was likely headed up one of the castle's towers—he'd often retreated to roofs or empty rooms in the week they'd been at Redcastle. He needed time alone to grieve his mother, whose body and heart had been interred at the Abbey of Dulce Cor near her grandfather.

To give him space, Margaret waited another hour before she went after him. She checked several rooms and a crenellated tower before going up a staircase turret of burnished red sandstone, atop which she found Malcolm at last. She put her hand on his back, and he jumped.

"I'm sorry," she said. "I can go."

She turned to redescend.

"No—" He grabbed her hand, pulled her back, and leaned his head against hers. "Stay."

They stood in silence for a while, and Margaret wondered what Malcolm was thinking. She didn't have any real memories of her own mother—just those she'd seen with Dante's astrolabe—since they'd parted just after Margaret's birth. Was it better that way?

Malcolm had spent years with Alice, but she'd been a redcape until the days leading up to her death. He surely had more bad memories than good—years of watching Alice struggle and kill, of being wrenched apart by her cape and the crown of teeth.

Margaret grimaced. Her throat thickened and she stroked Malcolm's golden-brown hair.

"In spite of her cape, she was able to love," he whispered as if he knew what she was thinking from the way she smoothed his hair. "She never turned her back on me or Ermengarde—or anyone."

He was right. Alice, even in the murk of Hermitage Castle, loved others and clung to hope. If anyone should have made it out alive, it was her—and that was why she didn't. She was selfless enough to die for others.

"She was stronger than the rest of us," Margaret agreed. "Like you. You both believed in me. Even when I sinned and my heart was dark, you didn't leave me alone."

He inclined his head to meet her gaze. "Then that's what we'll do for the redcapes. We won't leave them alone. It's what she would have done, if she..." His bereaved voice cracked. Even so, his eyes, though swollen, were less dull than before, ignited by the evening splendour or the afterimage of Alice's. "We will save them."

"How will we track them down?" murmured Margaret. "What if their hearts can't be saved?"

Malcolm wasn't in the mood to discuss the possibility of surrendering lost hearts or more Elliots. He said, "Don't worry about tomorrow; it will worry about itself," and he closed his eyes and took her hand. "Let's be at peace."

They embraced atop the castle and looked over darkening oak, ash, and beech trees, distant, roseate rain, and Beauly Firth hemmed by soft hills and brushed with warm highlights. A golden eagle soared freely over the water on wings of hope, radiant in the falling light.

More teeth might be pulled from the earth, more redcapes spawned and people corrupted by sorcery, but the sword would be there to try willing hearts by fire and water and, long after Robert and Margaret, Malcolm and Thomas were gone, whitecapes would be there to wield it.

Margaret watched the sun drip ever lower and, as love shines in the darkness, her white cape shone against a sky drenched in blood.

"For I will forgive their wickedness and will remember their sins no more." Hebrews 8:12

AUTHOR'S NOTE

I consider *Hearts Like Silver* a work of historical fiction; therefore, I tried to be as historically accurate as I could be while adapting the world to fit my story. I obviously invented the fantastical elements, but I kept the historical events as factual as I could (battles, reign of monarchs, birth and death dates of characters, etc.). However, there were instances I intentionally deviated from history, so I thought I would list those here, along with a few other notes and disclaimers:

- Margaret, the Maid of Norway, who might have been the last of the House of Dunkeld to rule, died at age seven on her journey from Bergen to Great Britain. She possibly died in St Margaret's Hope on South Ronaldsay, but in *HLS* her ship lands in Kirkwall on the Orkney Mainland. Her father, Eirik II Magnusson or Eric II of Norway, identified her body once it was shipped back. In my book, his identification is incorrect, as the body was that of another little girl—one who resembled his daughter—but, in actuality, Margaret was not kidnapped and turned into a redcape in Hermitage Castle... then again, only shreds of history are recorded.

- I chose to make the castles more modern than they would have been at the time. For instance, they didn't add sandstone (red or Devonian) to Redcastle until the 17th century when, according to Margaret Oag and Janet Skrodzka's *Killearnan: The Story of the Parish*, the younger son of the tenth Earl of Seaforth ordered the old keep to be rebuilt and expanded. I also made Hermitage Castle a bit larger than it actually is and I took out its ditches—Hermitage in particular has an in-story explanation for its sped-up appearance as it is the castle with the most page space, being the location of the Elliot clan.

- I used the modern-day Redcastle in *HLS*, which, to my understanding, is believed to be built on the site of the Castle of Edradour (Ederdour or Edirdovar, etc.). Edradour would have been the castle owned by Andrew de Bosco in the late 13th century to the early 14th century, not Redcastle.

- Hermitage Castle was possibly built by Walter Comyn, Earl of Menteith, but in *HLS* I've combined Hermitage Castle with the castle Ranulph I Soulis, or Ranulph de Soules, built on the east bank of the Liddel that no longer exists.

- Thomas of Erceldoune, or Thomas the Rhymer, has an ambiguous death date. Patrick Leopold Gordon of Auchleuchries refers to his death date occurring in 1307, but that reference appears to be uncorroborated. He may have died in 1298.

- Michael Scot's death date is also ambiguous, although he must have died before 1235. In *HLS,* Michael Scot was one of the many lives of Grimhild, and his death was faked in 1232.

- In the book, Isabella de Warenne is alive, unbeknownst to the Balliols and Comyns and Scots in general, though she died sometime before 1300 in actuality.

- Joan de Gray (of Codnor) may have been a nun at Aconbury Priory. She was not a nun or sister in London—but there is a Codnor connection to the Carmelites, so I didn't find it too offensive to place her at Whitefriars. In *HLS*, it's implied she is one of the White Friars.

- Goseck Circle, a Neolithic henge, consisted of four concentric circles, a mound, a ditch, and two wooden palisade rings. At one point in *HLS*, Margaret is in a stone circle in Germany, which I simply call a "Neolithic Circle." Although it's a stone circle, it's meant to be the Goseck rondel—made of stones, which are destroyed or swallowed by the earth when Grimhild is defeated, and the palisades are built later on. This of course did not happen in the real world as Goseck Circle dates back to Neolithic times, thousands of centuries before Margaret's story takes place.

- The three Burgundian brothers, Gundaharius, Giselher and Gundomar I, have many versions of their names and may have ruled together or separately depending on the source. I chose to make them co-rulers and used the versions of their names that I felt would be least confusing for readers, although they all begin with "G," so they and the other Burgundians may still be difficult to keep track of.

- The Knights Templar and White Guelphs of Florence were not related as they are in *HLS*.

- The tower Sigurd rescued Brynhild from is built where Burg Meersburg was and fell to ruin (a fictional tower that could have existed, the central tower for Burg Meersburg was built by a Merovingian king, Dagobert I, in the 7th century, and there could have been an earlier one).

- The Comyns acknowledged Margaret as heir and were likely honourable Scotsmen—but in *HLS* they participated in the conspiracy to have Margaret kidnapped in order to place John Balliol on the throne.

- Dante describes himself as "Dantes Alagherius, Florentinus patria, sed non moribus." Possibly "Dantes Aligerius natione florentinus, non moribus, magno Cani etc." (History of the Letters of Dante from the Fourteenth Century to the Present Day. Paget Toynbee. *Annual Reports of the Dante Society*, No. 36 (1917.), pp. 1-30.) I used "Dante Alighieri" for his name in *HLS*.

- Lists in the book are by no means comprehensive, there's so much I didn't include in *HLS*.

- I used first, second and third floors the US way. Ground and first floors are the same in the book, second is the UK first, third the UK second.

- I left out the prepositions in family names: Ada de Warenne became Ada Warenne, William de Soulis became William Soulis, etc.

- I also relied heavily on *The Life and Legend of Michael Scot* by Rev. J. Wood Brown, printed by T. and A. Constable for David Douglas, for my information on the real Michael Scot, who seemed to be, in reality, a scientist and philosopher. He was not a reincarnation of Grimhild of Burgundy and certainly not a wizard—though he could have studied magic and the occult, particularly in relation to astronomy and alchemy. He was a scholar who studied what subjects were viewed as serious in his time.

Again, I tried my best to be historically accurate, but we're all human—we all make mistakes and we all need grace—so please forgive me if there's anything I've forgotten or botched.

Translations:

I. Binski, Paul. 1995. *Westminster Abbey and the Plantagenets: Kingship and the Representation of Power 1200-1400*. New Haven: Yale University Press.

II. "I have her."

III. "He has come to see him again, His Royal Highness."

IV. "Yes because she could be an alpha. She is still on the side of Scotland and death."

Acknowledgments

This novel, and everything I do, is all thanks to God—the first and greatest storyteller and creator, who wrote the only perfect book in existence and is capable of redeeming the blackest heart.

Second, I would like to thank my father, who always believed I would publish novels and made my success sound inevitable, and my mother, who read books aloud to me as I grew up, bought me more books than I can count, and who now reads everything I write.

Thank you to my siblings, Ben, Bailey, and Seth, for listening to me ramble about my writing and worlds and all the strange (and sometimes gory) facts I discovered while drafting *Hearts Like Silver*.

Thank you to Raleigh, for being my first reader and proofreader, and to you and Missy for the gift cards and coffee shop trips and being so interested in the details of this novel on the first of those trips over a year ago. I always love hearing about your time in Scotland and all of your other adventures.

Thank you to Jon, for the long walks and the comparison of *HLS* to *Abe Lincoln: Vampire Hunter*, I really enjoyed that. And I'm grateful to you and Grandpa and Grandma Schaper for the candles and coffee—an essential for the morning writer.

And thank you to my in-laws, especially Grandma and Grandpa Lechelt for everything you've done for our little family and for this book.

To my husband Cameron, who embraced life with me—a writer who has one foot in the past while the other wanders far-off lands—thank you for sometimes wandering with me and sometimes drawing me back to the present.

If I were in a whitecape clan, I would recruit all of you first.

Thank you so much to my wonderful editor, Caitlin Faith Miller, for being the fire that refined *Hearts Like Silver*. Catie, you're the best, as an editor and as a person, and this novel wouldn't be what it is without you!

Thank you to Friel Black for editing the blurb; your input made it a hundred times better, you're just lovely to talk to, and I'm happy to have met you!

I'd also like to shout out the wonderful Instagram community; you're all so supportive and sweet. Even though I'm not on social media much these days, I'm happy to have met each and every one of you, and I'm still here cheering you on!

And last but certainly not least, thank you to all of my readers. I feel blessed every time someone reads one of my stories or signs up for my newsletters; it means so much to have people interested in my books and writing updates or supporting me in any way—even if it's just sparing a happy thought for me now and then. Thank you, I'm so grateful to have you on my side!

JAMIE SHEEHAN spent her childhood wandering through pine forests and dancing with faeries (who mysteriously vanished with her youth). When she's not exploring other worlds, she can be found baking buttery pastries, snuggling her fluffy kittens, stitching clothes with enchanted threads, and basking in the simple joys of everyday life. *Hearts Like Silver* is her debut novel.

authorjamiesheehan.com
Instagram: @authorjamiesheehan
The Ink-Dipped Trowel: jamiesheehan.substack.com

Printed in the USA
CPSIA information can be obtained
at www.ICGtesting.com
JSHW021631280324
59995JS00001B/15